PRAISE FOR *HEX-RA...*

"Steeped in the style of 1970s pulp detective fiction . . . Brimstone is cut from the cloth of the classic wisecracking detective, and Ridler peppers the text with perfectly pitched hard-boiled vernacular. The novel's wild mix of comedy and supernatural perils bodes well for its detective's future adventures."—*Publishers Weekly*

"Rollicking, exotic, and pulpy to the max."—*B&N Sci-Fi & Fantasy Blog*

"Terrific fun, dripping with rich period detail and nods to Ed Wood movies and Jack Kirby comics. Smutty, profane, and unapologetically slathered in pulp, *Hex-Rated* is a loving homage to all the musty, dog-eared paperbacks stuffed in the used bookstore's spinner rack."—Jason Heller, *NPR*

"The book inside is even better than the cover. . . . This is the first of the Brimstone Files novels, and I can't wait for the next one. Filthy, magical, and dangerous, *Hex-Rated* and Jason Ridler should both definitely be on your radar."—*Other Worlds Than These*

"Fast paced, clever, and a great example of world-building . . . it has everything you should be looking for in a supernatural-drenched thriller. And that cover art is sweet."—Bob Freeman, Occult Detective and author of *Keepers of the Dead*

"A contender for Best Book of the Year! . . . a page-turner in every sense of the word. The next book cannot come fast enough! Thank you, Jason Ridler, for sharing James Brimstone with us!"—*The Bone Breaker*

"This is the stuff cult movies are made of. *Hex-Rated* is a mash-up of *Magic Castle*, *A Boy Named Sue*, and *Lair of the White Worm*. . . . Overall, fun and appropriately tawdry as the cover implies."—*No Glitter Blown*

"Retro-pulp smut that reads like a cartoony *Rockford Files* mixed with a porno flick that's trying to ape Hammer Horror. . . . it might be cartoony, but it's nice to read something that delights in being so richly itself."—*10 Bad Habits*

Also by Jason Ridler

Fiction
The Brimstone Files
Hex-Rated
Black Lotus Kiss

Spar Battersea Thrillers
Death Match
Con Job
Dice Roll

Blood and Sawdust
A Triumph for Sakura

Non-Fiction
FXXK WRITING: A Guide for Frustrated Artists

A NEW BRIMSTONE FILES NOVEL

BLACK LOTUS KISS

JASON RIDLER

NIGHT
SHADE
BOOKS

Night Shade books may be purchased in bulk at special discounts for sales
promotion, corporate gifts, fund-raising, or educational purposes. Special edi-
tions can also be created to specifications. For details, contact the Special Sales
Department, Night Shade Books, 307 West 36th Street, 11th Floor, New York,
NY 10018 or info@skyhorsepublishing.com.

Night Shade Books™ is a trademark of Skyhorse Publishing, Inc.®,
a Delaware corporation.

Visit our website at www.nightshadebooks.com.

10 9 8 7 6 5 4 3 2 1

Library of Congress Cataloging-in-Publication Data is available on file.

Names: Ridler, Jason Sean, 1975- author.
Title: Black lotus kiss: a Brimstone files novel / Jason Ridler.
Description: New York: Night Shade Books, [2017] | Series: Brimstone files
Identifiers: LCCN 2017031335 | ISBN 9781597809351 (pbk.: alk. paper)
Subjects: LCSH: Private investigators—California—Los Angeles—Fiction. |
GSAFD: Mysery fiction. | Occult fiction.
Classification: LCC PS3618.I39225 B58 2017 | DDC 813/.6—dc23
LC record available at https://lccn.loc.gov/2017031335

Cover artwork by John Stanko
Cover design by Claudia Noble

Printed in the United States of America

Thanks to the following: Nick Mamatas for reasons that are Cosmic Top Secret; Cory Allyn and Jeremy Lassen for their continued support; and to the Amazing Kate Marshall for her many insights. And, of course, to everyone spending their cash and time to hang with Brimstone: thanks again. Let's do it again soon!

To James Gladstone Ridler. You watched as I injected my eyeballs with awful horror films, comic books, and pro wrestling, and politely enjoyed them from the sidelines. And yet you gave me a powerful lesson on storytelling. When I took you to see an X-Men movie, I realized you had no idea who the X-Men were but went anyway just to be with your son. "Dad," I asked, "did you have any idea what the hell was going on in that flick?" Your response? "Sure. Good guys were underdogs and the bad boy liked the redhead." *Plus ça change.* Thanks for all the love and support for your misfit son.

"Los Angeles is a microcosm of the United States.
If L.A. falls, the country falls."
—Ice-T

"Barbarism is the natural state of mankind. Civilization
is unnatural. It is a whim of circumstance. And barbarism
must always ultimately triumph."
—Robert E. Howard

BLACK LOTUS KISS

1

I CHECKED THE REARVIEW JUST IN CASE AN ANGRY member of the California Magi Rocketeers Sex Club had any funny ideas about leaving their clubhouse in upscale Inglewood and following me. But the reflection held only the tired wheels of Los Angeles on a Friday morning. I eased off the gas so Lilith hummed down Slauson at an easy thirty miles per hour, her brand-new paint job, detailed interior, and spotless windshield making her look like a million dollars, despite the fact that Dodge Darts weren't exactly in vogue.

Yet another reason I loved her. About the only advice my former mentor, the diabolical Edgar Vance, had given me that seemed to hold true once I was outside his thrall was: if you care what people think, they own you.

"Heinous," said the uptight voice in the passenger seat.

I put a little more heat on the gas because Cactus Hayes would never forgive me for missing a Legion event I promised to attend . . . even if I was finishing a case en route. I just hoped my suit from the good folks at Goodwill—a subtle orange and brown windowpane plaid—wasn't too wrinkled. Knowing Cactus, his dress greens would be starched to perfection.

"Sickening," said the lady's voice from the passenger seat. I tapped the scab on my right palm like Spider-Man slinging a web. The callus had hardened from where I'd stopped a bullet two months ago, when I'd nearly become a catalyst in a ceremony of dark magic and pornography. Sure, I'd saved L.A., but man, this callus was—

"Unbelievable."

Mandy Jefferson sat with photos in her lap, my straightest client since the nightmare of Tabitha Vance had come to life and attempted to birth a Nazi kraken on a pornographer's epic movie set. Mandy was normal. Normal looking. Normal pretty. Normal fears. But her husband—

Mandy's burgundy-nailed fingers plucked through pictures of Peter dressed in "wizard" robes: getting his prick sucked by a woman in black lace, hands tied behind her back, his glasses on the tip of his nose; next, he is anally penetrating another male wizard against a Stonehenge backdrop and wearing what appeared to be a fighter-jock's helmet, complete with oxygen mask that had been gimmicked to have its tube reach his submissive's mouth; and lastly, my personal fave, a third-class Jane Fonda in full Barbarella outfit, on all fours, receiving two gentleman in deep sea diving helmets at the same time. They looked like stills from a sexed-up version of *Plan 9 from Outer Space*.

"This is just sick."

I grinned. Lying to your wife about your time in a gonzo science fiction sex cult? Sure, that's wrong, and maybe even sick. But enjoying one? I chalked that up to personal taste, but that wasn't what Mandy needed to hear right now.

"The truth is weirder than fiction," I said. "That's how you know it's true."

Her lips pursed as she tossed the photos to the floor by her very practical stack-heeled brown shoes. "But this is twisted, perverted. Like some bad pulp novel."

"Wouldn't know; never read them."

I loved this case. Sure, it was a little twisted, but there was not one slice of magic I could taste. Peter and all of his gang were pretenders. All amateur-hour kids dabbling in magic but no threat to anyone, just people who read Aleister Crowley and think orgasms are the secret sauce to magic potions. The invisible scars Edgar Vance had dug into my aura had taught me many things—including that real magic was about suffering and slavery. Real magic was ugly as an executioner's heart.

The Rocketeer Sex Club was just that, a sex club with a fetish for Crowley's era of the Ordo Templi Orientis and an idiot's version of Vodou, but with a sci-fi twist and a hilarious newsletter called *Uranus Rising* that included porn stories with libertarian Martians made of Jell-O and willpower. Every paragraph made me spill my Dubonnet.

Mandy crossed her arms, as if to hold back the tears that would transform her thick eyeliner into dark rivers heading for her blushing cheeks. "I'm a modern woman," she said defensively. "But I can't stomach perversion. This stuff is not natural."

I smiled, nodded, and decided that sharing my opinion was a great way not to get paid.

"James, how do you live with this filth?"

"Live with it?"

"The cases you take, are they like mine?"

"How?"

"Unnatural. We seem to be living in an age of hedonism and perversion. What Peter's doing is . . . out of a nightmare."

And one woman's nightmare is another man's playground, I could hear Edgar saying in the back of my mind. My skull shuddered.

"I'm sorry," Mandy said. "I didn't mean to make you ill. You must see so many terrible things."

I exhaled hard and silent through my nose so it didn't sound as if I was contemptuous of Mandy's delicate sensibilities. "I've seen a lot of stuff, Mandy. To do what I do, you need to understand a range of human experiences, even ones you dislike, that scare you, or make you feel estranged. I try to be empathetic to all parties while serving my client's . . ."

Mandy had returned to the photos and was traumatizing herself with the Chinese finger cuff routine her husband and a buddy performed on a woman with a rocket painted on her back.

". . . I'll drop you off at your school. Do you want me to keep the photos for you? I can't send them through the mail without being brought up on obscenity charges."

"What? No . . . no," she said, eyes lingering on the dirty pic. "No. I should keep these. As evidence."

I kept my grin steady so as not to ruin the rational thoughts I suspected covered something darker flickering in her mind.

And that's when I *heard* it.

A cranky, revved-up throttle akin to the distorted saxophone on the Munsters theme song served as preamble before I caught sight of smoke in the rearview mirror. And in front of that smoke was a roadster ripping through traffic faster than the first sip off a drunk's flask.

"What in heaven's name is that sound?" Mandy said, then turned. "Good God! Is that . . ."

It was.

Ramming up West Slauson Avenue was a tricked-out roadster that would have looked futuristic when Peter started at the Jet Propulsion Lab back in the fifties: a pulsing red rocket car with wings and three wheels, smoke billowing out of a wheezy exhaust pipe above what looked like two rocket engines. Inside a glass bubble atop the contraption, manipulating the controls, sat the man of the hour: Peter Jefferson.

Jefferson's amplified voice punctured the L.A. afternoon like an electric whoopee cushion that had been taught how to speak.

"MANDY! STOP! DESIST! I COMMAND YOU!"

"Command?" Mandy said. Sticking her head out the window, hands still gripping the evidence, she shouted, "I command you to go to hell Peter, you dirty . . . bastard!"

I hit the gas to give her insult meaning and get some distance, but the rocket car was piercing through traffic like a crimson needle. The American Legion Hall—where Cactus had ordered me to be before noon—was only three blocks ahead at the intersection of South Harcourt. But I had to stop this mad scientist of sex before he killed us all.

"YOU ARE BOUND TO ME BY COSMIC FORCES!" Jefferson bellowed. In my side mirror, I saw him slipping past a yellow tow truck and a VW bug. "SUBMIT AND YOU WILL BE GIVEN PLEASURES KNOWN ONLY TO THE STARS!"

"It's over, Pete!" Mandy yelled, then stuck out the picture. "I've got all the evidence to sue you to death here on Earth, you pathetic egghead! Try commanding me again!"

The rocket car blasted forward to parallel me. We were going forty miles an hour with me honking everyone out of the way and Peter's voice still polluting the air. "YOU ARE UNDER THE INFLUENCE OF THAT NO-GOOD THIEF AND SPY! I WILL BREAK HIS SPELL!"

"I'm under no one's spell," she screamed. "I can do what I want, too! See?" Mandy yanked herself back in the car and planted an awful kiss full of teeth and tongue on my mouth, while mangling my hair from its otherwise bullet-proof quaff into a messy mound with her hand.

She pulled away and I stabbed the brakes as a yellow light turned red, throwing my right arm across Mandy so she didn't hurtle through Lilith's brand-new windshield. The Veterans Hall was just to my left. I'd, technically, made it in plenty of time. I just couldn't stop—yet.

Peter did what any pilot of a rocket car would do: hit a red button on his console and fired through the intersection like a comet, cutting in front of the onslaught of oncoming traffic from Harcourt.

Outside Veterans Hall, a protest group of longhairs waving placards stopped their slogan-chanting to goggle at the rocket car as Peter zoomed by screaming, "HELP! THE THROTTLE IS JAMMED! I CAN'T STOP!"

While all those eyes were on Peter, one pair of eyes was on me.

Cactus, standing on the steps to the hall in his dress greens, glared straight at me. His body language translated loosely to: "Clean up whatever this mess is you made, Brimstone, and get back here or I will parboil your flesh until your bones flee your meat sack and run screaming into the night."

Mandy's strident voice issued from behind her smeared lipstick, more or less echoing his thought. "Don't just sit here! Save him!"

I smiled, hit the gas, pressed my horn harder than a Swedish masseuse would a contortionist's back knots, and thought, "Why not? It could always be worse."

2

FRIGHTENED COMMUTERS PULLED TO THE SIDE TO get out of harm's way as we followed the rocket's red glare.

"Faster!" Mandy screamed, shoving my protective arm off her clavicle. "He's going to kill himself!"

I used my now-free hand to wipe the sweat off my dripping forehead, then swallowed the smear of lipstick she'd left on my teeth as we cleared another block.

The rocket's fire snuffed out. Smoke plumed.

"This is our chance!" I said. "Get in the back seat!"

"But I'm wearing a skirt!"

"Do it or he dies in his cockpit!"

She gave me a look that made my five o'clock shadow burn. Clunky heels hit the ceiling as she climbed over, belly first.

I'd like to say I didn't look in the rearview mirror.

But I did.

And I discovered Mandy Jefferson wore no panties. I found this glistening fact somewhat distracting, but still managed to pull next to the rocket car. In his control bubble, Peter was desperately pulling at levers and mashing pedals as we raced past Grace Methodist Church and headed for the curve at Overhill Drive.

"Jump!" I screamed and nodded at the empty passenger seat.

"I CANNOT ABANDON MY VESSEL!"

God, everyone in L.A. sounded like a movie script, especially when their balls were retracted.

"Peter, there's a dead-end parking lot with an old transformer station. Just aim the ship that way and get ready to launch!"

Peter glared. "YOU ARE MY ENEMY AND THE ENEMY OF MY ORDER!"

"Then jump in here and kick my ass. Just don't kill anyone to do it, okay?

"Do as he says!" Mandy said, sticking her head up from the back seat.

"Peter? Can I call you that?"

"MY ETERNAL NAME IS NOVA."

I honked to get a Chevy with a Nixon/Agnew bumper sticker out of my way. "Nova? You got about one minute to point this thing at the station and jump in here. That is, if you have the courage to do it. Think: what would Captain Kirk do?"

His eyes narrowed. "STAND BY, INFERIOR!"

My day could not get any better. "Standing by at fifty-five miles per hour. Move!"

Peter kicked a pedal and the bubble retracted from the throne . . . and got stuck halfway down. The wind jerked Peter as the transformer station came into view, but his gloved hands maneuvered the rocket car to the right so it would hit the gray structure.

"Hurray!"

He yanked open the cockpit bubble. "IF I PERISH, I WILL—"

"Shut your mouth and toss your ass!" I screamed, bringing

Lilith close, hoping I could turn her back to the street and away from the rocket car's certain doom. "*NOW!*"

Peter yanked out the last cable, stood on the precipice of the bubble, and dove for the window. His helmet came through and his gloved hands scrambled for something to hold as I peeled back into traffic. His boots dragged against the asphalt like a grindstone. "I'm slipping!" One gloved hand and then the other purchased only air as we crossed Overhill.

I shot out my right hand and grabbed him, but his weight dragged Lilith toward the rocket car's path. My left hand wound us back—

—and his glove slipped out of my right. "No!" I said as Peter slid out the window.

"Mine!"

Mandy's burgundy nails dug into the soft flesh of Peter's wrists, freeing me enough to pull a hard left. "You're mine! Now!" *BOOM!*

I slowed down and made an easy right on South La Brea Avenue. Mandy let go and Peter plopped out the window. I exited Lilith and saw the smoke cloud above the station's demolished walls. "Well, Pete," I said. "I'd say the maiden voyage of your rocket car will make the history books."

I walked around Lilith to find a throwaway scene from some B movie from the Parkway Drive-In of my childhood. On the concrete, Mandy cradled Peter's head as she pulled off his mask; the pictures I'd taken were stashed under her plaid rump. "Oh god, honey, can you breathe?"

Peter's sweaty, mustached face was free, his glassy eyes starting to focus as he sucked in air with a wheeze through clenched teeth. "It was written in the cosmos that you would save me, Mandy. And you have."

"Well, let's not fuss about that right now. What matters is you're safe."

"And I'm late," I said. It was nearly noon. "I hate to drop you off in the aftermath of a rocket launch, Mrs. Jefferson, but I think my work here is done." I nodded to the dirty pictures under her ass.

"Don't leave me, Mandy!" he said, gripping her shoulder with rocket gloves I swore had been stolen from a foundry. "Not for this *inferior*."

I smiled. Good on you, Pete. Fight for your gal. Call me names. Make me less of a man. Whatever you need to do.

"What, *him*?" She gave me a scathing look that nearly melted my eyeballs. "He's just an investigator. I was funning you, Peter. That's all. We can rebuild us. You just have to listen to me."

"So," I said. "About the other half of my payment."

"You'll get it in the mail, Mr. Brimstone," she said, sharp and swift as a career knifeman tossing his first blade.

I smiled. Hard. "No, Mrs. Jefferson. I won't. If I don't get the check I know you have in the inside pocket of your coat right now, I never will. The fire department and the cops are going to be sending out search parties for the person responsible for that explosion, and near as I can tell no one will fit the APB other than good old Peter, even without the bug mask. I have a spare pair of duds in the trunk that can replace his spaceman suit. Plus, I'll be happy to throw in a quick lift for the two of you to that school of yours if you'll be so kind as to hand over—"

She tore an envelope out of her coat and tossed it to me. "Help me get him inside."

I TOOK THE LONG WAY AROUND INGLEWOOD TO PS 109 WHILE MANdy and Peter got him out of his Commando Cody get-up and into a spare pair of black slacks and a brown shirt I'd worn while casing the electronics shop Peter and his buddies had turned into a HQ for their science-fiction double feature sex-and-magic club.

"Suck in your gut. God, Peter, what am I going to do with you?"

I turned the volume up to drown out her voice, but not loud enough to kill the itching sound of a siren on my tail. I kept things nice and easy, even knowing I was doomed to Cactus's wrath for being late with every minute I wasn't at the hall for his big event. When doomed, try to enjoy the ride. Waylon Jennings sang ol' Chuck Berry's "Brown Eyed Handsome Man" just as we pulled up to the school's parking lot. And I saw something that made me happy as hell.

A handful of black children were enjoying lunch on the school steps as the typical shouts and screams of public school littered the air. Turns out the L.A. Superior Court had a decent bone in its body. While I was hunting sex krakens in the Valley, they'd killed all attempts to keep these kids away and desegregated the schools of the city. The black kids looked wary as white kids ran around and controlled the jungle gym, the swings, and the baseball diamond. I'd fought in Korea and seen nightmares come alive that would scare the guts out of Audie Murphy, but looking at those kids enjoying their sandwiches, surrounded by kids whose parents, just two months ago, were up in arms about how integration was a tool of the devil— well, those kids on those steps were, for me, the emblem of courage in a world that wants us to be cowards by daylight and complacent by night.

"Ain't that a sight," I said.

"Yes. Nigger children. As if my day wasn't rough enough."

I had no idea how much restraint I possessed until I heard Mandy's voice. The voice of a teacher. The voice of someone preparing kids to be grown-ups. I swallowed the ice in my throat and she kept going. "How am I supposed to teach children with no letters or math?"

I rested my shoulder on the seat, turned, and smiled. "I will say this once. I'm friends with Gus, the janitor at this school.

We're members of the same bowling league. Real stand-up guy, Gus. Mentors black kids at the YMCA, teaches them boxing, like he learned it in the Army, back when they thought blacks needed a strong Southern man to push their platoons around like they were plantations, back when he wasn't considered a real American like you or me, just because of the color of his skin. He's a great guy to know, Mandy. I bet he'd help you start an after-school program to assist anyone who can't read and write as if they were taught in a white school. I bet he'd be a great ally in the challenge ahead."

Her forehead crinkled. "Why would I ever do that?"

"Just an idea. You don't have to take it. But if I find out that you're slacking, that you're not treating those kids as the future of this country, if you show the kind of race favoritism that makes our country a joke after liberating Hitler's concentration camps, well, then I might have to let your principal have the photos I took."

She grabbed her ass, then pulled out the folder. "I still have them."

I nodded. "And I have the negatives. I can make a wall mural of them if I want and hand them out with your address, just so everyone in Inglewood knows that Mrs. Jefferson's husband needs to get his shaft wet in the cosmos." Of course, I didn't have the negatives. The dark room I sent the film to was holding onto them until I paid off a debt I'd forgotten about thanks to getting Lilith's windshield fixed . . . but the vagaries of my fiscal life didn't seem prudent to share at this juncture.

She slapped Peter so hard I felt my own molars scream. Peter shook in my dark clothes, one size too small for his frame. "Don't just sit like a mole on a hill, Peter. Do something!"

Pete flinched, then tossed a right that looked like he was throwing a softball. He tagged my face and I winced.

I hissed. "Good shot, Pete. I deserve it. Now why don't you

help your wife out of the car and try and lay low before the cops drag you in for questioning about your use of rockets as sex gear."

Peter scrambled out of the car. "Come on, Mandy! Lunch is almost over."

Mandy bared her teeth. Some of her lipstick had smeared across them like blood. "Never took you for a nigger lover, Brimstone."

I sighed. "I never took you for a sexually regressive bigot who clearly wants to be her husband's mother. But, here we are."

She raised her hand.

"I owed your husband a shot. But if that racist hand hits me, I'll start the battle cry, 'Teacher has no panties.'" I covered my mouth with my hand. "What would your students think, Mrs. Jefferson?"

Her hand shook, Peter beckoned, and she clenched her manila envelope with her burgundy talons before rolling out of Lilith in a huff. I peeled out gently, knowing the fuse was lit for my ass-kicking at the Legion Hall, and worrying about the future.

By the time I'd circled back to Slauson and Harcourt, the fire department was already extinguishing the rocket car, two LAPD squad cars flanked the wreckage, and I was glad that all eyes were on the fiasco and fire and not the Dodge Dart that had run beside it. I pulled an illegal U-turn and replayed my drive to the hall, this time without dragging the tin cans of Peter and Mandy behind me.

The parking lot had become a mini-Woodstock of longhairs and megaphones. I pulled into the lot to find Cactus waiting. The fury of his gaze had dropped to sub-zero temperatures, akin to the Chosin River that gave our platoon frostbite.

Outside Lilith, the protesters chanted *"No more Nixon! Election Fixing! Cambodia bombing! Baby Killing!"*

I stepped out of Lilith. "I thought the bombing campaign was done."

"Kids are still dying," Cactus said. "So, they keep protesting. And you're late."

"Cactus, I would have been on time if I hadn't been chased by that amazing machine you saw blasting the street."

He stepped forward and I shut up. "Didn't ask for excuses. Don't care who popped you a weak fist, either. Come on. You need to bear witness." He marched toward the protesters. I followed.

The bearded man with the American flag T-shirt and megaphone blasted stats on casualties and horrors that were becoming fodder for gory headlines and evening news broadcasts, so much so that I was glad I still enjoyed news via the wires. But it wasn't just Vietnam that was bad. My last case before Mandy arrived involved a kid named Roger who had run away from San Diego to become a rock-and-roll star. His sister believed his taste in music was touched by Satan himself and found my ad in the *Free Press*. I hunted for the kid in the strip's motel alleys and gutter bars and found him with a girl his age, a needle in his arm, and downers down her throat: two beautiful corpses wearing black T-shirts with band logos and soiled flares. Not a taste of magic around it. No Satan needed to be a casualty in the aftermath of the peace and love generation. Then you read in the *L.A. Times* about Latino laborers murdered by the Sausage King's warehouse in East L.A., the rising tide of White Nationalism brewing around integration of schools, and the tired old lines about black violence, black rape, and black fears coming out of the children of GIs who broke down the doors at Buchenwald and you wonder, what in the hell kind of short-term memory loss does this city have?

A ripe avocado smacked my calf, and I turned.

Long-haired folks, some with mustaches, filled the ranks. All draft age or younger, some carrying placards high, armpits sweated to darkness on T-shirts that declared everything from KILL TRICKY DICK to LED ZEP, a British rock band that did a great job of exploiting black American blues. A couple of armpits stuck out because they were locked down by arms pinching skateboards to their ribs. They were younger, quieter, but no less present. Like kids following their big brother and sis into the fray.

The chanting grew, and I wondered if the radicals and freaks who hated the state would endure longer than those dropping out of the mainstream and finding the death blossom of youth in some sleazy motel named after a dead president or violent ends at the hands of cops who cause Latino and black mothers to mourn. Whatever else the 1970s were becoming, they were first and foremost a graveyard of idealism akin to what I saw in the 1950s, with hate for Freedom Riders tearing people apart. *Plus ça change*, the French say. Here's hoping the kids with megaphones and placards would keep fighting against war and the other horseman of the apocalypse I saw every day in this beautiful veneer of a city: bigotry, abuse, and damnation.

When a Honey Gold apple smacked my cheek harder than Peter's punch, I snapped back to the moment. The hall was a single story of gray brick but with nice, big windows up top that allowed the L.A. sunshine inside.

Cactus walked past a grizzled vet, a guy with hell in his eyes and fruit stains on his shirt, and his campaign medals attested he was, honest to god, a doughboy from the Great War, as well as the "good" one twenty years later. Made him seventy if he joined when he was sixteen. The disgust on his face could fill the sewers of hell. He looked at me—wearing an orange-and-brown polyester suit and brown-and-white wingtips, slightly scuffed—comparing my attire to his immaculate dress greens and spit-polished boots that had likely walked through more battlefields than anyone in a nuclear blast radius.

"Death merchant!" screamed a young woman who, I presume, lobbed the apple. Her dark wire-rimmed glasses hid her eyes. Freckles spread across her cheeks. "You're responsible for My Lai! War criminal!"

That stung. "Never served in 'Nam," I said. "But you're right. Charlie Company should be drawn and quartered for what they did."

"Charlie Company?" she said. "It could have been anyone created by the military-industrial complex!" Despite her vitriol, I was taken by the tall guy with a thin blond mustache standing silent behind her. His loose flannel shirt and smooth tan pegged him as "Native to Cali." Fit as a career surfer and stoic as a Greek philosopher, he placed one hand on the angry woman's shoulder. She quieted and sighed.

But his hands twitched as he touched her, with the precision of a metronome. Like his hand was a ticking stopwatch.

"Just get out! Stop killing!"

I turned back to the vet near the door but caught sight of something else that stuck out like weeds on a ceiling. Big guy, hard face with shark eyes, just standing in the middle of the screamers. Hair was long, but ragged. Scars on his arms. He was stewing in place, seemingly feeding off the rage of the protestors but doing nothing himself, like a doppelganger to the Gentle Blond Giant with the deep, dark tan.

A biker?

"You with them," the old timer said, "or you with us?"

I smiled. "I'm with Cactus." An orange crashed into my spine and I pushed my way into the dark of the hall.

I realized how strange it was that Cactus would ask me to witness his event. Maybe he just wanted to see me pelted with a poor man's Santa Fe salad.

3

CACTUS STOOD SOLID AS GRANITE ON THE PINE-
wood stage at the front of a room the size of a high school gym-
nasium. Next to him: a white-blond man in his twenties, also in
dress greens, who was stuck in a wheelchair but with what appeared to be both his legs intact. A victim of what I presumed
were the devil's playthings in Vietnam: Bouncing Betty mines.
Shrapnel in the spine can cut a man in half inside, leaving him
with legs but no way to run. The man in the wheelchair looked up
at Cactus with grit, not resentment or a thousand-yard stare. He
was *present* and *accounted for* at the front of a hall.

The stings on my cheek and spine from flying fruit soon dis-
sipated within the presence of so many mutilated hearts, minds,
and bodies. Soldiers from wars stretching back to the Argonne
and hunting bandits in the Philippines sat alone or beside
younger wounded creatures from Normandy and Okinawa and
my vintage from Inchon and Chosin, some with graying wives
wearing Sunday bests. The closer you got to the back of the auditorium, the younger the veteran, and the fewer the seats taken.

The copious amount of Brut 33 I'd splashed on that morning did nothing to reduce my sense of smell to such an extent that I could ignore the wounds of all the men who had experienced the hell of combat. Even though long healed, they always smelled like road kill baking on freshly laid tar in the Oakland sun.

But there was no taste of magic in the room. No flavor of ghosts or other abominations. I'd had reason to worry about such flavors since Tabitha Vance nearly served me as a crumpet at a sex kraken's breakfast. We hide the dead and dying, of course, in retirement homes, hospitals and cemeteries, alleys and dumpsters, psych wards and street graves. But in L.A., youth is god, and shines a light so bright that those who worship it want all evidence of the inevitable locked away. But those caught between worlds? The dead who do not die, the phantoms who find no peace, the in-betweeners who love to chitchat and seem to know me as if I had a neon sigil on my back saying: "Please, Creatures of the Abyss, Tell Me Your Problems!"? They all had largely lain silent since the craziness of the summer, and for that I was grateful.

I sighted what must be my intended seat sitting empty in the front row. A silver-haired major in dress with an Irish chin and razor-burned neck was at the podium, so I had no urge to make my way forward—smiling against the scoffing faces of men who had learned to kill, my vain attempts at mouthing "sorry" being as unwelcome as shit stains on a Gutenberg Bible—while he was speaking.

The major began belting out words that easily cut through the noise from the megaphone mouths of the outside youths, which were already muffled by the hall's walls.

". . . which is why we are recognizing the efforts of Sergeant Cochise Sandoval Hayes," he said, and I bristled at the pronunciation of all of Cactus's name. It had been a fact of life in Korea that no one called him by his Apache or Mexican names—hence his instruction to all of us upon hitting the frigid Chosin Reservoir valley that "so long as your white mouths are under my eyes, you will call me Cactus or I'll give you two language lessons, courtesy of each fist."

". . . on behalf of the Legion, in fundraising support for the widows of our fallen comrades, and for his substantial contribution to the Legion's oral history of both the Italian campaign and Korea. We award him this plaque for volunteering above and beyond the call of duty."

The applause was heavy, which had little to do with Cactus and everything to do with drowning out the faint calls of "baby killers" from outside the thick walls and high ceilings. I used the hand-slaps to walk forward fast and found that the left section was filled with most of the vets. My designated seat was in the "friends and family" section on the right. Cactus must have thought I'd come in civilian outfit. He was right.

My slacks hit the chair before the applause died and Cactus spoke clear and strong as if barking out our morning tasks. "Thank you, Major Armagh. I accept this today not for my efforts, but on behalf of those who have lost their loved ones. The bereaved are casualties as much as any of us. And today I'd like to dedicate the actual award to a special person."

Oh hell. Not me. It can't be me.

"Private Murray Arrows."

Whew, I sighed.

The woman next to me gave me an iced glance that was so disdainful you'd think she'd been born upon Mount Olympus so she could glare down at mere mortals and turn them to stone. The smell of money that came off her was pure Robber Baron Princess perfume and whatever the French were spraying on themselves this fall so they didn't have to smell their piss-covered streets. She wasn't born here, since she wore beige stockings with her cream pumps. She was a Connecticut transfer in tan skirt and sleeveless white blouse showing the kind of trim muscle you get from years of tennis and swimming. Hair a modified Jackie O tribute with a sliver of silver in her deep black locks. Around her bronzed neck was wrapped a gold necklace that could erase most of the national debt. Her disdain was dense enough to churn my guts.

I smiled.

The disdain congealed. And, sad to say, I liked it—until my brain smacked me with the name Cactus had uttered.

I blinked.

Murray Arrows? The name stabbed me in the chest, and I knew I was the one who was screwed.

"Get out of my husband's seat!" hissed the woman, and I hoped to hell this wasn't the widow of Murray Arrows. "It's reserved for him!"

Murray Arrows. Last time I checked, he was dead.

"And to accept the award on Murray's behalf," Cactus said, "his bunk mate, Corporal James Brimstone."

No one clapped. I made my way to the stage and Cactus glared as he put the award, a plaque with gold lettering framed in black, into my hand. "Do what I cannot," he grunted, sub-audible to anyone who hadn't been trained to hang on his every word. He stepped down and took his seat with the vets.

The blond man in the wheelchair nodded, grimly, as if he could feel the pain *I* was in, which made what I was about to say even worse.

The eyes of the soldiers bored into me, and all I could think was that I smelled like applesauce, orange juice, and overripe avocado.

"Uh, hello, everyone. Sorry about the duds, but I lost my formalwear when we demobilized, though if I knew there would be such a great crowd I would have at least worn green instead of brown and orange, which to all you fine men must look like camo for a pumpkin patch."

Silence.

Sigh. I was never one for speeches. "As Cactus . . . Sergeant Hayes noted, I served with Murray in Korea."

My stomach sank.

I wasn't sure if I was supposed to talk about Murray's death or his informal career as a historian. Because the last thing I wanted to do was discuss his life in the barracks. Arrows was a racist son of a bitch and viewed everything through the lens of the antebellum South. For instance, Cactus was a "warrior Injun," a phrase that earned him two black eyes. Talking with Arrows was useless since, like most amateur historians, he believed his volume of reading meant depth of understanding, and his ignorance of debunked racial theories was covered up by his refrain of "you've been co-opted." All of which made the death of Murray Arrows at Chosin that much uglier: his burp gun blasting so loud it deafened his shouting, "Die, you commie gook bastards!" before he was overwhelmed buying our platoon time to cross a frozen stream to find deeper cover to hold off the human wave of horror that was the Chinese army. Cactus wouldn't say a good word about him, because to lie that much would make him less of a man. But me? I was already a worm.

My silence insulted the crowd. So, I coughed. The beauty in the front row clenched her teeth so hard it would have turned pearls to dust.

"To his family," I said, "I can say this without any trace of dishonesty—" which sounded like shit as soon as I said it "—that Murray Arrows—" a hateful, self-righteous putz "—died saving my life and the lives of many soldiers. Chances are, I would not be here today if not for the last acts of Murray Arrows—" you racist shithook. "Thank you."

The Legion Hall filled with the sickly noise known as a "smattering" of applause.

I bowed, smelling of citrus and berry, then ambled to the

stage steps, passing the wheelchair man in glasses, who gave me his full attention. "Sorry about your friend," he said in a strong voice. Much stronger than mine, and I like to think my baritone can punch above its weight class. "And, please, you can have my seat." He pointed at the one next to the ice queen. He tapped his wheelchair. "I came with my own." He smiled at the self-inflicted joke. I wasn't sure if that took courage or sadism.

I grinned. "Thanks, sir." I offered my hand. "James Brimstone."

He took it and squeezed hard to make sure I knew that, with the exception of his legs, everything in his body was in its prime. For anyone who hadn't been trained in carny hand-torture or raised, as Cactus was, with men whose bodies were weapons of war and labor, such a grip would make them wince. "Alan Carruthers." I winced for his benefit, and he released his iron grip.

"Too kind," I said, nodding, then stepped down as Major Armagh spoke. "Now, our final award."

I took the seat next to the brunette. The platinum wedding band below a sizeable diamond solitaire on her left hand indicated she was Lady Carruthers.

Mrs. Carruthers' legs were clamped together, her posture stiff, and her focus dead on her husband. But every ounce of this woman's aura bathed me with contempt. If I'd read Marx as a street rat in Oakland, I would have said she was my class enemy at birth. But she was a princess of wealth from the rich lands of America, where you're never too thin or rich and you pay other people to make your life easier.

The Irish major belted on. "Private Alan Carruthers not only served his country bravely overseas, including being awarded the Purple Heart and Bronze Star," neither of which Alan wore, "but since his return and recovery, has led the charge for assisting wounded veterans of our nation's foreign wars with medical support from outreach programs created by Carruthers and Carruthers."

C and C? *C & C Pharmaceutical*? The drug giant, whose jingles for Relax aspirin burrowed into your ears and laid eggs that hatched while you were out and about, only to find yourself humming, "When pain begins to throb, and your patience is robbed, there's no time to delay! Take command of your day! With C & C—Relax!"

Ice Princess clutched her cream leather purse with a well-manicured hand.

"Alan has been instrumental in the success of the outreach program, visiting members who have since moved throughout California, and made sure that no stone was left unturned in finding them the best possible care on the home front. This is why he is receiving the Outreach Award for 1970."

Everyone clapped, washing the stain of my performance from the room and drowning out the protesting chants.

The chants turned weird. It sounded as if there was a tussle outside. The kind of noise you heard working an attraction tent, a rumble that wasn't the normal scuff of shoes on dirt paths or the swish of denim overalls and chinos: grunts and shoves sounding louder than they were, triggering the fear in the back of every carny's neck that someone would belt out a "Hey, rube!"—the Armageddon Call to Arms for those in the circuit to put up their dukes against the marks from civvie street.

"Thank you, everyone," Alan said. I kept my head straight and focused, lest his wife turn me to ice with one disdainful glare. "I'm accepting this on behalf of myself and my brother, Foster, who couldn't be here today, but wanted me to express his gratitude. If I am the wheels of the outreach program, Foster is the driver, and we're both honored to receive this award."

"Hey!" someone yelled from outside.

A pregnant second of silence followed before my reflexes jerked my head around.

A brick crashed through the high windows, shattering glass

over the back row. The people there scattered. Soldiers aged from twenty to eighty were on their feet, heading for the door with angry fists, but a dark spheroid came through the broken window. Before we could think, there was a chorus of a single word:

"GRENADE!"

4

ARMY-TRAINED REFLEXES MOVED FASTER THAN my active mind. I grabbed Alan Carruthers's wife in a bear hug, running hard from the predicted drop zone of the grenade. She screamed "No!" in my ear before I dived to the ground and pinned her to the floor, covering her with my male sprawl as I counted, *three, two—*

BANG!

The air sizzled with shrapnel, sounding like live blenders flying around the room. I hugged Alan's wife close, hands pinned under my chest. Every fiber of my body was itching to reach for a rifle I didn't have to return fire. My lungs crackled as I took in a huff, then I felt lines of pain perforating my back, and heard cries of horror around me.

I pulled myself off of Mrs. Carruthers. Her eyes were wide, hands shaking. "Hey!" I said, hard and firm. "Listen! We have to get you out. Can you walk?"

She didn't respond.

I flicked the bridge of her nose.

Her disgust with me returned while fresh pain and wetness drizzled down my back. "You!"

"That's better."

Her eyes shifted to what was behind me. "Oh god."

I turned.

All the vets were scrambled on the ground, but you could see the red-splashed epicenter. At the edge were the chairs we'd been sitting on, ripped by shrapnel.

"You . . . you saved me," she said.

I turned back. "Yeah, now do me a favor and keep living."

Up on the stage, Alan held his plaque. Shrapnel was an inch deep in his legs. Blood trickled down his face. "You okay?" I yelled over the groans of the dying.

He nodded, then dropped the plaque; it was studded with shrapnel that would have torn into his chest or neck.

Hazy, adrenaline blazing, I got up, yanked the woman from the floor. "Both of you, get out the back. Now!" I ran toward the horror.

Dead center was Cactus. Back shredded, body shaking, covering some old timer with liver spots and a ghostly countenance.

"Cactus!" I yelled.

"Brimstone!" he shouted back in a voice colder than a dead nun's heart. "Get the bastard, Brimstone! Now!"

I looked to the stage. Alan's wife had made it to her husband. She nodded at me, so I ran for the door. If the shithook who had wounded these men was out there, he would not find my backside.

My shoulder smashed the door open, but outside my lungs burned. The sea of hair and faces swirled with screams. I had no patience for their chaos. Words raced through my mind, as they always did when I caught a bullet.

Time for joyriding.

Concentrating on William Blake's poetic refrain—*Tyger*

Tyger, burning bright!—I felt the world become quicksand as my mind and body slid into each other and then—*crack!*

I entered a state of Transcendental Consciousness, what I called a joyride. The world slowed for a heartbeat, but I moved at my own pace, shoving, snaking, darting through the plaid flannel and tan leather head bands, the placards and bright-colored beads, moving fast as Kato on *The Green Hornet*, but knowing I'd pay a full and heavy price when I eventually got out of this dangerous Zen state.

Among the throng, the faces hadn't changed, but some had vanished, the crowd spreading out like a secondary ring of impact from the grenade.

The gentle giant with the ticking hand? He was gone. As well as the kids with skateboards. The angry lady with dark glasses was screaming, running toward the parking lot.

There was a motorcycle thirty yards away. Two bodies mounted on the chopper. Big. The arm of the one in the rear was thick and meaty, but I wasn't sure whether it was the calm blond or the manic beast I'd seen earlier. I ran while the world waltzed in molasses, gunning for the bike. I noted the motorheads had no patches, no insignia, not even poorly stitched nametags . . . and bikers were proud of their colors. Even for a hit and run.

I'd cut half the distance before agony flooded my brain. Joyriding this long was close to lethal. One stride, and the slowed cries behind me mangled the air while the driver of the hog revved his clutch, which, while joyriding, sounded like a long, wet fart.

Another big step and the world blurred. I was cutting the distance between me and the monsters who threw that grenade, but the colors of life began to melt and sponge around me. One more step, just two arm-reaches away from them, and reality fluttered through me like spoiled film running wild and melting from the projector until there was nothing onscreen but a blinding white.

Reality slapped back and hit me so hard I tripped over my own wingtips, crumpling to the ground with both nostrils gushing blood like a ruptured oil tanker. Face hit asphalt.

The screech of the hog's wheels burning rubber and ghostly exhaust pounded my face as I reached out into the smoke and grabbed nothing. The hog hit Slauson and bolted beyond my anger.

All my systems went numb.

The air was fresh with screams. My vision flooded with a darkness that stretched time like a hippo eating saltwater taffy.

I thought of Chosin. Ice filled my veins, then the shaking started. Behind me, men were holding their guts in with their own hands; medics were coming but would be too late. Cactus was the toughest thing I'd seen on two legs in the mortal world, but even an Apache warrior-Mexican guerrilla would hit walls they could not climb, fight battles they could not win. As my own pain switched to the "on" position, my ass hissed in anguish and my head pounded with the steady grind of a Soviet tank factory. My stomach churned at the cowardice of what had happened. The irony of it. Peaceniks throwing a grenade at veterans. L.A. was more vicious and deranged by the second.

Then, intense flavor bit my tongue. Sour and shimmering. My mouth involuntarily spat out the taste's name. "Magic."

Slick, sick, no-bullshit, premium-grade arcana. I staggered back up onto my feet and tried to rub the supernatural tang off with the back of my hand, but it clung to my lip.

A dark image fluttered before me.

A flower. It fell to the earth, soundless beneath the screams of the wounded and cries of the bystanders, petals as thin as bee's wings and supple as a harpist's fingers. Nine petals, one for each head of the demon dragon whom its gardeners worshipped— symbol of the dreaded Tiamat.

A single dollop of blood dropped from my nose. It raced with the flower, which won by some mystic means.

At my feet lay a Black Lotus of Cimmeria. Extinct for three thousand years.

"Well," said a voice as gravely as old concrete and familiar as a slap. "What a goddamn surprise. Jimmy Brimstone is present at another goddamn massacre."

5

THE VOICE POKED MY SPLEEN LIKE A TRUNCHEON.

I turned and slid my shoe over the lotus, weight on my heel, careful not to crush something rarer than a gryphon's feather or remorse from LAPD.

He wasn't in plainclothes, but instead dressed like a cheap PI on a pulp novel's shitty cover, complete with a stained beige raincoat that had been his father's back in his salesman days in Oakland. Richard Dixon stood before me while the same fire trucks and ambulances that had been sent to the rocket-car disaster switched to help a horror far worse. Cigarette cocked on his left ear, his short blond hair was pure football coach. "What happened, Jimmy?"

"Made detective, Dicky?"

"Surprised?"

"Nope. You were the smart one in the neighborhood. Which is why it was such a shock you became a cop."

"Smart mouth and a dumb ass. You've been a trouble magnet since Oakland Tech. Tell me what you know."

"Someone threw a grenade in the vet hall," I said. "My friend Cactus took the worst of it."

"He the Indian?"

"If any of the Apache Nations are near Calcutta."

"Christ, you know what I mean, Jimmy."

"You mean you think he's a no-good Indian, Dicky."

Dixon plucked his cigarette. "Tell me details."

A question was jarred out of my head. "Why would LAPD send a homicide detective to a protest site where things got ugly?"

Dixon tucked the cigarette into the right corner of his mouth. "Attacking vets is bad news for the department because it's bad headlines for Mayor Yorty."

"Can't have friends of Nixon looking soft on the peaceniks."

"Ain't nothing soft about a grenade tossed into a room of old men," Dixon fired back, then snapped out a Zippo and lit his cigarette.

"How is Traveling Sam doing, by the way? Starting to think he doesn't like old L.A. that much. Too busy playing the banjo on *The Tonight Show*."

"Yeah, yeah, he's a hell of a guy. Now stick to the point."

"Oh, about why you're out here? A new detective trying to make his name, slumming around a bunch of vets painted red by some unknown assailant. You got here awful quick."

"Stop playing connect the dots in the air, Jimmy. You're no detective. Just an idiot who bought a matchbook license for playing private dick—and you can best believe if you screw with me I'll make sure you're not licensed to eat the peanuts out of my shit."

Good thing I only had a PI certificate from a matchbook authority off the mainland. "Then give me one more dot and I'll tell you everything I saw."

Dixon snickered.

"How many other cases are there?" I asked. The dried blood on my back had started to itch.

Wind rustled Dixon's tiny hairs. "Don't know what you mean."

"Lousy liar, Dicky, just like the president. How many other cases of vets getting assaulted?"

"You're barking up the wrong—"

My foot remained a fraction of an inch above the lotus and I prayed to old gods that I would not crush it. "How many? Or I'll be on my merry way."

Dixon blew out a stream of smoke that covered his face.

"Two. In June, a veteran's picnic in Compton was 'interrupted' by explosions. Mailbox bombs. All the houses ringed around the park, like mortar shells. No injuries. But everyone was scared. Following month, a treasurer for one of the local legions was mugged and beaten so bad his face went from purple to black. Died of his injuries. And now a massacre." Two yellowed fingers plucked the smoke from his mouth. "That's escalation, those fairies—"

"Fairies?" I then realized he wasn't talking about the nastiest critters in the nethers, pound for pound. "Oh, the peaceniks out front?"

"You think they're so innocent," Dixon said. "Tell me what you know. Like what kind of vehicles took them away. No one already in custody will say a goddamn word to us."

"Yeah, since the Watts riots, it's almost as if you guys aren't taken seriously."

"Don't talk about Watts. This ain't about race."

"Funny how it's only white cats like us that ever say that."

He stepped closer. To many men, Richard Dixon would be an intimidating two hundred and twenty pounds of Oakland steel and attitude, but I'd seen him shit his pants when chased by an out-of-work longshoreman who wanted our milk money. Still, I admired the bastard's conviction. "What do you know?"

"It was a frag grenade. Something more modern than I've used. Got shards in my rump if you need them."

"Jesus," Dixon said, pointing to an ambulance in the parking lot. "Get some medical attention."

If I did, I'd lose the Black Lotus under my suspended sole. And something told me that a three-thousand-year-old flower might be a clue worthy of holding on to. "I'm standing under my own power, most of those guys can't. Let them have first dibs." Then I summed up the points I was willing to share with him: there were protesters, there was an award ceremony, someone threw a brick to break the window, a grenade dropped, I tackled a woman, took shrapnel in the rump, and then ran out here when Cactus ordered I find the monsters who did this.

Nothing about the gentle giant with the ticking hand and the rabid biker, or the handful of kids with skateboards who had vanished before I started joyriding. Nothing about the magic underfoot.

"And then?" Dixon said. His notepad was crinkled, black and white.

"And then I started looking for anyone who might be responsible."

Dixon glared.

"And I tripped on my own feet and boom, you appeared like a genie."

"The woman you covered?"

"Wife of one of the vets."

"These people have names?"

"Yeah, Carruthers." He kept talking notes, but his jowls shifted slightly. Good on Dixon for trying to hide his "tell," but I'd been reading card players and scamming marks longer than he'd been a member of The Thin Blue Line. I wasn't as good a lie detector as Edgar, but he had trained me to con and see cons in every walk of life. *Most of the sheep of this world are liars who, at once, think themselves cleverer than all, and also want to be caught and punished by Mummy and Daddy.* I shivered, hating how much of Edgar was still with me, denying me the total freedom I'd hoped faking his death would provide.

Dixon clearly didn't want me to know who they were, and playing dumb is so much easier when your interrogator holds you in contempt . . . and can't rip your fingernails or eyelids off in public without getting fired. "What about who you were running after here?"

"Nothing. All the activity I saw was at the transformer station that looked like it got nuked. Could that be the same people as the mailbox bombers?" I said and waited.

Dixon shrugged as if he couldn't give a shit. "That's for the beat squad. I'll look into it, though." Good. He didn't know yours truly was responsible. Not yet, anywho. "Anything else?"

There wasn't. But if I moved with his eyes on me I'd never get the Black Lotus from underfoot. He needed to leave of his own accord. Time for the simple art of deception and distraction. "Dicky, I've got shrapnel in my tush, a five-alarm headache from a grenade, and my best friend is keeping death's door open with one toe. Worse, my new wingtips are ruined and—goddamn laces." I kneeled, the storm of sick in my guts rolling with the fast drop, which surely made me look even more haggard. Dixon's gaze followed me down as my peripheral vision caught sight of Alan Carruthers and his wife beside the ambulance. I yanked my laces loose with frustration. "What about the guy in the wheelchair?"

Dixon turned, but not as fast my hands, which had been shuffling decks and rolling coins since we were rolling our own smokes outside the Oakland Public Library. I cup-palmed the ancient petals as soft as I could, but they still bit my skin like razors.

"Him? Just some vet who served his country." I was amazed at how poorly Dixon lied. He must know. "God, what a shitpile. Starting to think we should pull a Canada. Those Mounties are sending troops into that French capital of theirs to catch a bunch of ratbag terrorists. I don't like their prime minister much, but at least he has guts to get things done."

The newspapers had been running banner headlines about those actions from our friends to the north. Some French separatist group had kidnapped a couple of politicians and were now on the run. "I heard. Trudeau just declared Baby's First Martial Law. No habeas corpus. No reasonable doubt. Pick up anyone who looks guilty. If that's your bag, Dicky, why not follow the Soviet model, say, Hungary in fifty-six? Perhaps Prague sixty-eight?"

Slow as a last kiss, Dixon turned to me, face a shade paler than scarlet. "Don't even try to pull that liberal shit on me. You calling me a KGB thug? On my salary? Trying to find who blasted your friend into pieces? You think I'm still some ignorant runt from Oakland who joined the PD because I got mommy issues and need to beat people up because my old man beat her and I couldn't stop it? You think, for one second, that I ain't actually a cop because I want to *help* people, that I'm just a goon squad captain with a couple more letters near his name because I go to the library? How fucking dare you toss that commie shit my way, when I'm hunting for the guys who did this to not only those vets, but their wives and children, and even hurt those protestors, who, by the way, I think are cowards and idiots and full of shit but are *still* my responsibility." He exhaled so hard I thought I saw steam. "You get to call me these things, Jimmy, because you pretend to be doing my job. Only you do it alone, unaccountable, and can cast aspersions on me from the safety of your privileged position. Now fuck off. I'm sick of listening to your smarmy act. Go check on your Apache buddy, get the scrap out of your backside, and let the professionals get to goddamn work."

For a fifth of a fifth of moment, I was stunned, but played it off as if this was the kind of reaction I expected and gave a smug sneer in return before I let my shoes march toward the ambulances.

Dixon's words slapped my back.

"Just remember, Jimmy. You're in my house now. Best tread light. Especially in those wingtips, especially when they magically un-tie themselves." This war of words ended with Dix taking a victory lap, and me getting schooled on underestimating Detective R. Dixon—and how easy it is to do that with people that you hate. A temptation I've used to my own advantage more times than a rube loses his pennies at a five-and-dime.

I passed the paddy wagon, the back doors open as they hustled in another hippie, two lines of scraggly kids already inside, all of them shouting with hands restrained behind their back.

"This is a set up!"

"Fucking pigs fixed us!"

"I want my lawyer!"

The doors slammed. But the muffled voices still punched through as I passed them by and found myself in the circle of cops and medics. Reporters would be next, so I had to get busy quick. Last thing I needed was some crime-beat nobody shadowing my every move.

"James?" Alan said. He waved me over and I approached him and his wife, who was dabbing his face with alcohol and cotton, a first aid kit sitting on his lap. He sat next to an ambulance with its doors open wide, parked at the entry of the hall so they could ferry out the wounded. They'd leave the dead for the cops and, eventually, the morgue.

"Can someone help me get the scrap out of my keister?"

A tough old tank of a woman with face gaunt and monstrous stalked toward me, bandage and scissors clamped in her hand. "Let's see the damage, hero."

I presented my rear. "OW!"

"Stand still, princess. Now, drop your pants so I can bandage the boo-boo."

I did, but before I could cover the awkward silence by saying something clever, she grunted. "Rookie, I served in Sicily before joining the Peace Corps. Save the smooth talk for someone who gives a shit. Now stand still or so help me I'll nail this bandage in with a hammer."

"Yes, ma'am."

"Good."

Seconds later she was done, my pants were up, and she'd returned to her buddies in the ambulance pool, laughing at what I can only presume was my pathetic nature. "Just hold your ass!" she said over the laughter. "Bleeding will stop soon."

Outside of some cuts to the face and bandages on his numb legs, Alan looked the same. His wife's countenance, however, was altered—and strangely. Still carried the stiff and sharp presence of a former Connecticut debutante, but with runs in her stockings and disheveled hair, she looked like she'd finished filming a "roughie."

"You two okay?"

"Yes," Alan said, face taut. "Thanks to you. I . . . can't thank you enough for saving Veronica's life." For the second time today, a man with more courage and who'd faced more challenges than I had stuck out his hand and offered me a sign of respect, while I inhaled the scent of his wife's freshly spritzed perfume without making eye contact. I took his hand, and again felt his iron-clad grip.

"Some reflexes never die," I said, and instantly the iron turned to clay as Alan drew back his hand. I'd just told a man who could not save his wife that what I'd done was something all of us could do. "What I mean to say is—"

He waved away my awkward retraction. "I'm grateful, James."

"Yes," Veronica said, bringing her eyes up to meet mine. The ice had melted in those brown orbs, as had the serrated edge in her voice. "So grateful. I had no idea you were a veteran."

"Given the relaxed nature of my attire, I don't blame you. I was running late and god, I'm just glad I was able to make it."

"Me too," Veronica said. "James, your hand is bleeding."

Wounded by a petal, not a grenade. I quickly shoved the Black Lotus in my pocket. "Could have sworn I had a handkerchief." I removed my bloody hand and Veronica dropped to her knees, stretching her ripped stockings, and grabbed a bandage from the first aid kit before rising back up in a single, well-executed motion from someone who probably visited Montauk and had finishing lessons and probably kissed a girl in her college days, just so she had material for her class on short stories inspired by John Cheever. "Give me your hand."

"What? It's just dried paint from the horror show," I said.

"Let her help," Alan said. "It makes her feel useful."

She fired a look back at him that would have frozen gasoline. "We can all do our bit."

I stuck out my right and she took it. Almond-shaped nails on hands that were as delicate as the pink of her nail polish, but strong. My callus, the healed bullet mark in the dead of my palm, was an ugly rock cradled by her slender fingers. And I could almost hear her wondering, based on what she was now seeing, who the hell I was. She looked up. I quickly gave Alan all my focus because Veronica was now undressing me with her eyes right in front of her crippled husband.

"You okay, Alan?"

He nodded. "I was out of the kill zone, and the nicks I took didn't cut anything I was using." He smiled against the irony. "Cactus is still inside. They're moving him now. Sent in more medics than they know what to do with. They're being real gentle—"

A war cry that skinned a year off my life blasted from the building's doors.

Into the maw, my nose filled with the iron sharpness of fresh blood, bright and wet. I ran into a battleground nightmare, as two ambulance attendants hit the ground from one massive hammer strike. Cactus was sitting bolt upright on a gurney, streaked in red, dress uniform shredded, hair wild. There was only one thing animating his eyes: the warrior spirit of the Apache.

"Subdue him!" a medic screamed before eating a fist.

"Bad idea!" I yelled.

Five ambulance attendants and one plainclothes cop were slipping across the bloodied floor, dodging Cactus's bricklike fists as they protected him from the scourge of the white man who had taken his people and brutalized their elders and women and children, tried to break them from their past and stick them in the all-American blender so they could not resist what Uncle Sam and Company had to offer. The man before us had endured spits, fists, sticks, and guns on three continents—and come back to become a success despite the white man's hate by using the white man's weaknesses against him. Economic guerrilla warfare that would have done his family proud.

Of course, that didn't soften the blows he threw, one after the other, dropping the descendants of Custer and Cooke one by one. In the growl and froth of his mouth you could also tell this was the lineage of his Mexican roots, of Pancho Villa and Emiliano Zapata and their cadre causing havoc for maximum impact, of fighting giants with a smile, knowing they will lose and still charging into the fray.

On my best day, I might be able to flip Cactus on his back, giving me enough time to run the hell out of Dodge and take the first ticket to the Black Hole of Calcutta and hope he never finds me.

On Cactus's last day, which might very well be now, no one man could stop him without a bullet.

So, I would have to go with Plan C.

"Cactus!" I yelled as I approached the ring of blood and fallen medics.

He had one in his hand, held up off the ground, his teeth

bared and eyes so narrow you couldn't wedge them open with a dime.

"Cactus, this is Private Brimstone! Reporting!"

He snarled. Which, all things considered, was a good sign.

"We need an evac, Sarge! Ridgeway bought Easy Company time to cross the Chosin. They got artillery on this position, but we have to move. Now!"

The ambulance attendant dropped from his grip. "Brimstone?" Cactus said, wet and red.

"It's coming in hot here, Sarge. I've done the recce and we need out of this kill zone before they light it up."

"Brimstone, you contrarian shitbird." He lurched forward. "I can't . . . Brimstone, I can't move my legs!"

"Roger that. On it!" I ran behind him, and when the blond medic tried to stand I dropped an ax kick that gave him a broken nose and a first-class nap. "I got you on the gurney, Cactus," I said.

Then I saw Cactus's back.

Death by a thousand cuts. Blood was leaking out of wounds that should have been far wider than they were . . . until I tasted electric sand . . . magic . . . the kind that leaks between worlds when a warrior is headed toward the other places. Cactus was holding himself between life and death, past and present, and if he didn't get medical help soon, he'd leak into oblivion.

I pushed and Cactus's voice screamed, "Brimstone, you can't push a gurney by yourself, you fucking idiot!" The blood ran fresh . . . as if my lie was coming apart and forcing Cactus's wounds to burst, too. Given his people's religion, beliefs, and more, I asked myself: "What would Coyote do?"

He'd make a lie bigger so that it would hold and change the world.

"Arrows!" I yelled, then kicked another medic, a black-haired fella with two front teeth missing, out of the way.

"Screw you, man!" he yelled as I passed, so I looked at the far-thest guy, a rail-thin fella with glasses and red hair. "Arrows! You racist, no-account shitbag, grab the gurney or when we die I'm coming back to life just to feed your corpse to the Devil himself!" I winked, hoping to soften the blow and keep the con alive and, thank Glycon, the fake god of the ancient world and his love of luck and hijinks, the redhead figured out I meant him and found the mana in himself to stand up and grab the rails of the gurney while the others moaned around us.

"About time!" Cactus yelled. "Now, hustle, you goons! We ain't keeping Ridgeway waiting."

Like some live version of a horror-show rendition of *The Three Stooges*, we hustled our wounded leader through the minefield of blood from old soldiers and new vets, slipping and sliding and holding steady while Cactus chastised us like we were shavetails straight out of Basic.

In the glare of L.A.'s afternoon sun, Cactus came alive. His gooey red fist grabbed my lapels and pulled me close, his breath like death and fire. "Brimstone, you find them. You find the no-good commie bastards who snuck up on us. I don't care if you're out in the mountains for a month eating grubs and dirt. You find them, and you kill them."

I'd been ordered to kill before. By Edgar, my mentor. By Cactus, my NCO. I'd killed to save myself more times than most. I hated it. Every. Time. Because I knew enough about the nether-world to be scared of what happened when we weren't in charge of our fleshbags and brains. I possessed a deeper fear of what happened to those of us who filled those spaces with the spirits of the living, nightmare gods, and creatures of supreme darkness who flitter into our world for shits and giggles to remind us we are not only alone, but also insignificant. I knew the need to kill, but I was damn sure clear the price was almost never worth the cost. But Cactus had saved my life as part of his own code of honor and sense of responsibility to me—a guy he thought so little of he wouldn't want to be seen with me if he was driving his Rolls. Mother had given me life. Cactus had been the only person I'd met who would save it. And he was dying before my eyes.

"I'll do my best."

His fist clenched, and his breath was like dying coals. "Chickenshit answer. Kill them, or I will haunt you until the end of time."

"I'll do it." I pressed two more words past the gaps in my teeth, ones I loathed to offer. "I promise."

He nodded, then fell back on the gurney as we closed in on the ambulance where Alan and Veronica stood. When the redhead pulled Cactus away, I was dragged along. His fist held my lapel in a death grip. When I finally pulled free, my jacket was torn and bloodied.

The doors closed and that fierce taste of magic died. Cactus's people and culture had kept him from crossing over. Now, it was up to Western medicine to patch him back. There was a sick sense of mutation in the idea that made my stomach twist.

"Will he be all right?"

Veronica had walked within flight-or-fight distance and I'd barely noticed. I chalked it up to the fact of being so goddamn close to magic. The taste of the other worlds of this universe could sometimes startle me, which was a great way to leave our world by slipping on the banana peels of the mundane around me.

"James?" Alan's voice shattered the fantasy as he rolled up beside his wife. "Are *you* okay?"

I adjusted my jacket, surprised the rip was so minimal. The pattern even disguised most of the bloodstains. Quality polyester. "No. I'm not. Somebody just tried to ace my friend and killed or injured a bunch of old men and women. Nothing about this is okay."

And nothing made sense. It was a mess. Jagged pieces. One biker. Peaceniks with grenades. Strange kids with skateboards.

Big men who vanished. A rise in violence against soldiers and veterans. Blaming the longhairs. But the trail seemed to go to bikers. This was strange. Just like the Black Lotus in my pocket.

"James," Alan said again, and his voice was strong. "Cactus mentioned you were a private investigator."

I smiled. "He did?"

"Well," Alan grinned. "He said you were just starting out."

That was code for "stunk up the joint" when it came to my skills, at least compared to a guy who held tracking as a sacred art and was among the most feared members of the Counter Intelligence Corps. "That was kind of him."

"This was a senseless act, and if those who are responsible are left to roam, we'll never get justice." He reached into his pocket and pulled out a checkbook and a black pen with a gold circle around the body. It was engraved with the initials *AJC*. He wrote as he spoke. "I'd like to hire you on retainer. I want you to find the man who did this. And I want to give you all the resources you'll need."

He tore off the check, handed it to me.

I let it hang.

That check was a link in a chain to the rich, the mighty, the powerful. The people I didn't serve. The people whom Edgar wined and dined and plotted with, the power brokers and senior operators of avarice who made the conditions for a rotting underclass whom they played like pawns and worse.

Alan was not a bad guy at all. Everything I'd seen or heard seemed to say the opposite. But he was man of wealth and influence and had likely been trained at prep school and elite Ivy League trust-fund vacation schools to view a little guy from Oakland like me as a tool, a servant, a serf without land and a slave without chains.

I tried not to hate Alan. But Veronica's eyes were hungry for me to take the check. To be beholden.

I raised both my hands. "Thanks, Alan. I appreciate it. But I'm afraid I've already been hired for this case." I reached into my inside pocket and took out one of the five business cards Starla had made me when she wasn't on stage at the Thump & Grind Burlesque Club, which housed my office and apartment. She wrote out the details in an art-deco style:

ODD JOB SQUAD DETECTIVE AGENCY:
NO CASE TOO WEIRD.
J. Brimstone, Founder and Lead Investigator.

Alan pocketed the check and took the card. I hated to make him feel small in front of his wife for the second time that day, but I needed to let these two leaders of today and tomorrow know I wasn't their toy. "I'd like to enlist your aid in my investigation. You know the veteran scene. These old soldiers trust you. All the places you canvassed makes you the right man to ask questions. About anything strange. About anything out of the ordinary."

"Like hippies assaulting our veterans?" Veronica said, voice as smooth as aged brandy.

"That's one angle I'm trying to square," I said. "But we don't know what happened. And I plan to find out."

"You mean hunting through the longhairs?" Veronica said with the same tone of condescension.

"Why?" I asked. "Do you have enemies among the peaceniks?"

She smirked. "More like occult dropouts than drugged-out communist sympathizers. Right, Alan?"

Alan held my card in his lap. "I hardly see how this is relevant."

"It is now," I said. "Alan?"

"Veronica is just being jealous."

"Ha!" Her arms crossed with practiced power. She daggered one heel down and twisted it in a way I liked. "Of what? A runaway suburban nobody?"

"Just because Lorraine wasn't from our circles didn't make her a nobody," Alan said with the soft strength of a man trying to control an anger that made him uncomfortable.

"I believe she goes by 'Rain' now," Veronica said to me. "Be on the lookout for a dirty blonde who puts out and fears soap."

"That's enough!" Alan slammed his first into his dead leg. "She has nothing to do with this."

"Than what *does* she have to do with?" I said. "Alan, if she is any way connected to what happened today—"

He shook his head, then relaxed his fist before looking up at me. "Veronica? Can you give us a minute?"

"To discuss that wench? Happy to be absent," she said, and made sure her heels hit the ground hard with each step she took toward an ambulance.

"As bad as that was," Alan said, "it would have been worse if she stayed."

"A little pain now, a lot less pain later? I know that math, Alan. Now, about Rain?"

"Veronica hates her because . . . well, it's hard to say without sounding stupid."

"From what you both shared, I suppose Rain didn't join you all at the cotillions."

He smirked. "I hate it, James. The arrogance. The snobbery. The elitism. That's why I liked Lorraine."

I stifled a reaction I often have with the rich—gagging when I hear of their adventures slumming with their societal "inferiors." But Alan wasn't my enemy, not today.

"Rain's a local girl?"

"From Modesto." Hardly bragging rights, but, if I was being fair, Alan would be an incredible catch for someone trying to escape the long shadows of a desert town. "She was living in Long Beach, where her friends lived. I met her at an anti-war rally."

"Ah," I said. "And she took to a man in uniform."

"No," he said, rubbing the knuckles of his right fist in his left hand. "I took to the beautiful peace-and-love gal with dirty-blond hair. Sweetest person I'd ever met." I had no image of comparison beyond a panorama of braless ladies in headbands. My own "aesthetic" was wider than *Playboy*, Marilyn, and Ann-Margaret. Being a road kid with the Electric Magic Circus, where one sees beauty so wild and different that pin-up girls are but one variation on a theme, I had no single vision of beauty. But damn, it was hard to wipe the standard of Veronica from my mind, which made me think this Lorraine was a natural beauty, a desert rose Alan saw and had to pluck.

"So, how did you screw it up?"

He blinked. "What makes you think I screwed it up?"

"Relax, Al. You're among your own tribe. We always screw it up."

He smiled. "It's more like what I wouldn't screw up." The smile twitched. "I'm a modern guy, and I loved Rain, but she had a far more . . . open view of love and marriage than I did back then."

"Love of the free variety?"

He sighed. "It was both ways. I don't want you to think it wasn't both ways. But the idea of another man having her, even if I could have someone else . . . this sounds hopelessly old-fashioned, but I only wanted her. Sounds young and stupid, doesn't it?"

Damn. I was actually starting to like this rich bastard. "She stayed in the Land of Golden Copulations and you signed up?"

His jaw clenched. "Before I got my draft notice. And married Veronica before I shipped out. Her family, the Weathers?" The name hung to allow me time to fill in the blank, but I played ignorant, though I damn well knew the Candy Barons of the West Coast. "They're longtime friends of my family. We'd known each other since childhood and there was always the assumption . . . Well, we were seen as a good fit. I shipped off a week later."

Old story, going to war to avoid the pain of love. Alan really was an old soul. And Veronica seemed so hard and prudish that she was the warped mirror image of Rain: controlled, not free; hard, not soft; austere, not easy. And today shook her up hard. "The folks who were here today? The protestors of many colors? Were these Rain's people?"

"They might be. They seemed, I don't know, stranger? Everything in the city seems stranger since I got back."

"Couldn't agree more."

We chatted more about Rain's appearance. Her one identifying mark: a missing canine tooth in the right side of her mouth. "But it made her even prettier."

I grinned. "You still have a soft spot, huh?"

"For our first true love, don't we all?"

Izzy came to my mind like a hot blast of jungle air, my beautiful Filipina who had killed more fascists by the time she could legally drink than most American GIs, and who had kicked away my proposal as the childish whim of the young of heart before vanishing into America. "Veronica's not a fan?"

"Of anything," he chortled. "I'm being rude. Veronica has every right to her feelings."

"So, you didn't invite Rain here? She didn't know you were going to be here?"

"I haven't had any contact with her since I . . . came back. Besides, her group wasn't radical. Except about sex, and, well, skateboarding." He started laughing. "Can you believe that? What's next, a gang of kids on mopeds? Armed with sticks?"

I logged the detail in the honeycombs of my mind, filed under "skateboards," a category with nothing else in it, and carried on. "This group have a name?"

He closed his eyes, searching, then muttered. "Tumbledown. They had a ratty crashpad in Dogtown on the border of Santa Monica and Venice Beach called Tumbledown. They always rode along the Boardwalk, picking up pot and trying to recruit people to the cause."

"What cause was that?"

The approaching sound of Veronica's tip-taps tickled my spine.

"None that I saw or knew," he said. "Beside getting their founder laid." Veronica closed in as Alan added, "Blond asshole called Sonny Ray."

"Alan, Foster sent the car," Veronica said, placing her hands on the handles of his wheelchair. He didn't turn to look at her.

A black limo pulled into the still-chaotic Legion Hall parking lot and took the space that had last held the ambulance that carted away Cactus. A hulking fellow emerged from the driver's side, walked around the car, and opened a back door with ticktock precision, then moved toward us. Framed like a linebacker, it was clear he was security, driver, and a spare pair of arms for his disabled patron. "Are you ready to go, Mr. Carruthers?" he said without a trace of urgency.

"Give us a moment, Dexter," Veronica said. Like a dutiful dog that knows it will get a snack or smack if it doesn't follow doctrine, Dexter turned around and waited by the car like a Beefeater guarding the Tower of London.

"We can't thank you enough, James," Veronica said, enjoying the chew of my name on her lip. "I'm sure Alan will help with your investigation, but we have another engagement."

I didn't exactly ignore her, but it was obvious my attention was solely on her husband. "Please, see what you can gather from the vets and their families, Alan. Call me as soon as you have anything that seems out of the ordinary, no matter how insignificant." I considered the Black Lotus in my pocket. "Even the smallest thing can mean everything."

"You got it," Alan said. "Be safe."

Veronica pushed his chair toward the limo. "Take care," she said, letting her eyes linger on mine.

Dexter hoisted Alan out of his wheelchair like a ventriloquist lifting his dummy into a trunk, legs hanging limp as wet noodles, and gently deposited him in the back seat. Veronica rounded the back of the car and looked at me, lips pursed, then breathlessly open as she mouthed, "Call me."

The Carruthers pulled away from the mess of the massacre and I realized I was now working pro bono to find the shithooks who'd brutalized good men for no good reason . . . and my only clues were a sex gang in Dogtown and the Black Lotus in my pocket.

It was time to hit the Boardwalk, so I turned to the lot where I'd parked Lilith before the madness began, hoping the tear in my tush wasn't fatal . . . when my guts sank beneath the last dungeon of hell.

Lilith was gone.

6

I SAT AT THE BACK OF THE 108 MARINA DEL REY BUS, heading south, my butt wound itching as I played with the little green ring on my right index finger, a throwaway piece of flash from my carny days that always felt good when things went bad. The afternoon ride was filled with a mix of people and smells. Old black women heading to choir practice, discussing Psalms and smelling of sweet perfume. Farther down the aisle, a handful of Mexican construction workers clutched the reins overhead and shared the sweat of a hard day's labor with the rest of us while they spoke in Spanish about their sons' soccer games and if they were going to a union meeting. Hands hardened to thick leather gripped the handrails and held lunch pails that had held large meals for rough work under the sun. Near the middle of the bus, a couple of black teens were whispering to each other about whatever secret adventures were on for the day.

The public transit system of Los Angeles has long been the envy of no one. Or at least no one who has ever taken bus, rail, or street car, but that had nothing to do with the people who needed it. It was another way to make reaching the next economic rung difficult. When your daily commute for a ten-hour job was two hours each way, trying to make your life better was like running uphill on quicksand. L.A. was car country. A car was more than transportation, it was possibility with chrome trim.

And a car was something I did not currently have. Because someone had stolen Lilith.

Someone who would have to pay. Just not now.

She was gone, but perhaps recoverable. I tried not to think too much about Lilith. I needed to concentrate on finding who on this astral plane would target a bunch of veterans, or, maybe, a specific veteran.

"Ladera Heights," said the driver, a red-faced Scandinavian with thin lips and deep pit stains. The bus stopped. The choir ladies on my left stood and headed toward the side door.

"Afternoon," I said.

"Afternoon," they responded with varying levels of enthusiasm, each one looking like respect incarnate, but wary of a kind remark from a scruffy-looking white man. I could not blame them. They descended the steps. My thoughts ascended.

Cactus had enemies, of course. He was security at a casino. He'd pissed off more than one member of our platoon with, well, being in command, even if he suffered in the mountains and basins with us. Most of the WWII fellows could have enemies, too, because being a soldier didn't mean you were a hero. But the highest value target for a hit was Alan Carruthers, a Vietnam volunteer and millionaire heir. And yet, the assault was so wild and unfocused you'd think it had been planned for three months by the Gang Who Couldn't Shoot Straight.

"I have the toll!"

His voice was rich with the street, cigarette damage, and screaming for your life. The grace of the black women was soon replaced by a gray nightmare. At the front of the bus stood a dirty white dude, six feet straight up, hair and beard wild and battle-ship gray, wearing a once-brown poncho aged to the color of burnt tobacco. He placed each of his coins in the box, muttering as they clinked. I couldn't help but think of Charon and the River Styx as the gray eminence of the gutter turned to the back of the bus . . . and the stink of him rose to full volume. Dried urine, old and sharp, flecks of feces for good measure, and the deeper moist tang of someone whose open sores were leaking onto their clothes.

Knees were pulled in and faces averted as he walked to the back of the bus.

He gazed from side to side as if to part the commuters, Moses of the Metro, leading no one out of bondage but looking like he'd been wandering the streets since the Spanish called it home.

Working with carnies, you learn how to treat people differ-ent than in civilized society. I had heard every possible stripe of racist, sexist, degrading, and debilitating venom come out of the mouths of people who looked far better than this lost soul. While training me to be a stick—the "local" who would challenge the pros—for Hercules and the other circus wrestlers, Dr. Fuji once told me that kindness must always be your first attempt, since "everyone is fighting secret battles." Edgar's approach was a tad different: "All people are tools or fools unless proven otherwise." Me? I needed cause to be a shithook.

Thus, the partition of disgusted faces along both sides of the bus didn't really register with me. I'd smelled worse, seen filthier, and didn't judge this lost soul whose story I couldn't know. But as he strutted closer, I felt antsy.

I closed my mouth and rolled my tongue. The flavor of this sad man was hard to pin down . . . magic? If so, it was the barest of morsels, far less than Cactus as he walked between this world and the next.

The man grumbled, grunted, and swayed. Bushy eyebrows twitched. Then he sniffed *me*.

His wrinkled lids rolled with eyes hidden, until a cracked and black iris was revealed to me and, so it seemed, to me alone.

"You . . ." the voice echoed as if from a rusty sewer drain.

"Me?" I said. "Hey, old timer, happy to give my seat." I stood.

"You taste of chaos."

I sat back down. "Uh, groovy. I prefer Beat poetry, man, but whatever floats your boat."

A dark-haired Latino kid in a tri-color T-shirt and brown cords so worn they'd likely been bought by his grandpa pointed and whispered. "That's Weasel. He's always giving sermons on the bus. You know him?"

I shook my head.

"I know you," Weasel said, low and jagged. "They said you'd come."

"Afraid I don't know this 'they' of yours," I said. "I'm a free-lancer."

Weasel shook his fists. "Gods from the cosmos above said a man would come who tasted of chaos, of death and plague and misery, who would walk across the lines of the past and the future and herald the coming Armageddon which will set this world ablaze! And in the maelstrom, as civilization falls, as buildings crumble and snuff out the living, there will be a new age for the strong, as everywhere others will be bound in chains, a period of rapine abuse and slavery that will erase our world like a head wound and in its graveyard a new Babylon of blood and thunder, of rape and mutation, of sundering of all we hold dear, an age of barbarism heralded by the coming of the man with the Black Lotus!"

The barest flicker of recognition caught Weasel's attention.

"Yes! It is you! I am a seeker and before me is the grail of oblivion, as the great god Tiamat births herself from the cosmic ocean womb and casts us into a shadowland of horror the likes of which died in the lost ages of Cimmeria!"

"He's talking about you," the kid whispered, smiling. "Man, I love these rants."

That made one of us.

Weasel loomed above me. "Listen, Herald! Listen as I invoke the call to arms for the damned!"

"I'd rather not," I said. "My name's not 'Harold' and you're disturbing these people's ride."

"There is but one ride, Herald! And it is the final one."

He flung his arms out in a Christ-like posture, his eyes rolled back in his head. The language that rolled out of him predated the birth of the Nazarene by more than two thousand years.

"We are the servants of the demon goddess, of her terror brood, we are born to build on the graves of our enemies and make palaces of bones to worship the rape of creation, we taste the blood and death and crave to suckle more before the fires of our burning die out in a chorus of the damned! Let the days of blood and sword rise! Let the magic of ruin transform our world into a new Babylon, fit for the end of time! And the sins of the fathers will be bled dry by the sons! And Babylon will welcome us home!"

Weasel ranted and shook with the lost language of Babylon rolling off his lips as easily as English from the queen's tongue. Lost in his exultations, he didn't notice when a vial fell from his poncho. But as it rolled to my wingtip's toe, its belly full of rattling pills, Weasel stopped raving and tracked the sound. The prescription stopped, hidden by my shoe.

"No! That's mine!"

Doing a little trick best done with juggling pins, I flicked the bottle with my toe into my lap. Weasel's sunburned hands reached for its afterimage, but the vial was already safe in my hand.

He retreated, but barely. "Give it back!"

"Not until you tell me where you learned that language. It certainly wasn't The Strip."

"I am a seer!" he said, desperate, and everyone looked at us as if we'd started performing an off-off Broadway play. "I must have visions to keep out the nightmares."

Weasel was a desperate critter and it felt bad to push him, but he'd made a correlation between me, the Black Lotus, and the world of ancient Babylon. He was connected.

"Who taught you those words?"

Weasel's split lips pursed. "I swore an oath!"

"Hey," the kid said. "Give the guy his medicine!"

"Throw the old guy off the bus," a black teen said. "I think he crapped his diaper."

"Why don't I throw *you* off," said an old lady in pressed pink polyester slacks and a floral blouse.

"Silence!" Weasel said. "Give back what is mine, Herald, or I will call upon my gods to set horrors loose upon you!"

I tossed the bottle to him, but I could see the label as it spun through the air. Faded, it was hard to make out what the prescription was for, and Weasel's name, though in bolder black letters, had been intentionally scraped away.

Damn it.

Weasel snatched the meds and shoved them into the folds of his gray mess. "You bring death, Herald. When the masters arrive, you will be the first they devour under a blood-red sun."

That's when I caught it. On his right wrist. A jangle. Medical bracelets. You'd have to claw those names and numbers off with sterner stuff than yellow nails and gummy teeth. I stood and held out my hand. Needed to be closer to see it.

Weasel recoiled.

"Look, I just want to apologize and give you my seat."

"You are a trickster."

"I've been called worse by better, but if you're right and the big nasties of the world are looking forward to my demise, then I might as well try and make amends before the L.A. skyline goes crimson. Please?"

Everyone held their noise, except a sleeping old man with flabby cheeks who snored gently like a gas leak through a tin whistle.

Weasel shook his head but looked at my outstretched hand. "I can see . . . I can smell the aura."

I grinned against his dread. Every once in a while, I'd meet someone touched by magic, someone who could sense it like I did, as colors, as a smell, or textures. They were rare, tortured, and often lost souls who'd lived on the sharp margins of the world, and slid off into oblivion, but Weasel was schooled. He had arcane knowledge you don't find in the gutter. He was connected, somehow, a casualty that fate had put in my way.

My hand was steady while Weasel, who had called me "enemy" and "Herald," did the math in his head of what he could or should do with me.

A pothole shook the bus. The snorer woke. And Weasel's hand slid into mine.

Every crack, crevice, and tendon was gnarled, but the shake he gave me was formal, the kind you're trained to do somewhere better than the gutter. As I pumped back, I twisted my hand to toss the chain around his wrist so that its heaviest part, the ID tag, landed on his wrist.

"Z. C."

Initials alone, but Weasel took the look at his wrist as sacrilege. "Demon seducer!" I let him kick my stomach with his sandaled foot, the big toe's overgrown nail gouging me in the abs. My ass hit the seat as he ran to the front. "Stop! Stop this chariot! You carry an abomination! We must all flee!"

After arguing with the bus driver, Weasel fled, alone, no one heeding his call as he ran into the street wild and free—and utterly broken and depressing.

"You're like a celebrity," the kid said while I poked my gut, hoping that toenail hadn't infected me with whatever Weasel had. "You got jumped by a member of the Merry Pranksters!"

"Weasel runs with Ken Kesey?"

"He did," the kid said, big smile on his face because he was schooling a grownup. "They kicked him out. Too wild even for those freaks. Now he preaches on the street and speaks in some crazy language, selling poems and offering wisdom."

"A modern-day prophet," I said.

"We get the prophets we deserve," the kid said.

I chuckled, seeing I had not added much more than a bruise to my growing collection of wounds. "You've got a hell of a good eye for detail," I said. "Anything else you can tell me about the Master of the Toenail Stab?"

The kid lit up. "Oh, yeah! Everyone has a story about Weasel. Some said he was at Pearl Harbor and lived, and that drove him mad because all his buddies died. But I don't think so."

"And what do you think . . . sorry, my name is James."

"Manuel," the kid said, and shook the hand vigorously. "I think he was a professor. One of those guys who reads so much he goes crazy. I know soldier crazy. I know crazy, period. And Weasel, man, he talks like Dr. Strange, and Dr. Strange is smart."

I nodded. "Thanks, Manuel."

"What do you think, James?" he said, which surprised me. No one talks to anyone they don't board the bus with, but Manuel not only wanted to talk, he wanted to listen, a trait seemingly removed from the genes of his generation.

"I think you're onto something."

He stood and pulled the cord for the next stop. "Don't be rough on Weasel," Manuel said. "He's nice sometimes. When he's quieter. Tells crazy stories."

"About what?" I said as the kid with answers ran to the doors.

"Monsters! Dungeons! It's like Johnny Quest meets King Kong!"

Then Manuel was on the street, running through pedestrians as if he owned the block.

"You were too nice to him," the pastel-pink grandma said. "Kid like that needs discipline."

"Kid like that?" I said.

She grunted and looked out the window as we headed south, and all the weirdness fell into the normal sluggish speed of the L.A. afternoon haze, with me heading into the unknown, searching for anything that might make this puzzle more complete so I could get a good look at the picture and grab the guy who hurt Cactus.

"Find him, Brimstone. Find him and kill him."

"Next stop, Crenshaw. Transfer here for the Metro 806 for the Boardwalk."

I made my way to the open doors and stepped out.

Cutting through yellowed sandwich wrappers and the greenish pall that made L.A. such a lovely garbage heap on the good earth. I looked around at the young and old, black and white, brown and pink, and tried to think of how the hell I could keep my word without taking a life.

My stomach sank as I realized Cactus might already be dead. And promises to the dead are ugly business.

7

I RAN TO A PHONE BOOTH, FISHED OUT A DIME, AND made a call to Veterans Hospital.

"I'm calling regarding my colleague, Cactus—I mean, Sergeant Cochise Sandoval Hayes. He was brought in today with severe shrapnel wounds and blood loss."

"Are you a family member?" Her voice was so smooth I expected there to be a sexy robotoid on the other end.

"The brotherhood of arms."

"But not a blood relative."

"I'm the closest thing to family he's got left, thanks to General Cooke and the Trail of Tears and . . . Look, I just want to know if he survived the ambulance ride."

"I'm afraid we don't give out that information over the phone, sir."

"And I appreciate that, because most people are human garbage, but this case is rather extreme and I really need to know if he's alive or dead."

"You should contact a family member—"

"But not a next of kin? So he's alive?"

A pause. "I didn't say that, sir. It is protocol for those with a concern about friends to contact family members first. Otherwise, I'm afraid I cannot help you."

"Wait! Look, you seem like a professional woman. What's your name?"

"I will not—"

"James Brimstone. I know you've been trained to keep abusers and worse away from their victims. By your standards and training I might very well be the person who caused the grief. You are absolutely right in not assisting me in finding out this information. You've saved lives doing this, right?"

Silence, but she heard me.

"So, what I'd like to suggest is something that will protect the sacred trust you have with your patient, but also allows me piece of mind. Doesn't that sound good, ma'am?"

"Miss Geary."

"Miss Geary, thank you. Here's what I propose. There was an ambulance attendant who took Cactus inside. Rail-thin redhead with a short haircut. Strong, but wiry. I helped him get my friend, Sergeant Hayes, on the gurney by calling him a name he knew. Can you ask that redheaded ambulance driver to pick up the phone?"

"We do not provide access to ambulance attendants."

"Naturally, otherwise you'd be setting the hospital up for all sorts of legal problems. You're vigilant, Miss Geary. That's great. I don't want anything to be compromised, especially for Sergeant Hayes. Here's what I suggest: ask the man if he wants to talk to the guy who called him 'Arrows.' I called him that while he helped get Sarge in the ambulance. He was the only one who heard that name and I'm the only one who knows he knows it. If he doesn't remember, or has no time for me, fine. But if he wants to talk to the man who helped him save a life, tell Arrows that I am on the phone."

Silence held me like Cactus's hands around my throat.

"Miss Geary?"

Silence.

"Hold, please."

My ears filled with Tijuana Brass from some station left of the dial as I watched the shadows of the afternoon grow, cars moaning and coughing as my throat constricted with smog, strain, and fear . . . A promise to a dead man made everything harder. Death changes everything. That promise could lasso me to a fate that might never be fixed as I struggled to make Cactus's ghost rest. Kill "them" might mean "kill all of them" or "kill myself" if he saw me as responsible.

Metro brakes squealed and I knew I didn't have long before missing the connection and having to walk to the Boardwalk, since waiting for the next bus would take even longer.

The bus clanged. My ears popped. A click came from the receiver.

"Yes?" I said. "Arrows?"

Silence.

"Come on, man. My name is James Brimstone. You figured out what was going down with my combative friend at the Legion Hall when I yelled 'Arrows.' We got him on that gurney together. Please, just tell me, is he—Sergeant Cochise Sandoval Hayes— alive, or is he dead? If you don't want to get in trouble, just say 'cabbage' for life or 'prunes' for death."

Silence.

"Come on, man!"

A cough. "Cabbage, but it's going bad, quick. Might not last the day. Shit, Geary's coming."

"THANK YOU!"

I slammed the receiver into its cradle, yanked open the door, and ran like hell after the bus as it pulled out and off, ignoring my frantic waves, because the Mayor Who Never Visits said he would make the buses run on time.

"Damn it," I said, then looked down the road. No one but a few kids in denim and a couple of winos in evening dusters on the sidewalk. Cars zoomed by.

I decided to stick out my thumb and await the fate of the road and the kindness of strangers until a half-hour passed. I'd been hitching and riding with danger since I'd run from Oakland, grabbed a train in Richmond's Iron Triangle, and headed out to parts unknown. For conservative types I'd look like an out-of-work lounge singer. For lefties, I'd be seen as a threatless—if somewhat tattered—member of the power elite.

But no cars stopped. In a city in perpetual motion, I was as motionless as a concrete curb. My mouth was half road grit, half chewing on thoughts about the day.

Knowing I didn't *yet* owe a promise to a dead man eased my nerves some, even with the shrapnel wounds in my ass itching like I was covered in ticks.

I plucked the Black Lotus from my pocket, careful to avoid letting the edges of the petals cut through my skin again. But I needed to see this clue, this amazing slice of antiquarian relic from the deep Cimmerian past that had ended up in L.A. for no goddamn good reason.

The nine petals were ebony and sharp and, despite being snipped from whatever stem that it once called home, the monstrous flower was exceptionally vibrant and healthy, which begged the question: how long had it been free from its mother root? How many blooms like this are around L.A.? The world?

I placed the unbelievable flower back into my pocket, then stuck out my thumb again and let my mind wander. Weasel's rants . . . they'd been littered with Cimmerian and Babylonian references, if jumbled through the coffee press of his own delusions. If I couldn't grip his psyche to shake out what he knew, who could I ask?

His talk of a fallen world in which we reverted to some

natural state of barbarism made my shit swirl. It was the kind of world Edgar lamented, where everyone was under the thrall of horrific creatures of tremendous power, beasts that Edgar thought he was better than. *Ethics and morality were invented by the weak to make the powerful feel guilt and to galvanize the cockroaches of this world against their natural superiors. There were times when such words were meaningless, where power, dominion, and mastery was all that saved us from unending chaos and madness. Now we have a world of debauchery for the meek and heroes made of musicians who shoot drugs in their veins. All empires fall, and it will be for the strong to take what they can when decadence erases these pathetic peons from the soil. Take what you can from this world, my dear apprentice. Feel no guilt, no remorse, no regret. Such feelings are holes in your armor for letting the cockroaches invade.*

I squirmed against the memory of Edgar's hedonistic philosophy as a burnt-orange station wagon pulled up.

Behind the wheel was a woman with a beehive she'd been maintaining since the last decade was young. "Hey slugger," she said from dark purple lips, a perfect shade to go with the catseye glasses and pounds of caked-on makeup. "You going my way?"

I grinned. "If your way is near the Venice Beach Boardwalk."

She chewed a green chunk of gum that had likely lost its minty flavor—overcome by coffee and cigarettes—ten miles before. "Close enough."

I walked around the front of the car. She reached over and popped the door open so I could slink into her world. "Much obliged," I said, closing the door. "I'm James Brimstone."

"Harriet Pinkerton."

"Oh, like the Detective Agency?"

"Ha!" she said, peeling off. "That takes me back. Most of the boys I pick up wouldn't know a Pinkerton from a G-Man." She winked. Here she was, dressed as if the galas of the Rat Pack in 1960 were still the rage, yet Harriet Pinkerton was what I would call one-hundred-and-ten percent her own self: confident, sure, and not giving a damn.

I liked Harriet Pinkerton immediately.

Thanks to her lead foot and inability to distinguish yellow from red, Harriet was catching up on the bus I missed, all while sharing her amazing life story, which was a novel unto itself: part romance, part horror story.

"But that's what you get for marrying a makeup man. Don't get me wrong, Don was also a great lover, but you become his Guinea pig for every monster face he thought the folks at Universal might think could be the next Wolf Man and it wears you down. God, he went through a fish-critter phase where I was a squid-faced demoness, head like a giant clit with tentacles."

"Think I missed that one at the Parkway Drive-In."

She patted my arm while pulling out and dodging anyone who used their brakes. "Well, it's sweet of you to think he had a chance at a drive-in monster movie, but his specials—that's what he called when he turned this pretty face into a walking nightmare—his specials weren't worth a damn. Nobody liked monsters anymore. He had to settle with what he was almost good at: backstage showgirl makeup."

"Ah, you were queen of the floor show."

She slapped my knee playfully. "Get too fresh, James Brimstone, and you'll get a bruise! No, I couldn't dance more than a few box steps before both feet were making left turns. I was a singer, which is a fancy way of saying I wasn't pretty enough to show up and do anything else. 'Pretty enough to sing' is what the bookers used to say."

I grinned, enjoying this respite from a day of broken men, bloody bodies, and a friend in a coma.

But relaxation invited reminiscence. These kids coming back from the Mekong Delta are haunted. So are we Korea vets. We didn't get a hero's welcome either when we came home from the

Korean "police action"—like Vietnam, they didn't even call it a war. Mostly we were ignored. As were any nightmares we were dealing with . . .

A wrinkled hand with a heart-shaped ring waved in front of me. "Hey, Earth to James, Earth to James, you read me?"

I laughed. "Sorry, Harriet. Guess I just drifted off for a second."

"Bored you into a coma, huh?"

A volley of cold hit my spine. "It's not the company. Just thinking about a friend in the hospital."

"Well, look at me being an inconsiderate slug. I haven't asked you boo about yourself. Your friend down near the Boardwalk?"

I had to change the patter. I wasn't going to share any of my life story with Harriet, though I hoped that when I was her age I wouldn't mind being as free and easy as she was with her personal life. "No, just going to search down there for something that might cheer him up."

"If his style is Venice Beach," she said, "I like your friend already."

I smiled, until I looked in her rearview.

It was a black Lincoln Continental. And behind the windshield was the face of a woman, skin taut, thin lips frozen in a rictus.

She wore a red bow tie. In its center was a voice box.

She rolled down the window and stuck out her head. The speaker sputtered to life with the voice of a damned bastard.

"Brimstone!" Shanks said. "Alicia Price sends her regards!"

Wonderful. Just what I didn't need: an encounter with the undead putz of a powerful sorceress, both of whom had already made a few attempts to send me to oblivion.

Shanks was Alicia's favorite heavy. She kept his brain in a jar and gave him a new corpse to re-animate when needed. Shanks was bad enough, but Alicia was pure evil.

She was the bitch who'd broken Lilith's windshield.

8

DEL REY WAS AN EVEN WORSE PLACE FOR A CAR chase than Inglewood, since it was a tourist trap hiding a black hole. Plus, Harriet was an innocent, a bystander, and not touched by magic. But this secondhand zombie-brain-in-jar henchman was going to try and kill us both.

"What in the hell is that?" Harriet said, looking in the rear-view mirror at the corpse lady with the male voice made out of static and frustration. "An ex-wife?"

"No way," I said. "Harriet, just drop me off before he . . . she . . . it catches up with us. That driver is first-class bad news and you've been a saint."

"Nope," Harriet said, then swung a wide right that burned more rubber than napalm in the jungle. "I know good people, James. Mother was a fortune teller and was right nine times out of ten. And I'm my mama's daughter." She adjusted her bouffant as we jetted down Redwood Avenue. "I'd bet my back fillings that you need a friend who won't bail on ya. Sound about right?"

I grabbed the oh-shit handle as she gunned the Ranch Wagon, feeding the distance as Shanks's burning tires hit our rubbery shadow and came for us. "I can't ask that of someone who I've just met."

"You ain't the one asking," she said, taking another hard right at Washington Boulevard. "I'm asking you. James, will you let me show this two-bit gal who the real queen of Marina Del Rey is?"

My only other option was jumping out of the car and breaking my neck before Shanks ran over my ribs and tap-danced my skull to splinters. "Harriet, I'd be grateful."

The next four-to-five minutes turned the blur of grays at my sides a whiter shade of death. Harriet's plan, near as I could tell, was to screech as close to corners as possible while keeping all her turns right, and Shanks's plan was to keep up with this woman who drove like she'd been born on the Indy 500.

"Damn you, Brimstone!" Shanks screamed. "Slow down and meet your certain fate!"

"James," Harriet asked, spinning the wheel so we fishtailed, "why does that girl sound like a throwaway horror flick from Val Lewton?" She then peeled away and shot us toward Shanks's car.

"Guess she's a fan of the classics." The danger of the situation suddenly hit me because I could see Shank's mind working in that corpse face. "Uh, Harriet, don't, he's going to play chicken."

"Good," she said. "I don't flinch!"

Then she gunned it.

But Shanks was undead. If we crashed and died, he'd get a new body and a full paycheck. "No, pull right! Trust me! Please, Harriet! *Now!*"

Slicing our chances of survival into shreds, we turned, but not hard enough. Shanks nailed the rear end of Harriet's wagon and shattered the tail lights. Harriet turned with the impact, nerves and skill on autopilot. "She would have crashed into us."

"Yes," I said. "We need to lose her, not confront her, because she doesn't care who gets hurt, including herself."

"Goddamn, James. I thought you were smarter than that."

"Smarter than what?"

"Putting your willie in crazy chicks!" I laughed, but she was dead serious. "Suicidal lover, huh?"

"She has a hard time saying goodbye."

"I can understand that." She took a left that honest-to-god threw Shanks for a loop after all her right turns, and then punched the pedal. We sped like a bullet through a chamber, honking to keep the innocent bystanders and drivers out of harm's way.

"Gangway! Hot stuff, coming through!"

"Who the hell taught you to drive?" I asked.

"Don's best friend was a stunt driver." She smiled, and let the implication hang like a dirty joke between old friends.

A garbage truck the size of the Hulk turned into our path and saw us coming at full strength before they hammered a foghorn to signal our doom.

"Brace for impact!"

Tires screamed before the beast of a car skidded toward the green monster. Behind us, Shanks revved up.

"Get out!" I screamed, but Harriet already knew the drill, and both of us piled out of the vehicle two seconds before impact.

Harriet's car jolted forward and crashed into the garbage truck. Shanks's car crunched like an accordion into the orange rear fins of Harriet's once-pristine 1960 Ford Ranch Wagon. Harriet tucked herself into the dip of a shop's doorway. The rush of wind from the crash puffed over my wounded back. Under the polyester, it was hotter than hell's gate.

Shanks's head smashed into his windshield, and a crackling spider web distorted the unmoving smile. I wasn't a betting man, but even the Pope would put it all on Shanks's rotting corpse body being broken but not done.

The driver's side door opened.

I placed one wingtip on the accordioned bumper and leapt, then slid like I was stealing home base just as the .38 Special became visible heading towards Harriet.

"She's got a goddamn gun!" Harriet said. That was more than the garbage gang needed to reverse engines and pull out.

My foot slammed the tiny wrist of the dead girl Shanks inhabited, and sent the revolver spilling behind.

The icy grip of the dead claimed my ankle. "Brimstone! You were foolish to get this close to me! You are now in my clutches!"

With a single yank, the monster from Staten Island pulled me inside the car. The taste of Shank's magical nature, and that of his master Alicia Price, was like sucking smog made of spoiled milkshakes: thick and vile. I tumbled into the back seat like a sack of bruised potatoes. And when I saw the shattered windshield, I couldn't help but think of Lilith, my stolen beauty, whose windshield I'd only recently replaced, and how trivial it is to attach so much importance to things, which, as the Fat Prophet of the Bodhi Tree says, is the root of all unhappiness.

And yet, watching Shank's girlish head turn, rictus grin at a hundred watts and static laughter hissing from that charmed bow tie, I decided it was all right to be petty when faced with the absurd. "Nice digs," I said. "A dead chick's body suits you."

"Laugh all you want," he said, hitting the ignition. "When I'm done with you, Alicia Price will give me any body I want to claim as my own, full possession. *Including yours!*"

The car reversed, which was good, because it kept Harriet out of the danger zone. Even if it brought me closer to hells of infinite suffering.

I snapped out a kick that jarred that once-living head and received only laughter for my trouble. "Try and fight me, Brimstone! Try and beat a dead man who—"

BANG!

The windshield shattered as a strong voice screamed.

"Duck!"

I rolled into the fetal position.

Four shots rang out, accompanied by Shanks screaming "no!" each time bullets smacked his chest and neck, propelling out that gray-green ooze Alicia's patchwork resurrection man used to provide Shanks with one of the bodies he'd been hoarding since Edgar first set me against him. Shanks head dipped over the seat, hands shaking. "No! No civilian can stop—"

I shot my hand up, grabbed his bowtie, and yanked.

"NO!"

Tearing off the magical contraption killed the body from being his ride, but it didn't eradicate the sound of Shanks' annoying voice.

"HOW DARE YOU!" the box screamed. "I WILL RIP OUT HER EYES, BRIMSTONE! I WILL EAT HER BRAIN AS YOU WATCH BEFORE I—"

"Shanks?" I said to the bow tie. "Nap time."

I smashed the receiver against her skull and static slashed through the air before dissipating.

I reached for the passenger side door, but it opened.

Harriet, with a smoking .38 in one hand.

"Thank you," I said.

She shook. "You were not kidding." She sneered at the mess of the body that was Shanks's no more.

"Don't look, Harriet."

"I was a WAAC, James," she said, giving me her hand. "Let's go before we're blamed for this mess."

We abandoned the crash site, which was sure to bring heat because city trucks (as opposed to the workers) might have been hurt. While running, Harriet tossed the gun onto a rickety pickup filled with fence posts, a far better destination for our innocence than a sewer or a garbage can, which even greenhorn recruits straight from the academy would put under the magnifying glass. Under the awning of a fruit shop, the fresh taste of strawberry skin parching my lips, I caught my breath, "What about your car, Harriet?"

She dropped a dollar into the shopkeeper's hand, said "Gracias," and took a pound of strawberries. "My car? It's in Long Beach. I'll pick up another one for the ride home or rely on the kindness of strangers."

"Kind strangers are starting to be a rare breed in this city, my dear."

She tore a strawberry apart with a single bite. "Beautiful, everything has a price. You could have been some master pervert. Could have passed you by and missed one hell of an event, James. Life is too precious to be spent playing it safe all the time."

She held out a strawberry before her face.

I leaned forward, and found her red, rich lips instead. She gave a hell of a passionate kiss with my adrenals still on fire, and I pulled back for air before she KO'd me in the first round. I gulped air and realized that her five o'clock shadow was peeking out of her makeup. Once immaculate, the pancake had now started to melt.

"Does that bother you?" she said.

I smiled. "No, Harriet. It takes all kinds. And I'm glad the world has your kind in it."

I kissed her again, and she received me with relish before pulling back and handing me the strawberries. "See you around, James," she said, then cut her way down the street with the bearing of a queen, her shadow long and true.

I ate three strawberries as cop cars drove past without sirens or lights, hazy black-and-white Belvedere beetles running down the street. If Shanks's hijinks had caused a stir with the police, there were no evident signs.

I looked west. It was a long walk to Venice Beach, where I hoped to find a link to whoever hurt Cactus.

I tossed in a strawberry. It was overripe and melted like soggy cotton candy as I handed the box to the shopkeeper. He threw up his hands and shook his head, thinking I was trying to return them.

"I want to share one with you, Uncle."

Shock widened the eyes of his weathered face. *"You speak Cantonese?"*

"Poorly. These are good. Please?"

He plucked one out, bowed slightly, then took a very small bite, the kind of bite that said he'd had to split a handful of rice for a lot of mouths over the years, the kind of living that says a whole strawberry is only fit for gods and emperors. I realized my appetites, no matter how varied or expansive, how much they sang from the gutters, were quintessentially American and bloated.

He handed the strawberry back, and I took it, bit a small piece, and handed it back.

We did this, smiling, as if it were a game, and as good as those first four were, the last tiny bite, green stalk and all, was delicious.

"Thank you, Uncle."

He nodded, a gentle smile on his face, then waved me off. He was a working man.

And so was I. Venice Beach, I thought, I'm going to work your Boardwalk until you spill your secrets about the Black Lotus and skateboards and hippies that use grenades. The Boardwalk was still a good half-hour walk away.

It was a pleasant enough stroll but would have been faster without the wounds in my back. At least I had plenty to think about. I was almost to Shell Avenue when I saw something a half-block away that jarred me back to the here-and-now: there, preaching next to a crate of stacked grapefruit, stood Weasel.

9

AT ALMOST THE SAME INSTANT, WEASEL SPOTTED
me and abandoned his citrus. The homeless prophet was fast.
He'd obviously been building up the capacity to sprint short dis-
tances thanks to endless desperation and the law of the street.

We cut through a gaggle of tourists and locals, the buildings'
shadows getting longer and the vista of the ocean like blinding
gold on the horizon. Parents with long sideburns pulled their kids
close while freaks and pushers with maps to the stars swore under
their breath for screwing up their sales. A handful of kids whose
faces were a blurry mess of hair and braces screamed for me to
"kick his ass!" as if fighting the homeless was some kind of spec-
tator sport. I hoped I'd never live to see the day when beating the
unfortunate became common.

I was lamenting signs of a new dark era, just like Weasel.

"Weasel! Wait!"

"Herald of DOOM!" he screamed, leaping over a poodle with
a rhinestone collar. The dog's platinum blond owner yanked its
leash to pull Fido out of my way, but I jumped all the same. Didn't

want to slow my momentum toward the fleet-footed critter who could speak ancient Babylonian. And, as if reading my wish list to Santa, Weasel actually pumped his legs straight toward the shimmering ocean.

"I just want to talk!" I said.

"You speak doom! Go back to the Abyss that sprung you!"

"How dare you say that about Oakland!"

Weasel threw back his hand and I raised my guard, but he was aiming lower.

Marbles slid under my wing tips and I tap-danced with gravity, trying to get my bearings before falling down like a career failure at the roller rink. Shouts from others joined the chorus of swears in my head as Weasel threw another handful of Vacor Trébols, straight from Mexico, causing havoc on the streets of Venice Beach.

"Hey, these are classics!" I yelled. "Why not save them for your collection?"

"Doom!"

"Am not! You are!"

We ran until I could see the haze of shadows on the horizon . . . the Boardwalk. Packed with people paying attention to nothing but novelty. Weasel would vanish like tears in the desert.

The street was filled with screeching tires as we ran through traffic. I closed some of the distance I lost thanks to his fistful of marbles. (A trick I would remember in case I ever found myself in the role of L.A.'s most hunted.) Brief slices of shade from palm trees and telephone poles cut across us as the street curved like a racetrack, and I wondered if anyone was betting on the contest between the Gray Disaster and the Polyester Nightmare.

"Weasel, please. I need your help!"

"You help no one, Beast of Lies!"

"Black Lotus is back."

For a second, he slowed down to a trot.

"Do you know where it grows?"

He shot a look back, then bolted faster than I could breathe.

On we went, until the sidewalk thickened with the crowd for the Boardwalk, locals coming home for a respite, and hand sellers looking for a better corner for this time of day. The strawberries were now ashes in my mouth as I sped up to match Weasel, who clearly knew more than he let on about Black Lotus. He either knew where it was, or why it had come back, and that was a hell of a lot more than me this fine day.

"Save me, Tiamat! I will do your bidding! Just save me from this human monster!"

And, as if a genie were granting the last wish from a lamp-rubber, Weasel started to slow. His breathing was labored. The miles of life on the street seemed to catch up with him as I got closer and closer.

A curious sound curled in my ears. It took a second to place it.

Behind me, the gritty grinding of wheels on pavement neared.

Wheels.

Skateboards.

I looked back and saw an inverse-V formation: three shirtless kids, beach-bronzed skin, muscles taut and toned, slamming their feet against the pavement to push their boards like waves propelling surfboards. The concrete was their ocean and, judging by the litter of white scars and bruises against the tan, just as cruel a mistress as the sea.

Effortlessly, I was flanked by two cinnamon-haired boys. Behind me was a blond kid with wide eyes . . .

. . . one of the protesters who'd been outside the Legion Hall.

10

I WAS TORN IN TWO DIRECTIONS. AHEAD WAS THE madman who may have an answer, and behind me was a kid who was at the massacre. I couldn't grab both. I needed information and Weasel probably knew something, but so might the kid. And he had the benefit of not being cocobananapants in the cerebral cortex.

Also, I was tired of running with strawberry breath.

I stopped, jamming my heels, as the two flankers slid forward, popping their boards up, making a horrible screech. I started to swing a haymaker at the leader, the kid I'd seen at the Legion Hall, but he'd already shifted out of striking range by pivoting first on one set of wheels then the second, moving to the side with dexterity that would have made any acrobat jealous. They reformed their V formation faster than fighter pilots, the crab walker in the front.

Weasel nowhere in sight.

"Afternoon, boys," I said. "Mind getting out of the way? I have a meeting with old Weasel."

"Sounds like the meeting's over," the lead shirtless wonder said. "Maybe find some other kind of action besides harassing the less fortunate."

"Since when were questions harassment? And don't think I don't know the irony of asking a question to make this point."

My wit was lost on these young, hazy-eyed athletes, but I was acquiring a larger audience. The grinding sound of more wheels on concrete heralded the arrival of ten more teenagers, all beach-bum bronzed. They circled me like a shiver of sharks. The smell of sweat, grass, and tanning oil clogged my nostrils. Eight guys and two girls. The boys, if shirted, wore striped tanks or t-shirts. One girl filled out a gold bikini top, the other sported a too-tight Micky Mouse. All wore cut-offs or shorts. Back in the day, we'd say this crowd was spoiling for a rumble, a gang ready to make good on its rep. Yet this cavalcade of sidewalk surfers had been protecting a homeless guy.

"How do you all know Weasel?"

The leader sniggered. "You a cop?"

"Not with this fashion sense. I'm a private eye. And you were at the Legion Hall."

Body language from several kids silently signaled "caution." The leader waved them off, even though worry was etched on their golden foreheads.

"Yes," he said. "I was protesting."

"Mind telling me when you left?"

"After the explosion."

"Kevin, don't talk to this pig," said a tall, chestnut-haired fellow with a mild sneer. He stood about half a foot taller than Kevin.

"I'm no pig," I said, but all my attention was on Kevin. "That explosion? It damn near killed a friend of mine and may yet still."

"Good," said Chestnut. Kevin zapped him a glance so sharp it cut off his oxygen.

Kevin looked back at me as the rest of his gang saddled up behind him like a bronze wall. "I'm sorry about your friend," he said. "I had nothing to do with it."

"Do you know who did?"

Kevin shook his head, but his face said, "I don't trust you with ANY information."

"I know, I know, I look like the fuzz or your dad or a narc," I said, "but I just want to find the creeps who would assault a bunch of old men and their wives. I think someone is trying to hook the blame on the protestors, but that doesn't smell right to me."

Kevin showed no discernible change in attitude, except for the slightest softening of his jaw.

For a moment I thought of bribing them, but they looked righteous enough to see any cash transaction as an insult and proof of my untrustworthiness. Trust needed to be earned. "What can I do to prove to you fine citizens that I'm not the enemy?"

"Dragon kiss!" the Mickey Mouse girl said.

A half-dozen lighters emerged from waistbands and pockets. I was just glad there was no taste of magic in the air, that no real dragon might be summoned by one of these miniature torches.

Kevin took a Zippo from the chestnut kid. He flicked a flame, and then I saw the darker patterns across all of their forearms: burns.

"Ah, a test?"

Kevin smiled. "If you can last longer than me, it'll prove you're no cop."

"How so?"

"Cops won't mutilate themselves," he said. "Makes them look like they joined a gang."

"Not a bad test," I said, taking off my bedraggled jacket. "Have at it, Kevin."

Using his name jarred Kevin a mite. "What's your name?"

"James Brimstone."

They all laughed, and Kevin chuckled. "I would have pegged you for a Horace or Mortimer."

"I get that a lot. Now quit stalling."

The gang laughed and snickered at my genius comeback and then the Zippo blazed right under his forearm.

Kevin's eyes steadied on mine, but he wasn't looking at me. Judging by his breathing, someone had taught him some pain management techniques. The flame licked his skin, but he didn't register the damage.

At first.

As the gang counted to ten, his face shook and finally, at fifteen, it was too much, and the light snuffed out as he exhaled.

"Fifteen!" Chestnut said. "A personal best!"

They were in awe of their leader, who wouldn't let the tears leak out of his shaky eyes. "Your turn, Brimstone." Again, titters at the old-man name, obviously the underdog in a young man's game.

I'd folded the orange jacket neatly across my forearm, then rolled up my sleeve. Outside of the bullet-catch scar on my palm, the usual bumps and grinds from life on the road, a clean bullet wound received in Korea, and a few reminders of run-ins with Hells Angels, most of my scars were invisible to the naked eye. Edgar made sure the true damage he'd done could only be witnessed by me. The torture of my years as his right-hand man was never seen by the waking world. My arm was just another hairy beast with a speckle of gray.

Kevin tossed the lighter and I caught it, awkwardly, to again put a show on for the righteous youth. "Hope there's enough fluid left," I said. Kevin smirked and his friends snorted.

I flicked the Zippo open and hit its wheel. "Let there be light," I said.

The flame lapped my arm with heat and agony, but I focused on my breathing and sang Don Ho's "Tiny Bubbles" to the starry-eyed crowd as five seconds became ten, ten became twenty, and then thirty.

"I don't believe it," said the Mickey Mouse girl.

"He's tricking us somehow," Chestnut said.

Kevin shook his head. "You can stop."

I shrugged. "Your call, Kevin." I snuffed the Zippo and tossed it at Chestnut, whose hand scrambled with it like a hot potato, much to the enjoyment of myself and the girls.

I examined my smoking flesh. Burnt-marshmallow ugly. Smelled like burning garbage. But if I'd done my breathing right, it would also heal quicker than a bug bite over the next few hours.

"So," I said to Kevin, "did I pass this ordeal?"

Kevin smiled. "Ordeal?"

"That's what Germanic warriors called it when they had to perform a feat of painful endurance to earn back trust that was lost: an ordeal."

"This blows," Chestnut said. "He talks like a teacher."

"A hot teacher," said Mickey. I let it slide.

"I'm just a friend looking for justice for an old army buddy."

"You fought in the war?"

"Not this one," I said, cool. "The other one."

"Korea?" Chestnut said. "That was just a prelude to Vietnam. This guy is bad news, Kevin, even if he ain't a cop."

"I know, don't trust anyone under nineteen," I said. "Hell, I'd hate me if I was your age. But I'm me, and my friend is sitting in a hospital holding onto his life. Kevin, you were there when some coward tossed a grenade to kill a bunch of people grateful to be out of war zones."

Kevin considered my point, and his crew. I was struck by what a natural leader he appeared to be. They were waiting for *him* to make a decision. I hated authority in every possible permutation, but that meant I was even more impressed by someone with the born talent to lead. Like Cactus or, in a much tinier way, Kevin.

"Like I said, we were protesting. But there was a mix of people."

"So, who is 'we'?"

Everyone stared at their shoes or boards, shuffling with the "oh shit" countenance of kids caught out after curfew.

"I'm not here to rat you out to the *federales*. You're from Tumbledown?"

"Kevin!" Chestnut said, then yanked him. "Let's go."

Kevin just looked at his arm and Chestnut begged off. "You're the one making a scene, Austen. Cool it and shut up." Quick as a bullet he yanked the board from Austen's hand. "Or else you're walking back."

Austen took a step back, glaring at me, then his confiscated board, as if someone had torn Excalibur from Arthur's hand right before battle.

Kevin tossed his head to get the hair out of his eyes. "We are from Tumbledown. But that wasn't all who was there."

"You rally some like-minded souls?"

"Not of our doing, man," Kevin said. "We've been protesting ceremonies to remind people of the blood behind the ribbon, that people are getting awards for killing babies and families in their own home. We run into other groups. Mostly college kids, though some Chicano groups are solid, like the Brown Berets. But none of those were there, beyond the usual UCLA loudmouths. Loudest on the street, laziest behind the scene."

"There were two big fellas I saw there," I said. "One looked mad as hell. Agitated. As if he'd spent the night up on black beauties. Think he ended up on the back of a Harley after the place went boom."

Kevin shook his head. "We don't run with freaks like that. But I remember him. Dude was all elbows and shoulders, glared like he wanted us to melt."

"There was another tall guy, big as our friend with the need for speed. Looked like he could have been your older brother."

Kevin shrugged. "Rings no bells, Brimstone." His voice got lower, the tone holding a fine edge of disdain. He was lying, and bad at it. That blond lumberjack must have been their leader. "What did you want with Weasel?" Kevin said, redirecting his "tell" so the onus was on me.

"Good question, Kevin. Weasel said something troubling. You ever hear of anyone pushing dope called Black Lotus?"

His face scrunched. "We don't deal dope."

"But you've heard the name?"

"Just in the air, man. You want to know about Black Lotus, you'll have to talk to Billy Mars."

"Should I check the phone book or do you have his place of employment?"

"He works the Boardwalk now, and yeah, we can take you to him. We were heading to the Boardwalk when we found you."

"Lucky me."

They all smiled and laughed. It hit me like a brick that these kids might be young, but they were strong, organized, and working silently together like a gang. Kevin tossed Austen his board. "Snake Race in ten minutes. You better hustle to catch Billy Mars before I make him eat my dust."

Ten bullets on boards bolted toward the Pacific glare.

My wingtips chugged slowly in their wake.

11

TEN POUNDS OF SWEAT AND TEN MINUTES LATER,
my soaking suit approached the resplendent glory of the Venice Beach Boardwalk. Street-side buildings were painted in sun-
bleached versions of primary colors. Pacific Avenue was alive and
reminded me of the Electric Magic Circus: street musicians scop-
ing out corners and presenting wonder and protest in competing
packages. The air was sickly sweet with saltwater taffy and popcorn. A scraggly-bearded twenty-ish beach bum in a gray shirt and
bell-bottoms juggled on a corner, old bowling pins served as his
clubs. At first blush, you might assume he was a bored hippie who
spent most of his free time mastering the fine art of scrounging
bowling alley garbage until he found his true calling, one pin at a
time.

And you'd be dead wrong.

His hands were thick, long-fingered, and strong. He did not
juggle so much as dance with the pins as three separate partners.
The jugglers I'd known were all failed *others*: failed magicians,
failed broad tossers, failed coin men, failed pickpockets. A juggler

was about the lowest rung you could fall to on the entertainment ladder, and yet here was someone who created vistas of spins and plucks and knocks that had most of the oglers of the Boardwalk in a trance.

A girl on the other side of the street strummed a nylon-stringed guitar and spoke poetry that smelled a little too close to Weasel's rants.

"These are the days of blood and needle
When L.A. slumbers God will hide
When dreams are all kept in empty bottles
And the gulf between us all will become a void."

I crossed between two pillars and approached a circle of bodies surrounding three people. One was Kevin, who looked as if he hadn't expended an iota of energy. The other was a muscle-bound rock of average height with cut abdominals and hulking arms, but without the trademark chicken legs of many new muscle-heads. His blond-white hair was bleached and scraggly like Rastas I'd seen in Jamaica, his beard reddish. His body was covered in welts, easily seen thanks to his fashion choice of cutoffs and a shirtless chest.

But that wasn't the scene-stealing sight of the Boardwalk.

That was Billy Mars.

Ghostly white with black hair slashing his face and swaying down the back of his lean, serpentine frame, Billy Mars wore a blue-and-white jumpsuit that seemed better fit for a Marvel comic cover than the waking world. But who was I to judge? Around Billy Mars's pencil-thin neck was a silver Yin Yang medallion. The sunglasses may have been John Lennon, but the mascara dripping down his face like veins revealing themselves under a hex was pure Johnny Thunders—a popular cross-dressing guitar player who sometimes stumbled into the Thump & Grind to throw up in the bathroom stall. I poured him into a cab once and he just kept saying "Take me to the Lincoln," as if naming a president could get you to a nice hotel.

Billy Mars had that drugged-out disdain chic that Thunders was riding to an early grave. He and the rest held boards in their hands or under their arms. I pushed through the crowd with the career expertise of a carny, resisting every urge to liberate coins and cards and bills from these awestruck rubes staring at a bottom-rung rock star.

I made it through the circle and Kevin looked embarrassed, like a son watching his dad crash his secret birthday party.

"Just found out about the Snake Competition. I understand you're the man to talk to?" I said, approaching Mars, who faced me with a practiced indifference that made me presume he was British.

"Conformist," he said and, sadly, instead of Oxford-posh or cockney, I was treated to the nasally bleat of a born Bostonian. "We're starting as soon as I'm done with my smoke." He produced a joint from behind his ear. "And I prophesize that this day, the victor will be the one who is most deserving."

"Oh, I don't want to race," I said. "I just wanted to chat. Word on the street, as the kids say, is that you're a man who knows a little about Black Lotus."

The pretense that controlled Mars's visage itched before being replaced with fresh smugness as he placed a joint between pompous lips. "Sure thing, grandpa," he said as a boy with buck teeth and a Grateful Dead shirt lit his idol's doobie. "Tell you what. You win this race, and I'll tell you everything I know about anything and more. I win, and you fuck off from the Boardwalk and head back to the squares that produced you."

The chuckles of the crowd confirmed that this was what passed for wit in these circles.

"He ain't got no board," screeched the musclehead, sounding

like a wheezing George C. Scott, his diaphragm clenched by his surging physique.

"Yeah, you heard Jack Lumber," Chestnut said, with an attitude reserved for those who worship rules. "He's not one of us. He ain't from the Boardwalk."

"Kid, I've walked more boardwalks than you've bummed smokes, just not this one."

I caught the flash of motion from Kevin's hand just before he launched his board, and I caught it with one hand. Didn't look too shabby, though everyone from Tumbledown was groaning. Then Kevin looked at the chestnut-haired boy. "Give me your board, Austen."

Austen saw he was stuck. Refuse an order from his leader, and he'd lose. Give in and he'd fully accept Kevin's actions. Frustrated, he erred on the side of loyalty and tossed him his board.

"Fine," Billy Mars said. "Race starts in sixty. Riley is at the end of the line. He'll throw the prize to whoever makes the jump. That clear, old man?"

I'd already gotten one of my wingtips off and was pulling off my brown sock to reveal my milk-white flesh.

"What are you doing, grandpa?"

"Oh, are there any rules about going barefoot? Would that not be too groovy?"

Billy Mars scoffed. "Whatever turns you on, gramps, but it won't make a lick of difference." He smiled at Kevin. "We all know this is between you and me, Little Mister Sunshine."

Jack Lumber stood between the two like the Hulk's shorter brother: no less intimidating, but a little more ridiculous with all the muscle he had packed on a five-foot-eight frame. Even standing up straight, with pecs as big as watermelons, he was leaning forward.

"You counting me out, Mars? I'm the baddest thing on this beach. And that prize is mine."

"Keep your shirt on, Jack." Mars said. "At least with the fossil in the race you won't end up dead last!"

Jack gripped Billy Mars by the neck and lifted him a foot off the ground. "Take back the smart talk or I'll send you back to Mars, first class!"

Both my bare feet tasted burning asphalt, and as I strode toward them I realized there was something in Jack's intonation that rang familiar. He was built like a bodybuilder, boulders of muscle and veins welded to joints that best be made of steel, but his wild eyes and hair, his bold choke and brag—all were practiced and familiar.

"Well if you kill him, hero," I said to Jack, "we'll never know who the better concrete surfer was. Why, we might even think old Jack Lumber fixed the race like some crooked wrestling show."

Mars hit the ground and Jack Lumber jabbed a finger at me that looked like it was drawn by Jack Kirby: thick and dangerous. "You say wrestling is fake? I'll take you on right now, bubba, break you in two before all these little fans, and then win this board competition so that everyone knows Jack Lumber is the god of the Boardwalk." Then he flexed down with a Charles Atlas pose that exposed even more muscle and spiderwebbed veins. Jack's face was red as an unwanted stepchild.

"Then maybe we should race."

We all looked at Kevin, cool and serene, waiting for the adults to get their shit together.

Billy firmly planted his black sneakers and straightened his lean body. "Enough of this jive. Zoey? Get ready to drop the flag!"

A wild-haired brunette in an army jacket took ten paces backward from where we stood, the crowd parting with military precision. She dipped her hand into her shirt and yanked out a small flag with a peace sign on it, and then raised it to the sky. "The only rule," she said, in a smoky voice, "is whoever gets to the end first and grabs the prize is the winner. The rest? Losers!" She dropped the flag. "GO!"

12

ALL THREE OF THEM BLASTED OFF AND SET SAIL
along the Boardwalk. I gripped the board with my feet like Dr.
Fuji had taught me back in the Electric Magic Circus—not that
the good doctor envisioned grasping anything like a skateboard.
But holding the board as if I had talons seemed to work. Then I
shoved off, feet grazing the ground, swimming in their wake as
my body tried to balance the complex configurations of being a
middle-aged man on a teenager's wheeled weapon.

Pretty sure I was going five miles per hour.

My only experience with skate wheels was at the roller rink.
It was nothing like dealing with these flat deathtraps. I chugged
on harder. The stuttering ripple created by the Boardwalk planks
gave me a headache before my mouth had time to go dry and
holy Christ did I feel all of my forty years banging into each
other as we slapped our feet to the ground to project ourselves
forward—Billy and Kevin vying for the lead and me clawing my
way through sweat and struggle to catch up with Jack Lumber's
insane quads, pumping him forward like pistons. My only saving

grace was my grip on both the board and the world. Jack wobbled with the staggered confidence of a man who rarely thought he was wrong (even when his failure smacked him in the ass), and that overconfidence, step by step, allowed me to creep forward. Our soundtrack was the ocean crashing against the ambient sounds of the Boardwalk: the cries of gulls, the screams of kids, the electric static of rock and roll, the strums of battered acoustic guitars, and the hoarse cries of locals and tourists for all of us to watch where we were going.

About a third of the way to the end, Boardwalk attractions thickened and narrowed our passage. We passed booths filled with posters, cards, charms, and the bric-a-brac of the love generation: dream catchers without a flick of magic, because they were not made by any indigenous person, but by two stoners from Pasadena who had a vision quest while tripping at Woodstock.

Tie-dye and sun-tanned faces blurred past as one foot cranked the earth and the other grabbed the board with the strength of a dozen monkeys perched on the last branches of survival, Jack Lumber's ridged and blistered back coming closer. For all his curls and lifts, his cardiovascular system clearly took second place to his gold-medal physique. He was struggling to catch his breath while I avoided crashing into a sun-burned tourist family in matching Hawaiian-print shirts and a kid in Spider-Man tee. Two more thrusts of my earth-gripping feet and I was neck and neck for last place.

"Ain't no way!" screamed Jack as we circled around a mass of teenagers dancing in the center of the Boardwalk. "Ain't no way some mark is gonna ruin my race!"

Mark? I smiled. He *was* a wrestler. Their slang is rooted in old carny code familiar as Edgar's voice teaching me all about rubes, scabs, and freaks.

"Sorry if my healthy living is equal to all your days at the gym, Jack."

The son of a gun growled at me. Two more thrusts and I was a solid six feet ahead. Mars and Kevin were in a dead heat in front of me. Mars looked back, his face etched in sweat and malice.

Then I had a Eureka moment: Jack was a tool meant to cripple Kevin's chances so Billy could win. But the distance between the two frontrunners was growing by the second with Kevin shooting forward and Billy falling behind while Jack was focused on me.

A flicker of magic flavored the air, dark and cold, wafting from the back of the head of Jack Lumber, whose legs now pumped the ground like he was auditioning for the role of a taxi driver on *The Flintstones*.

He cut through a crowd of musicians, to the horror of their small audience. "Get the fuck out of my way!" Jack snarled, voice a primeval horn filled with gravel.

None of it was natural. His speed. His stench. His voice. It was all augmented by the twilight coil of stink that he'd somehow gotten into his body, the same kind that was in my pocket.

Jack Lumber was in the grips of Black Lotus, a berserker on the Boardwalk flying high on a skateboard, an unguided missile in a public theater of war.

There was no way to catch him, so I looked to the sides for something I could use to even the odds. One of the shack outlets on the left was selling useless trinkets, peace buttons, sacks of dice, and my weapon of choice: a sun-bleached blue pack of Bicycle playing cards.

I tore into my front pocket, which was sweatier than a prostitute in church, and tossed out a fistful of coins as I swerved close. The coins rained on the merchant, a steel-haired Mexican with sharp eyes.

I snatched the pack. *"Sorry for the rude gesture,"* I said in Spanish. *"But thank you for the cards."*

His response was a swift flurry of swearing about this four-wheeled gringo. I'd have to make it right somehow, but first I had to take care of the drugged maniac tearing through the Boardwalk. As I doubled my pace, Jack's helter-skelter transit threw two women into shack-shops and everyone screamed. This sucker had to go down.

People now scurried for safety as he plowed hard and fast to cut the distance. I weaved and wobbled as I chugged forward, hands tearing the pack and unleashing the crisp, fresh cards. They instantly, if briefly, brought back the hours spent with such, mastering their weight and feel, practicing every trick in and out of the book, firing them into watermelons with the intent of an assassin.

I didn't want Jack Lumber dead; being an asshole has never been a crime in L.A., but he was already too big for his bones.

Which meant I was going to have to throw cards faster than I was traveling on a skateboard and with pure accuracy.

There was no way I could pull this off without getting into the zone of the immortals.

The world blurred on the corduroy path as my mind whispered: *Tyger Tyger, burning bright!*

13

EVERYTHING SLOWED. I FELT AS IF I WAS SWIMMING through molasses; the pain pierced through my skin and nerves like barbed wire. Edgar had warned me never to "travel to the ethereal plane that maps our own" more than a fistful of times in a life. I'd done what I call joyriding three times in the past month—once earlier today—and if this electric bone sizzle was any measure, I'd best stay the hell away from it until I was already dead.

Against the tsunami of agony, the Boardwalk stood awash in dark and moody colors thanks to a slice of cloud killing the sun's rays, the darkened landscape dampened into a depressive reflection, almost a negative afterimage. I wondered how much the pain burning through me had to do with the tone of the joyride, but I didn't have time for pondering.

My right foot hit the ground three times and I rushed forward against the near-static images of the Boardwalk, closing in on Jack. He had the pallor of a corpse and his whole body was shaking. The death-ash tang of Black Lotus oozed from his sweaty flesh.

I flicked out a card from the deck, an ace of spades, but I had no desire to drop the death card on Jack—who was many things, but not worthy of murder by my fine hands. Instead, I flipped out the queen of clubs, the Lucky Lady of Freedom and Movement, which seemed more apropos.

Blood began running from each of my nostrils as if a tap had opened, so I stopped the mental appraisal and let the queen fly with a snap of my arm and flick of the wrist. The card sang through the air, fast as lightning. Pain magnified behind my eyeballs like balloons made of broken glass being inflated in my brain.

Tyger Tyger, burning bright!

Chains of pain whiplashed my skull, knocking me back just as my grip on the board died. Left leg up in the air, head heading south, I shot out my arms to deaden the fall—totally forgetting the cards in my hand. Smacking the earth, the cards emptied from their pack as the pain of impact rumbled my bones. Then Jack Lumber's scream reminded me of fates worse than myths.

"Argh!"

Everything felt like lead, and the Boardwalk's planks were hotter than a branding iron. I brought my knees up to my chest, inhaling blood and snot before executing a perfect kip-up. A gaggle of heads *wooo*'d as I went from horizontal to vertical just in time to see Jack grabbing his bloody ankle, dancing on one leg like he was on a pogo stick. Then Jack was jumping in my direction with industrial-grade fists ready, the stink of Black Lotus billowing from him like cheap cigar smoke from the poor side of Hades.

"I'm gonna enjoy bashing your melon!"

Dizziness and exhaustion ate my equilibrium as I raised my guard, hands open and palms out as if in deference. "Easy, pal! You were going off the rails. No one gets bonus points for hitting women and old folks."

"*Rawr!*"

The fists struck at me, clumsy and thick. I pulled a little wushu magic trick by inviting a punch to my face, then bending the momentum by twisting his wrist. Jack's fist landed directly on Jack's face. Goddamn, but that monster hand had speed and power. Add accuracy and he'd be dangerous.

Jack staggered back to the roar of laughter from the crowd, favoring his ankle, dripping blood and sweat all over my cards.

"Hah! He punched his own face!"

"This must be part of the Olympic Auditorium wrestling show."

"Ah, this is fake! Bullshit! Bullshit! Bullshit!"

Calling these tough guys fakes was an invitation to trouble. The clarity of rage in Jack Lumber's eyes confirmed it. He shot a hand out and grabbed some gawky teen, choked him, then lifted him in the air. "Call me a fake? I'll be fucking your mom on your grave tomorrow, you goddamn rube!"

The crowd whistled, thinking it was all part of the show, but the kid's purpling face spoke to the life being choked out of him by this musclehead. Enough was enough.

"Put him down, Jack," I said. "Or can you only beat up kids a third your size?"

He jerked his head around, tossed the kid like a bag of rotten eggs into the crowd, and hobbled toward me. "You screwed my race! So now, I'm going to rip off your—"

I threw a spinning back kick to his face. Hit him right on the button, under the jaw, with the force of three uppercuts.

Jack shut up, then fell down, then was out for the one, two, three . . . thousand.

A roar of applause came from the crowd.

"This must be a new movie!"

"Where's the camera?"

"Hey, mister, do you know Bruce Lee?"

I smiled. I did, but that story was for another day. "Show's over, gang! Thanks for watching rehearsal for our new hit cop show, *Boardwalk Beat*, coming this fall to CBS right after *Hawaii Five-O*. But autographs to anyone who can fetch my wingtips from the end of the Boardwalk."

A few of them ran off and I scrambled, feet burning, over to Jack.

He was out, but his body seemed to still be running like his foot was stuck on the gas, chest heaving like a bellows. The taste of magic was so bitter, it was as if it was coursing through his veins and its waste product pumping out as exhaust. In short, his body was a pollution factory, strong and deadly and working overtime to reach death.

I turned to the horizon just in time to see a silhouetted figure run off the pier. Someone tossed what looked like a bag into the air and the shadowy figure snatched it like a hawk, then descended over the edge.

Panting on hands and knees a few yards from the edge was Billy Mars.

Kevin vanished over the edge of the Boardwalk, followed by a splash.

I smiled, took off my brown paisley tie, and tied a strong tourniquet around Jack's cut ankle, tight enough to staunch the bleeding and to make sure it hurt with each step he took. I ran through his pockets, and found a joint, keys, and a twenty-dollar bill. At least he was solvent. Also, an empty dimebag that stank of ashes from a lost age.

Black Lotus had been in there. But how had he taken it?

The mob of kids from Tumbledown and other assorted spectators were now running, many of them cheering "Kev! Kev! Kev!"

I put back Jack's belongings, then checked his pulse. It was tapping like a speed freak in detention. I pulled back his ruddy lip.

Between his stained yellow teeth and bleeding gums were flecks of black. One poked out and seemed thin. Dried. A petal that had been cultivated somehow or way.

"Kev! Kev! Kev!"

I let the huffing Jack's lips fall closed and grabbed my board, careful to keep one eye on Billy Mars in case he, too, had some kind of magic, or perhaps a transporter like *Star Trek,* and would vanish from L.A. the moment he knew someone was onto him.

"Kev! Kev! Kev!"

Two girls approached, the bikini-top and Mickey Mouse duo. "You forgot your shoes," Mickey said.

"Much obliged."

"We heard there was a reward," said Bikini. They each playfully hid a shoe behind their back.

Ugh. I never understood men who liked young girls after they got done being young boys. Sure, these two were cute, but something grilled into me from the circuit always proved true: girls you need to teach, women will blow your mind, so don't creep backwards. Go around the block long as I have and you realize the best women are a challenge, and the best challenge comes from experience.

I held out the board. "Trade! One, two, three!"

I tossed the board in the air. Both girls launched my wingtips, heels first, at my chest, all to the sound of Austen moaning, "That's my board!"

The girls laughed and ran off; Austen chased after.

Shoes slipped on without socks, I turned and saw Mars running into the oncoming traffic, clearly tired of the spotlight without a championship belt.

Until he looked up and saw me.

I smiled. "Looks like we both lost." He sneered. I walked toward him and nodded at Jack. "Sorry your insurance policy didn't pan out. Nice way to rig things when you know you're going to lose."

"And what would you know about anything, square?"

"I know our friend Jack's about one gram of salt away from cardiac arrest with your product in his mouth."

Billy snarled, board shaking.

"And if you think you can swing and hit better than Jack, hero, be my guest. But if you'd like to avoid naptime with your friend, why don't you and I get a Coke and you tell me all you can about Black Lotus. Or else, when the beach cops ride in here, I might remember your name as I report this sad little adventure."

Billy Mars lips pursed. "Let's get this over with. I can't be seen hanging with the enemy."

I smiled, and we headed for a burger shack called Caveman, which featured a dinosaur eating a burger made out of screaming cavemen, which I thought was a clever reversal. "Your treat," I said with relish, because when it came to the smug, I always enjoyed adding insult to injury. Helped them learn humility.

Two lukewarm Cokes in hand, Billy and I walked off the Boardwalk and into the little maze of "backstage" areas for shacks and stands, where the sizzle of grills merged with the ocean's roar and the cacophony of human banter.

"My prophecy came true," he said. "The most deserving won."

"Funny thing about prophecies," I said. "You keep them vague and you can justify any outcome. Where'd you learn such hackwork? The Boardwalk?"

He snickered. "I'm in the Magic Circle!" He sat his Coke down on the wooden walk, then flashed his hands and did a series of junior coin tricks that would impress anyone who wasn't me. "I'm not some back-alley carny fixing dice and doing the Paris drop for idiots. I'm legitimate!"

I raised my hands in surrender. "Sincere apologies. But I'd hate for that professional gang to think its main face on the Boardwalk was involved in illicit goods."

His bravado retreated into an icy stare. "I don't sell anything."

"You mean 'not anymore.' Stop stalling, Billy. What do you know?"

His sour puss contorted more. Hoping to mask his reaction, he picked up his drink and took a slurp. "So, sure, I used to sell some. Still got friends in the concert world." His brag indicated he was, apparently, a musician—and that I was supposed to be impressed.

"I made little mints here and there selling grass, uppers, coke, even H." Then his nostrils flared. "But junkies, man, they're like leeches. They'll follow you around. I'd be doing my prophet routine and they'd be jonesing in the crowd, scaring away my daylight patrons and generally being a drag. God, that drug is going to ruin our good time, you know?"

I thought of the jazzmen I'd met, black musicians who were gods on the chitlin' circuit, and how dope infected their lives and careers. So many dead from a drug that helped take away the sting of a world that said they were lesser men, of an America that enslaved their grandparents, then dropped the chains of the plantation and put on of those of Jim Crow. Heroin was another form of slavery. And this little putz was talking about his good time getting ruined? "Save the philosophy for the acolytes. You were slinging dope."

"Yeah, until those zombies kept creeping me out. So, I sold my end of the business to another candy man."

"Who?"

"A cat named Mick Butler. He'd been a roadie for the Pretty Things but was finding night work groovier. Man, what a sleaze."

"What earned him that epitaph?"

"Pretty sure he was doing porno before he saw there was more money in hustling dope. Guy just . . . let's just say I wouldn't leave a girl alone with him, maybe even a boy. Has a big, creepy nose with a waxed moustache like some lost member of a barbershop quartet. Whatever, he bought me out good, and all my zombies belong to him. Which is a relief."

"Gone? Do they have a junkie HQ or squat where they all hang at?"

"That's just it. They did. All of the junkies dropped in on abandoned clubs downtown. But they got torn down so they could put in a few more tourist traps. I haven't seen one of them since. It's like they vanished."

No one misses junkies when they're gone. They're just relieved. They don't ask questions. "Addicts stick to where they've got access. Is Butler still hustling here?"

"If he is, it ain't smack. Though word was he also had contacts in the Golden Triangle. Asian gangs and revolutionaries all too happy to sell dope to the USA to fuel their revolution against Uncle Sam."

"Gods of war love irony. Where can I find this Mick Butler?"

"Don't know, never asked, got no clue. Know he's never around the Boardwalk. I wanted nothing to do with that creep once he bought me out."

"Then who do the kids here buy drugs from?"

"Weed? Everyone's got it. Man, you need to buy a clue."

"I mean something stronger. Something like speed. What some call Black Lotus." Billy pursed his lip as if to keep more words from spilling. "Your buddy Slumber Jack? Pretty sure he was enjoying a particular variety."

Billy raised his hands. "Look, I never heard of Black Lotus till you mentioned it, man. It sounds like Spanish fly for those with an Asian fetish. If it's something Jack is into, hey, bodybuilders and wrestlers were among my best customers, not for smack, but other shit. They're all at the Muscle Beach Gym or the Olympic Auditorium, but that's as far as I go and as far as I know, dig? Can I go now, officer?"

I nodded and he turned to leave, then looked back. "But if you go poking around Mick's clients, be careful. He's not just a creep. He's tough. Not like Jack, not pretend tough. Carries a long knife and always smiles when he touches it." He shivered. "Fucking with that dude is a funeral waiting to happen."

"Thank you for another prophecy," I said, and Billy *tsk*ed and left for the Boardwalk.

I followed him back to the Boardwalk and watched fans swarm around him as he proclaimed Kevin the winner. Jack was, incredibly, already on his feet, stumbling toward a toilet, tanned body covered with the grit of the Boardwalk like a pox. My tie around his ankle had slid off . . . and he wasn't bleeding.

I hadn't done *that* good a job. That wound had healed in minutes.

The wind had scattered the Bicycle deck like giant confetti. A few cards were still slipping and sliding, spinning and tripping. One came close to me and I snatched it between two fingers:

The Joker. I put it in my front pocket.

Kevin, riding on his board at the pace of the crowd, was grinning ear to ear, a dripping-wet bag of weed tucked in his jean shorts, hair soaked but skin quickly drying. I stepped out, waved. "Hail to the king of the Boardwalk!"

Kevin stopped and the crowd lurched forward. He was blocked from view until he silently communicated for them to part the way. "Not if you hadn't been so good at chasing for last place."

Everyone laughed, but only he and I got the joke. "Kid, I've been the last in line since before you were born."

"Still, thanks, man. You ever need a place to crash, we have it for you at Tumbledown."

"Much obliged," I said, and Kevin and his bevy of fans wheeled and walked off down the Boardwalk, then turned and headed into the city.

With them gone, I strolled down the Boardwalk, and took inventory:

My feet ached from gripping the earth like I was on a balance beam above the River Styx. My nose was crusted with blood from joyriding for about two seconds; I was pushing myself toward the edge of the grave if I kept it up.

Black Lotus seemed to be tied to the Boardwalk drug culture and this scuz Mick Butler. Jack Lumber had used it, and the smell made me positive it was the same kind that got dropped at the Legion Hall. Jack was a wrestler as well as a musclehead. Billy Mars had sold to both and Mick Butler had taken over his clientele. If Mars was telling the truth, Black Lotus didn't come into play until Butler was on the scene. Whoever put Cactus in the hospital was tied to Black Lotus and, as of now, that meant Mick Butler, wrestlers, and bodybuilders.

I knew where to find the muscleheads: here on the Boardwalk at the open-air gym. It was time to find some denizens of the squared circle and maybe Mick Butler.

But first I needed to check how the wider world was doing.

Passing a shack selling crystals that would cure cancer with energy that had no "chemicals," I came to a phone booth that hadn't been busted or used as an outhouse. Plastered on one side was a poster.

FRIDAY AT THE OLYMPIC AUD! WRESTLING
ACTION!
SEE THE MOST DANGEROUS MEN ON EARTH
COMPETE IN THE RING!
PLUS, LOCAL ROCK SENSATION WITCHIE POO!

Scrawled across WITCHIE POO was the word CANCELED.

The picture featured a supermensch with a buzz cut crushing the world in his colossal hands and standing on tiny legs. Wrestling and rock and roll? Well, even without the music, I guess I knew what my Friday night was shaping up to be.

One dime and seven digits later, I had access to my message service. Which I was not looking forward to.

"Thump & Grind Burlesque Club and Review."

"Hey, Lace," I said. "It's James."

"Of course it is," she said. "I just started my period and hadn't had enough of a cramp in my gut yet, so you're right on time." And yet, all I could see on the back of my eyelids was the dynamic, buxom thirty-year-old bottled-scarlet whose command of beauty was second only to her ability to dance in high heels with fans, a combination that made every man in the room beg for more, knowing none could have her.

But they didn't live in the storage unit of the Thump & Grind, where some nights a girl just wants to relax with a man who will treat her right and ask no more than to make her feel good.

When it came to dating, I was simply tragic.

"I know, I know, I'm sorry I had to cancel our dinner reservation, but I was—"

"On a case. You know what James? You *are* a case."

"Lace, please, listen, you're right. I sullied my honor as a gentleman and I'd like to make it up to you."

"This better be good," Lace said.

"The Bijou Lounge. Lobster. Champagne."

"Keep talking."

"Bananas Foster."

There was a pregnant silence. "How did you know that was my favorite dessert?"

"Unlike most men, I actually listen when a beautiful woman talks to me."

She snickered. "Okay, you're out of the doghouse by a paw. Even though I *know* we aren't going anywhere near the Bijou. Now what is it you really need?"

"What? No, Lace, I was—"

"You've buttered my muffin just fine, and you'll be doing it all night to make up for abandoning me at Clio's. What do you want, James?"

"I need you to see if there are any messages on my answering machine. If so, you need to play them and hold the receiver over the speaker so I can hear them."

"You don't mind me listening in on your business?" she was practically salivating.

"I trust you, Lace. Plus, this is important. One of my friends was almost killed today."

I told her about the Legion Hall.

"I heard about it on the radio," she said. "Protesters attacking veterans? I think I prefer the sixties, thanks."

And I would prefer the future, since most of the sixties had me running around trying to stop Armageddon cults from turning the peace and love generation's happenings into mass graves. "Will you help, Lace?"

"'Course I will. Call me back on your line."

"But my door's locked."

"Oh, James, everyone has a key to your fucking office."

She hung up.

I fished for another dime while an old man in a sunhat pulled down across his face circled the booth. He tapped on the glass. "How long you gonna be?"

"Can't tell until I hear from the other side," I said, vaguely mysterious, hoping he'd assume I was strange and not worth mucking with.

"Then can I make a call first?"

"Sir, on any other day, sure, but right now a friend of mine's in the hospital and—"

"Oh, save your bullshit stories, James."

The man raised his head and glared into my eyes. Any courage I possessed fled faster than a gambler from a bookie.

Edgar Vance's face was ghost white with sun cream, his eyes black and red with magic that I could not taste because my mouth was dry with terror. "Dead men have no time for such tales," said my mentor.

14

EDGAR RAISED A MELTING ICE CREAM CONE TO HIS leering mouth. The cone almost duplicated the deformed shape of his never-noble Roman nose. "I see you can take the kid out of the Boardwalk, et cetera. Prithee, James, what pathetic problem are you calling a quest now?"

When scared to the bone, try banter. "Thought you liked playing dead. Alicia Price is still sending out goons for your skull."

He licked his lips. "Ah, she is a feisty piece of ass, is she not?"

"Whatever floats your boat, Edgar. What do you actually want?"

"Same thing as before." His eyebrows raised. "My offer still stands."

It wasn't an offer. It was a death sentence, complete with indentured servitude that didn't end until I wound up splattered in some mage war I didn't care about. Edgar had freed me from my previous bondage when I helped him fake his death. Now, for the second time since his "death," he was trying to get me to volunteer myself back into slavery.

"No," I said. Not brave and bold, but clear and terrified.

"You know, James," he said, then took a long lick of vanilla ice cream with his cratered pink tongue. "Mmm. Vanilla. The most boring of flavors to those who crave novelty every second of their life. But there are layers of flavor in vanilla, a flavor that stretches back in time to the days of . . . well, you tell me, my charge."

"I am not your charge," I said as politely as my fear and anger would allow. "And vanilla is rooted in Mexican and Mesoamerican culture and traditions."

"Full marks, but do you know what you must do to make a flavor this profound and deep?"

"Is this question rhetorical?"

His gaping grin hitched higher, and I knew my smart mouth had overplayed my anxious hand. "It must be done in stages. First, you pluck the young flower from its home."

"You mean kill it."

"Then you sweat it until it reveals to you all the power and flavor it has."

"Charming."

"Then you dry it. Force it to become the best it can be."

"I'm seeing a pattern here."

"Then you condition it to be even better than its potential." He took another lick. Lace was waiting, but if I fucked up here, I'd be dead, or worse. Edgar would take great joy in ruining everything in my life just to make me suffer. "You're wasting your time. I could help you catch those you seek."

My lungs froze, not wanting to breathe the same air that carried Edgar's promise. "How?"

"Oh, I forgot, you are a lousy detective. You barely solved the riddle of those rocket-ship sex idiots. Really, James, picking up coins on cases involving that idiot Crowley? I raised you better than that."

"Those aren't who I seek," I said. "You're bluffing."

Again, the words fell faster than my common sense could grab, and this time I saw the cinder in Edgar's eye flare.

"Careful, my charge." He tapped a yellow talon on the glass. "I could hex this box into a first-class ride to the nethers and leave you on burning sand littered with the eyes of those mad enough to cross me once upon a time. Does that sound like a bluff?"

All hydration in my body vanished. "No."

"Good boy. Now, about the Indian who's fading into the Pale. Oh, fine, I can read your face. The Apache warrior whose back is now a slaughterhouse buffet of blood and guts. You want those who did this to him? Fine. I'll take you to them. I'll help you stop them. And if Geronimo falls, well, maybe I know a trick or two to drag him back into his carcass, though I suspect he'll find a way to kill himself because of the pain of being a cripple. Any-who, that's what I'm offering."

"What's the price, Edgar?" I said.

His finger cut a single line in the glass. "One day in my service. One day doing real magic, not this dimestore variety which, I must say, you're even getting worse at. That 'joyriding' nose bleed was pathetic."

"Why so little time?"

"Because you know that's all I need to convince you that you really want the Big Time. One day, and you'll volunteer the rest of your life. I've plucked, sweated, dried, and conditioned you, James. You just need a taste of the Big Time . . . then you'll forget about these rubes, marks, and *civilians*."

If he'd stopped at Big Time, he might have had a deal.

"No."

He blinked and the eye turned molten before returning to its "normal" green hue. "As my hearing is perfect, I take it that declining my offer had something to do with my disdain for your clients. Really, James. The world is made of those who rule and those who serve. The better quality the servant, the much greater the ruler." I kept my lips shut as he shoved the entire cone into his large, gray mouth. He crunched down, almost giving me brain-freeze by proxy. "Suit yourself," he said, chewing through his food and words like a slob. "But as I told you before, you're a terrible detective. When your Injun friend dies because you were too stupid to find his killers, my offer will have expired." He swallowed, then held out his finger as if to flick the glass. "And your guilt will eat you alive."

He flicked the line he'd etched in the glass and the entire panel shattered around my feet.

Edgar was gone.

I kicked the debris off my wingtips, though being sockless meant I had to take each shoe off and shake out glass ground to powder. Passersby gave me the stink-eye and families pulled their kids closer as I fetched another dime, grateful that no one wanted to harass the freak who'd destroyed public property and then stood in its remains. I started to dial Lace.

. . . dies because *you were too stupid to find his killers . . .*

I stopped, my finger still stuck in the dial.

Edgar had said that if I didn't find the villains who had attacked the vets, Cactus would die. I would help *cause* his death.

Me. Responsible. Whatever Edgar knew, whatever secret fate he implied I was tied to, was gnawing at my courage and moral code.

The answers I needed were hidden middle of a Black Lotus-flavored, three-layer magic shitcake and, so far, I had barely even tasted the frosting.

I finished dialing with a quivering digit.

Three rings. Four. Five.

Click.

"I swear to Christ, if you hold me up any more than you already have I will take it out of you in flesh."

"Even angry," I said to Lace, "you sound sexy."

"Oh, you're not getting any action that easy."

"Lace, you're absolutely right. A woman of your quality needs better. And I aim to give it to you. As much as you want."

"What I want is to get back to my book."

"What novel you reading these days?"

"Not that you care, but it's a short story book."

"I should have figured you for a more refined reader."

"Keep the compliments coming and maybe I won't tear your head off. Some guy named Beaumont. God, so creepy. Used to write for *Twilight Zone*. You finish one story, and you need to read another to get the scare out."

I'd had enough scares to last me a lifetime; didn't need to chase it in books. "Sounds great. Say, are you near the machine?"

"I've been sitting at your desk for ten minutes while you were jerking off in that booth."

"Great. Is there a—"

"Flashing light? Yeah, it's brighter than the Bat-signal."

"Great. Hit rewind." The reel-to-reel whizzed in the arcane manner of machines talking backwards until there was a click. "Okay, now, hit the big blue button."

Thunk.

A hiss.

Then a scratch before a voice I wasn't expecting.

"Mr. Brimstone? James? This is Veronica Carruthers."

"Who?" Lace said, but I shut up and listened.

15

"I . . . WANTED TO SPEAK TO YOU, PERSONALLY, BUT I understand if this is the best way to do so." Her velvet voice sounded as if it had marinated in a flask of gin and seasoned with one long Pall Mall. "Alan has been doing as you asked, and from what I've heard they're all blaming the . . . hippies who were outside the place."

"What a witch," Lace said.

"But that's not all. I went to the hospital to check up on your friend, the Indian fellow, Cactus? Our families are donors, so I hope you don't mind that I asked some questions. Now, normally I'd never do such a thing, but your friend saved us all. Just like you saved me."

"Oh god, James," Lace said. "Is this your latest twist?"

"She's a client," I said. "Now, please, *shhh*!"

Lace groaned.

"It appears he's in a coma. They've stopped the bleeding, given him a lot of blood, removed the shrapnel, and stitched the wounds up. He has not regained consciousness. He's on an IV for hydration, medication, and nutrition. One lung has collapsed, so he's on life support for now. But, well . . . there's another complication."

She paused like she was preparing to deliver bad news.

She delivered it. "An attorney showed up with some legal documents. They stipulate that if Sergeant Hayes is in a coma for more than a day, according to his wishes, they are to take him off all medication and life support. That would be tomorrow morning. It's all quite legitimate and the hospital doesn't dare go against such documents. I'm . . . I'm sorry, James."

During the pause, Lacey was silent while my heart clenched like a baby clutching its rattle.

"I thought you should know. I . . . I also, well, wanted you to know that you've been on my mind. I treated you so poorly, as if you were a common—it doesn't matter; what matters is that I judged you harshly and I owe you my life. And . . . I can't stop thinking about you."

Lace huffed.

"I understand you are working in Venice trying to find who committed this awful crime. As it happens, I'll be in Venice, too, at the Hilton. My family has a suite that we rarely use, but if you should need a place to work . . . well, I'll be there. And thank you again, James, for saving my life."

CLICK.

"'As it happens?'"

"She almost died today, Lace."

"So, you going to see her tonight instead of me?"

"As much as I'd like to see you tonight, babe, I'm not seeing you or her or anyone else tonight unless they can lead me to the coward who shoved a grenade into a room full of old men and ladies."

"Okay, James," she said, a tad softer than usual. "But one of these nights—right?"

"You bet. Thanks, Lace."

"You're welcome. Sorry about your friend."

She hung up first. She always did.

Now there was a ticking clock in the sky. Connected to magic or not, Cactus was dead in the morning. I wanted my promise to him done before he passed into the nethers.

I pulled myself out of the booth as sirens tore up the main drag. I looked up the beach to where they were headed.

Damn.

I chased the ambulances. They were headed straight for the outdoor gym.

A ring of spectators surrounded the fenced-in gym filled with bronze giants and bleached hair. A collapsed man lay in its center. Most stood stock still while a brunette in a bikini kept hammering his chest. "Come on! Come on, Jack!" She pulled his mouth open and breathed in as if he'd been drowning, as if mouth-to-mouth could replace the breath of life that was escaping.

Two men leapt out of the ambulance, the driver with short salt-and-pepper hair, the other a redhead . . . Arrows! The red-headed guy who'd helped me drag Cactus, kicking and screaming, from death's door, whom I'd just chatted with.

They reached the body and pulled the woman away. "Let go of me! He's my husband!"

"Then let us save him!" said Salt and Pepper, shoving her away, and I had half a mind to release the Joker from my front pocket and slice off his eyebrows, but his hands might be needed to save the poor sap on the ground.

Red was already injecting something, maybe adrenaline, into Jack's veins. We watched the rushed attempts to bring him back, but all of it failed.

When Arrows checked the pulse again, I knew the answer.

There, like a frozen slab of inflated meat, lay the body of Jack Lumber.

"Is he dead?" a kid asked at my side. He and his gang all gawked.

"Of course he's dead. He's not moving."

"But he's bigger than the Hulk."

"If the Hulk was five-eight."

"Easy," I said to the scraggly kids.

I wiggled my way through the gawkers. "Hey! Arrows! Arrows!"

Red looked up as the ghoulish sightseers shoved him in the back. "You?"

"Yeah. Me. Do you have a sec? Please?"

"Call it in," Arrows said to his buddy. "This guy might know him."

"Sure," said Salt and Pepper, yanking a cigarette from his pocket. "This dude's not going anywhere." He opened the ambulance door, got in, shoved the smoke between his lips, and slammed the door.

A muscled behemoth was holding the brunette. She was hysterical. "No! He can't die! He's in perfect shape! Perfect!"

I pulled Arrows away from the crowd, but he tore away from me and went toward the woman. "That lady was the last person to have seen Jack alive," he mumbled as I followed.

"Ma'am," the redhead asked, "are you his next of kin?"

"Don't talk like he's dead!" she said, scarlet fingernail jabbing an inch from Arrow's eyeball. "Don't you dare! He's a machine of health." The behemoth who held her wore *Easy Rider* Ray-Bans and a T-shirt on his head like a Boardwalk sheik with a bald spot. "Let go of me, Achilles."

The name suited him, if the ancient Greeks cared more about bench presses than hacking guys with short swords. "Calm down, Sam. They're trying to help."

"You ain't helping shit!" she said. "Unless you let go, I'll get a cop!"

Achilles released his grip and held his cultivated arms up in surrender. God, his biceps had to be twenty inches all the way around, as if his thighs had gotten misplaced.

It was only when Achilles backed off that I understood why he was holding on. Sam was beautiful, and that distracted from the power of her build: round shoulders, strong arms, hard legs; this woman was a career athlete and gym rat, not some bunny doting on the boys doing curls. She walked with the force of a hurricane and grabbed Arrows by the shirt with two tanned mallets. "What happened to him? He was fine this afternoon."

"Ma'am, I can't say. But his heart stopped, and we can't resuscitate him."

Then Arrows's feet were dangling above the ground. "No way. Not Jack. He was in perfect health. He was a perfect specimen." I admit I heard the Bard whisper in my ear, *the lady doth protest too much*. She needed to believe her husband was a paragon of virtue and good living, but something told me the Black Lotus he chewed on the Boardwalk had not been his first taste.

"No need to strangle the nice fella," I said. "He's trying to help."

"He failed!" she said, shaking Arrows, whose face was now cherry-red below his carrot top. "He was too weak to save my man."

"Especially after he lost to this guy." Goddamn it. Austen, that miserable toad, was smiling from the Boardwalk, his skateboard hugged to his chest. "He damn near ran him over."

Arrows hit the ground and I found myself a foot taller as Sam the Bereaved Amazon lifted me closer to heaven than I would ever get on my own. "You were in that race?"

I nodded.

She sized me up. "*You* . . . beat my husband?"

"More . . . like a tie. Draw at best." Her hands shook as the crowd waited for her next move. "Didn't mean harm," I said. "Especially to such . . . a great wrestler."

Her eyes softened.

My ass landed next to Arrows with a thud that lanced pain up my spine.

Sam dropped to her knees, chest shaking, tears streaming from her blue eyes. "This was supposed to be his big match. He was getting over with the fans. He was main eventing at the Olympic. Sasha would get her medicine." She crushed her hands to her eyes. "The child is so sick she can barely walk!"

Pain turned to guilt and it was getting hard to swallow air I didn't think I was entitled to. Arrows got up, offered his hand. "Please, come with us to the hospital."

"I can't! Our babysitter—"

"We'll drive you to your home," Arrows said. "You can get your daughter."

She reached out and clasped his pale and freckled hand. Arrows steadied her and helped her to her feet, then looked at me. "No news on your friend."

I nodded and knew pressing for details on Jack was not going to gain me any favors. I might even end up in a headlock. As Sam was taken away, the crowd dispersed, including Austen, smug as the cat who got the cream.

"Hey, you!"

I sighed, turned, and stared at the boulder of a human being who went by Achilles. "You knew Jack?"

I nodded, and an idea bloomed in the form of a lie. "From the Northwest wrestling territories. For a big guy, he could wrestle."

"You heard what Sam said about this being his big night?"

"Sure, brother."

"Then I'd suggest you do the right thing."

"You need to help me out, Achilles, I don't speak Californian."

My stunning sense of humor was deflected with a smug look that made it clear I was yet another rube until proven otherwise. Achilles bent and picked up a green gym bag. He handed it to me. "Jack's trunks. Costume. And mask."

Uh-oh.

"Before you start making excuses, Jack was doing two shows tonight. But in the main event, he was wrestling as the Assassinator." He looked me up and down. "Scrawny, but you could make Sam her payday and make sure Sasha gets her medicine." Around me all the lifters, pullers, and curlers were vanishing to the beach, abandoning what was now a death marker for a "healthy" man whose heart must have exploded thanks to Black Lotus.

I wanted to run in the other direction. Sure, wrestlers had carny roots, but the modern variety was a brotherhood unto themselves. They kept their lives in shadow, secret, and bullshit. If they found me out, they'd chew me up. But that show was the only connection I had to Black Lotus. Maybe Mick Butler would be drumming up business before the big match.

I reached out and took the bag, heavy with gear. "What time?"

"Eight-thirty. Tell Hector that Achilles said you were cool with kayfabe and doing a double for Jack."

Kayfabe . . . that took me back. It was carny slang for maintaining the illusion that a con—like wrestling—is real. "You going to be there?"

Achilles scoffed. "I'm just security, rube. Now go and make it right."

Something told me that Achilles's interest in Sam and Sasha wasn't strictly humanitarian, and that Sasha likely had the eyes of Achilles. But who was I to judge?

I had two hours before the bout to try and gather more info on Black Lotus. I needed to know what it did. Where it came from. How in hell it had crept out of the Cimmerian age and what in hell it foretold.

Standing on the blistering Boardwalk, a cool breeze shook me. I wasn't close to any esoterica shops worth a damn. Venice was never a hotbed of magic like the heart of L.A., and what occult roots were buried here were, to the best of my knowledge, dead and gone. And, frankly, herb lore was never my scene. Edgar's greenhouse was filled with enough poisonous roots and psychedelic worms to make Timothy Leary run home to his mother's tit before he "dropped out." I hated when Edgar had me steal flowers from the graves of his former enemies from the worlds of real or stage magic—filching freshly planted marigolds or impatiens under a waxing moon—just to make sure Herb "The Magnificent Moroccan" Harrak had a harder time ascending to whatever afterlife he'd be performing in for all eternity. As for the lore of plants—from witch hazel to woad to Black Lotus— well, that was as enjoyable as reading a terrible pulp novel: both were packed with ancient rites and warrior traditions filled with blood, guts, and glory.

But what this stuff did? How Jack could chew on it like an acid tab and become a berserker of the Boardwalk? What it did to your heart, your glands, your turds? Pretty sure I cheated on that exam. And Edgar didn't mind. Which meant he knew, he *knew* I didn't know shit about Black Lotus and its properties, but *he* did. And would have shared. And helped me find the bastards who put Cactus in a coma . . .

I spun and ran down the Boardwalk to cat calls of "fruit" and "fairy," which bounced off me like rubber hail on a rhino's hide.

In the sea of lobster-red faces and tanned bodies with ass cheeks swinging away on roller skates, Edgar's sour puss was nowhere in sight and there wasn't a flicker of his magic in the air.

Until I heard a familiar giggle lofted on a cryptic wind.

"You're doomed, James. Without me? You and everyone you love are doomed."

It wasn't the veneer of malice that coated Edgar's voice like tar on a jazz singer's lungs that pushed my button. It was a word that Edgar used, a word that had no meaning to him personally but that he could wield like a hammer against others.

Love. *Everyone you love.*

I fished through my pockets because I needed another dime for another dame, and without anyone as the middleman. All I had was two hundred from the Rocketeers Sex Club, all in twenties.

Breaking a twenty was as easy as buying a Coke, but—hoping to banish the taint of an odious brush with Edgar with a good deed—I chose a harder way.

In the shadow of a shack selling shaved ice stood a small card table and the world's oldest waste of money.

"Another winner!" said the dealer, a career beach nut in bronze skin and a tie-dyed tank top that hung off his skinny body like rags on a skeleton. "Michelangelo, if I didn't know any better, I'd say you were scamming me!"

The man in front of him was an innocent. A creature born simple and sweet, a child destined to never grow up but, unlike that little shit Peter Pan, not granted magic powers. The air around him tasted of cotton candy, not conjuring.

The asshole with the cards was using this big kid's good nature as a means to fleece him.

I walked up, face all "gosh-wow" as if this cat in the lounge-lizard suit had never seen such entertainment. "Wow, you must be doing great!" Big Kid looked up at me and smiled, eyes huge, face burned, a badge around his neck telling the world he was "Michael G," from St. Christopher's Center for the Mentally Retarded. "I'm lucky!" Michael said, but his eyes kept being pulled to the shack where stuffed animals were displayed. The apple of his eye? A dingy version of Underdog—his red shirt bleached pink—tied with other tacky prizes to a board behind the table.

"Three times," the asshole said. "Three times he's doubled his money. That's a lot of gum drops, Michelangelo! That's a lot of paint and canvas. One more and you could buy that prize without having to play a single game." Then the asshole stuck the cash out so the bills fluttered in the ocean breeze. "Or I could give them back—"

"No! Again!" Michael stared at the black cloth on the table as if it was staring back.

This was bad. Conmen rarely let a mark win *any* hands at three-card monte. But this big kid looked like a payday, so he was playing high risk with a victim in waiting.

The asshole fidgeted with three cards. Each was bent down the center like the roof of a log cabin. He put them down side by side with the care of a master craftsmen laying brick. "You know the rules, Michelangelo. Follow the lady with the nice dark hair—" He lifted one card and revealed the queen of spades. "—and she will grant you your wish!"

"She granted mine," said a surf dude standing nearby. He flashed a fistful of cash.

"You'll eat me out of house and home!" the asshole said. The beach bum was surely his shill, building up the idea that this game was legit. Michael glared at the guy with the big wad of cash, as did I, but I focused my peripheral vision on the conman. As we gawked, the dealer made his move.

He palmed the queen of spades and pried one card apart, revealing a second.

"All right!" the dealer said and, with Michael back at full attention, shuffled. "All you gotta do, my friend, is find the lady with the black hair. That's it. That's all there is. Which explains why I'm still working the Boardwalk and not in Vegas."

He was good. Smooth. But I could smell the finger moistener on his tips, the stuff he'd used to stick the cards together and that allowed him to palm them like a magnet on lead.

"Fun game," I said to the dealer.

"Not for me, I gotta feed my family!" He kept hustling the cards like a juggler.

"Care to make it more interesting?"

His hands never stopped moving. "Always. That's why it's fun to be alive!"

"Terrific!" I took out a twenty-dollar bill, creased it like the cards, and placed it on the black canvas with a single finger stabbing it in place. "I bet I can find the queen of spades while you're still moving your hands. Double or nothing."

Michael's ears perked, but all his attention was on cards that weren't the queen.

The dealer snorted, which had to be a signal. "Wow, never heard that one before!"

He was using a pattern called the Hindu Diamond, which looked pretty but was meaningless because the queen was now tucked on the back of a shaved card. No matter what Michael picked, he'd be wrong.

But not me.

"Just say when," the dealer said. I could feel the shill's shadow on me, in wait, ready to do something stupid in case the dealer had to run.

I smiled. "When."

As quick as this dealer was, he was low-rent compared to the hustlers who trained me, from Edgar to every talented shill in Oakland working Chinatown to the docks. Plus, Edgar's isometric training and Dr. Fuji's muscle-control regimen meant my fingers were spring-loaded triggers for cards, paper, coins, and more. Before our dealer realized he was in a jam, I launched the twenty at his face with a flick.

Even for the most hardened conman, money in the face is impossible to resist. He brought both eyes up to catch the bill as my hand struck out faster than an asp at Cleopatra's breast, bent the glued cards in half with thumb and index finger, and sliced them back so that the queen of spades was resting on her back in the sun.

When the dealer plucked the Jackson from his eye, the gig was up. He didn't clench his jaw, but he didn't laugh about needing a new day job, either. He just held his face, then blinked twice. "Wow. Ain't that a sight?"

Michael looked confused and sad. I felt like an ass. "Sorry to interrupt your win," I said to Michael. "Tell you what, since I changed the game, you can get my winnings, minus a dime." I looked at the dealer, who just realized I'd flushed out his reserves beyond the cash in the shill's pocket (which might well be counterfeit). The dealer's eyes were tiny calculators running the odds of escape. I placed my finger on the queen, in the exact same launch position I'd used for the bill. At this distance, I could slit his throat or shave his forehead. "You do have enough to back up the bet, correct?"

The dealer stole one glance at my finger and saw my little green ring. A slice of flash to distract the rubes, and, right now, make it clear that if he screwed with me he'd be in a world of hurt. He smiled and nodded. "Of course. I'm a legitimate businessman."

He reached into his back pocket and I kept the card on the launch pad until he fingered out my earnings—my twenty and another twenty dollars in smaller bills and change—into Michael's hands. Michael was shocked and a little scared, but as the money piled up, his smile grew. "Why?" he said, then looked at me. "Why, mister?"

"Like I said, I was rude to interrupt your game, Michael. To make up for my rudeness, I wanted to help you. But we all know you would have won this round anyway, right?

He smiled and nodded.

"Great, now how about that dime?" Michael plucked out a coin, and proudly handed it to me along with my original bill. "Now, go and save Underdog from that awful leash around his neck!"

Michael crammed the money in a pocket and nodded just as his caretaker—a harried woman in her sixties cramming two hundred pounds onto her five-four frame and into fuchsia capris, a blue blouse, and rhinestone sandals—arrived. "I told you not to veer away from the group! The bus is waiting, it's almost craft hour!" Michael grabbed his prize before following the woman. I had no idea what craft hour entailed for Michael, but I was glad that Underdog was tucked safely under his arm, ready to smash evil should it invade the city.

"You fucked me up the ass," the dealer snarled, gripping his table so hard the veins on the backs of his hands swelled like a junkie's itching for a needle. "Who sent you?"

The shill's presence behind me was as annoying as a winter coat in Aruba. "No one. I'm a freelance do-gooder, and you, good sir, were ripping off someone who wouldn't hurt a fly. Where I come from, that makes you a shithook."

"Where you're from don't matter as much as where you going," said the shill. The point of the blade in my back was more annoying than his presence or his threat. "Come on. We're going to take what you stole."

I sighed. "Boys, I'm proud to say I swing in many directions, but I don't entertain shithooks, so listen up clear. You can murder me here, run, and let L.A.'s finest cops follow you to whatever hole you're squatting in. Or you can admit defeat, grab your table, and find a fresh stretch of property. Anything else, and I'll show you my favorite card trick. The Cyclops."

The dealer snorted. "So, you're a sharp. Big goddamn deal. What are you going to do with that? Slice a watermelon at twenty paces?"

"Hmm. Not a bad trick. But not as fun as this."

I let fly. The card launched in the air like a ninja's shuriken but spun with just a hint of magic to fuck with physics. The queen sliced a gash across the dealer's forehead before taking flight, bouncing off the telephone pole with the wrestling show poster plastered on it, ricocheting back, spinning, and planting itself in the shill's eyebrow. All in less than a speed freak's heartbeat.

Screams followed as both men reached for their faces and the shill dropped his switchblade. "Someone help them! Killer bees! They got hit by killer bees!" The great thing about cutting the head is the amount of blood that ensues in seconds, but no permanent damage is done. It's the kind of wound you see on real wrestlers, not bodybuilders like the late Jack Lumber, whose ears had barely turned to cauliflower.

Everyone stayed away as the two rotten bastards bled across the Boardwalk, heading north. But the shadow behind me was annoyingly familiar.

"You know what, Jimmy?" Dixon said. "You're starting to make my ass itch."

16

DIXON LOOKED BAD. LIKE, ALL-NIGHT-COFFEE-and-cigarettes bad. But I'd last seen him at the Legion Hall only a few hours before. "You look lovely, Detective. New shampoo to make your buzz cut shine just so?"

His jaw was chewing itself, cheekbone stronger than iron. "Why is it if I'm looking for trouble all I have to do is follow the glare of your awful suit?"

"High fashion has never been a criminal act in L.A., and you know it."

"What the fuck was that ruckus with the Boardwalk trash?"

"You know, if West Oakland had had a boardwalk, we would have been its trash."

Shoulders hunched, he spoke with contempt. "Knock off the memory-lane bull. Just because we went to school together doesn't mean shit. Who were they?"

"Confidence men. A rather rotten breed of street thug, related to jugglers by marriage, if I'm not mistaken."

He poked my chest with intent to do harm. "What do they have to do with the bombing?"

"Nothing."

He pulled his jaw back and laughed. "Oh my god, Jimmy. You got a friend dying in the hospital and you're wasting your time on trash hustling the idiotic?"

I smiled. "Haven't you heard? I'm an awful investigator. But as bad as I am, you're here, looking for me and asking questions. So, as bad as I am, you don't have much better. *Detective*."

The smug smile sank into the recesses of his face. "You're involved. You are. I couldn't find any ties to that goddamn porn actress going missing. But I know you were involved."

"Can't help you there. She was something of a free spirit." Meaning Nico, a.k.a. Tabitha Vance, Edgar's daughter, a hellcat by any other name who I hoped would take a short eon to recover from the nightmare she'd put me through.

And Dixon had been on my heels then. Bad news. He might be a rotten human being, but he had the determination god gave mamma bears to protect their cubs. The cub in Dixon's case was his pride. The little rat from Piedmont had made detective, and now his major case was going so poorly he was hassling me. "But I was going to ask *you*, Detective, if there was any word on the people who attacked the hall." My tone was calm and aggravating. If his shit itched before, it was now sweating with friction.

"The investigation is still ongoing," he said. "We're tracking down several leads."

"Well, I hope they lead somewhere," I said. "Cactus will be yanked off life support tomorrow if he's still in a coma. So, take your time. Wait until your assault case turns into a homicide. Me? I actually want to catch the guy before my friend goes from vegetable to corpse." I walked off.

His fingers bit into my shoulders almost a second before I could flex, breathe, and not allow those fingers to cause pain.

"Watch yourself, Jimmy. The only friend you got is almost dead. But I will tell you this: there's something . . . bigger at work than hippies having a psychotic break."

I matched his stare. "Something more organized? More planned?"

He held still. "Let's just say I'm getting the push to mop this up, pin it on the freaks and heads, and call it a day. I don't like being pushed, Jimmy. Not by anyone."

Which is why it amazed me that a guy who said "fuck you" to the army would end up a cop. "Thanks for the tip."

"It's more like a warning. Something's behind this. Someone with influence. Watch yourself." He shoved me. "And don't come back here."

I raised my arms in surrender, just as a little bus drove by. In the front window was Michael and Underdog, watching me getting pushed around. I smiled, but it did those two heroes no good.

Rat or not, I had to take Dixon's warning seriously. As for the Boardwalk, I was sick of it. Maybe I couldn't avoid it in the future but for now I could at least place some distance between its planks and my presence.

I headed into town to find a payphone, one that I prayed didn't have Edgar hiding in its glass. I strolled a few blocks and stopped at one near the red-tile-roofed Venice Post Office. I doubted that official U.S. government property was any protection against Edgar, but at least Windward Circle is a pleasant neighborhood.

I dialed.

"Pet Palace, where your pet is king."

"Dr. Isabella Caylao."

"Who should I say is calling?"

"Anyone but James Brimstone."

"Oh, you. The guy who ruined her office."

"I tried to save it! Look, just patch me into Izzy, okay?"

The familiar sound of dismissal amongst Filipinas was a *tsk* that sounded more like *chit*.

Phone cradled on my shoulder, I saw a weak reflection of myself in the glass. My hair, as always, looked fantastic, even if a bit mussed. (Dad's thick Irish mane was the only gift that sack of violence and lies ever gave me.). But my suit looked worse than worn and tired, and it wasn't even happy hour. I adjusted my shirt, then licked both hands to reform my mane into a slicker version of its wilder cousin.

Then a *click*. The liquid in my voice turned to sand.

"This better be anyone other than James Brimstone."

"Hi, Izzy."

"Because James Brimstone still owes me an explanation for the riot in my waiting room."

"See, about that—"

"And James Brimstone owes me two dinners and a movie of my choice, which will be in Tagalog because he needs to improve his own, which is awful at best."

"That's mighty fair."

"And James Brimstone better not be asking me for any more favors, since I've never received so much as a thank you for the one that, if he is still alive, saved his life."

I sighed. "I'm alive, Izzy, thanks to you and that anting-anting charm. I would have returned it, but in order to save the world I had to let a monster eat it."

"You . . . destroyed a good luck charm?"

"Yeah."

Izzy's laughter was warm, even when served cruel. "Of course you did, you stupid American *batang lalaki*. I give you one thing to save your life and you destroy it!" She cackled at the irony of my idiotic existence. "Oh, James. This *is* you. This is you in a peanut shell."

126

"Just so we are clear, I also saved the universe."

"No, you didn't!"

"Well, a part of the universe."

"A very small part, but I live here, so thank you. And this is why you call? Because you're not thanked? You don't come back to my store and face me for what you've done and what you've broken and what you've ruined and wrecked. You are many things, James, but I didn't take you for a—"

"Cactus is in a coma."

Her tone changed quicker than a switchblade retreating into its handle. "Awful. Who did it? Who *could* do it?" Izzy liked gambling and had met Cactus numerous times at his casino, the Filipina and the Apache both enjoying the games that sucked the white man's pockets dry. I tried not to think of what happened between them after hours, since Izzy was a modern woman and took what she liked in love and romance and, in my case, left it behind. And, well, Cactus was five times as handsome as yours truly.

"That's what I'm trying to find out. My trail is warming up, but I need someone who knows a lot about herb lore and plants. The kind that haven't been kicking in the dirt for two thousand years."

"What kind of plant could fell Cactus?"

"A kind called Black Lotus."

"Hold on." She left me hanging. I heard her heels clack and the ruffle of papers. Izzy's main vein was animal magic of healing, but she dabbled in florae, which had been her mother's trade back in San Juan, north of Manila, in the highlands of Luzon. Her grandmother had been a master of bug magic. Both had died under the sword of the Japanese when MacArthur ran away to Australia and left girls like Izzy as the front line against nationalist, racist shitbags who viewed the Filipinos as a bastard race and slave labor.

Her heels clacked louder and tickled the old wound in my heart. "Cimmerian flowers?"

"Exactly."

A *woosh* of flipping pages. "They're . . . tied to early days of magic and blood. Sumerian . . . tied to Tiamat, mother of gods and monsters."

Weasel's rant was fresh in my ear. "That sounds lovely. But what does it do? What if you eat it?"

"This is not my field, James. What I have here says warriors ingested it before battle to have no fear and fight like gods. You're saying this flower is alive and in L.A.?"

"Yes. And one flower was found where Cactus was almost blown to hell and back. There's someone selling it on the street. I think it strengthens people, but it may ruin their organs."

"The age of Cimmerian warriors was short and bright," Izzy said. "It would not surprise me if they bargained for strength in battle for a short life."

"Killing you to make you invincible? I'll take an old-age home and hitting on nurses until the light winks out, thanks."

Izzy giggled and I wanted to hold her. "There's that bravado that charmed all the girls along the carnival trail. I'm sorry, James, that's all I know. The masters of plants were even more secretive than you magicians."

"Damn it. Is there anyone you know who might have answers?" As Samuel Johnson noted, there were two kinds of knowledge: that which you had, and the kind that let you have more. "And anyone in Venice Beach."

"Venice?" she said with a mild tut-tut of disgust. "You can take the boy out of the carnival, but—"

"Not everyone hates their carny days, Izzy."

Which was when I fell for her. Got her a ring made from a spoon and a diamond I'd stolen off a woman who liked fifteen-year-old boys to rub her back for a penny. Presented it and my love, only to hear laughter and have her vanish the next day. "You're still a stupid romantic," she said.

"Only for you."

I could *almost* hear her smile. "There is a girl who worked for me. She was awful with animals, but her calling is the herb and plant world. Her name is Margarita Diaz."

"And she's in Venice."

"Yes, she left contact data. Very upscale place, so you better buy a better suit."

"You don't even know what I'm wearing."

"Whatever it is, you picked it, so you'll need a *better* suit. Ah, here it is. The store is called 'El Dorado.'"

"Great. Address?"

"Hilton Hotel in Venice. I suspect there's only one."

Yup. And inside was a married woman waiting for me like a tiger ready to strike.

"James? I prefer silence while I nap. How about a 'thank you' instead?"

"Thank you, Izzy. I owe you."

"Again." She sighed. "I wish I had some charm to keep you from getting into trouble. But then, you wouldn't be you if you lived safe and sound."

"You've already done enough to make my life worth living, Izzy."

"Stupid romantic."

"Always."

She laughed, then hung up, never saying goodbye.

I squeezed out of the phone booth and waited to hear Edgar's cackle across the wind. But if he was paying attention, he did it in silence.

At my feet was the bag Achilles had given me.

In the shade of a juice stand's awning, I unzipped the bag.

Jock sweat, gym socks, and old blood greeted my nose as if released from a canister filled with biological waste.

Inside there was a full-body suit in black that looked like it would hug my muscles like pythons. Canary-yellow boots with long laces up the calf featured daggers going through a skull on each side, a riff on a popular Marine Corps tattoo. Fugh. Did he serve? Vets were dying around me like I was a walking sack of mustard gas.

And then, at the bottom, in shimmering silver and gold, was a wrestling mask that a man I helped kill today wore. Guilt and logic socked each other in the jaw as I lifted up the mask, the thick glitter sharp around the eyes and mouth. I'd done carny wrestling for years on the circuit. Hercules and Dr. Fuji taught me how to take a bump and perform basic holds and reversals, but I was almost always the "stick," pretending to be a boy in ragged overalls covered in coal dust or farm muck or whatever other grime was pertinent to the place who would volunteer to fight Herc. The fans would writhe as Herc tossed me around and got the first fall, then I'd fight back for the second, and then everyone was on their feet when he finally got me in a blood choke made famous by Ed "Strangler" Lewis. (After he ripped it off of Evan "Strangler" Lewis, keeping the tradition of theft, hoodwinks, and charlatanism alive and well in the squared circle.) We made a mint with this routine, and I rarely went off script unless I was "shooting"—wrestling for real—for a couple of bucks at a work camp or parking lot. But I knew pro wrestlers improvised, and if you fucked around they could turn the match real in a heartbeat, sticking you in an ankle lock that would cripple you for months. Thankfully, Dr. Fuji taught me legitimate martial arts, too, so I could protect myself.

Staring at the mask, I wasn't sure if I'd need to. But something told me this outfit was also unfit for entering such rarified air as the El Dorado at the Hilton. And while I looked amazing in my subtle orange-and-brown windowpane suit, they might think I was the piano man arriving early for the five o'clock lush set. Albeit one with a hole in his ass.

And every move I made without finding the murdering bastards brought Cactus closer to death.

I took a breath and centered myself, exhaling deep from my chest: I had a lead, and it was at the wrestling match. Knowledge was power, so I would go to El Dorado to arm myself.

For this to work, I had to wear the outfit of a masked goon in the ring, and—to get to the ring—finer duds than I was ever used to owning, let alone wearing. In my line of work, your outfit generally won't last a single case.

I fingered my cash.

Two hundred and no change. Enough to buy something more than decent. But this was laid-back, bohemian Venice. Where could I find upscale duds in a hurry?

I hit the main drag and caught sight of a cab. I whistled hard enough to break glass and the yellow beast skidded to a halt in front of me.

Behind the wheel was a teenage Latino in a well-worn denim workshirt, hair just a smidge too long for the army and a smidge too short for the revolution. "Where you headed?"

I hated the words that followed. "Martel's Magic and Costume Emporium. You know it?"

"Yeah, it's that closet in Mar Vista where all the kids hang out."

Yeah. Kids. And Shirley Martel, the Rockette who became the face of women in magic back in the day.

And who took the virginity of one James Brimstone.

17

TRAVELING THROUGH MAR VISTA WAS LIKE CHANG-ing channels on the TV and only finding commercials. Dress shops. Mechanics. Designer Jewelry. Hardware. All the parking spaces were filled with the cars of the rich, who walked streets without a hint of weed in the air.

"You a magician?" said the driver, who, according his license, was Francisco Machado.

"Just for birthdays and weddings. These days I'm wrestling."

Francisco smiled. "You mean like the guys at the Olympic?"

I nodded. "Yup. I'll be there tonight. You like wrestling?"

"Of course. My family used to wrestle in Mexico City. My uncle was famous, like Santo." Most of the waking world in the USA had no idea who Santo was, but the masked *luchador* was a folk hero in Mexico, and his B-movies—in which Santo and the Blue Demon fought werewolves, aliens, and communists—were so popular that there was talk of the Pope making the king of the *luchadores* a saint.

"What was your uncle's name?"

"El Grand Diablo! He had a waxed mustache and hair like horns. Everyone hated him because he was the *villain*, but they'd pay through the skull to see some *luchador* crush him."

"Being hated is a good way to make money."

Hector looked back. "Only in wrestling. So, you going to do some magic in the ring?"

"I need to update my costume."

"Well, if they don't have what you need, I could wait. Take you someplace else."

"Much obliged, but I think she'll have what I need. But I'll need a ride afterword, if you don't have a fare."

"No, *compadre*. I'll wait for one of the men of the ring to return. First three minutes for free."

I shook my head. "That's too generous. You're a working man. I can cover it. Just hang outside and I'll be out as soon as I can." I flipped him a twenty. "Here's insurance against anything weird happening inside."

He smiled. "Okay, *lucha*." He plucked the twenty. "Working men must band together."

"Unite, brother," I said, then opened the door. "I hope to be back before long." I tried to make every meeting with Shirley Martel nice and short. Just like the first time.

On the sidewalk, two kids with unkempt hair and freckles were hanging around a teen in an orange T-shirt who was doing the rolling knuckle and making his novelty coin disappear.

"Wow!'

"Who taught you that?"

"Wendell, man. He's the greatest. Dude could make a roll of quarters vanish if he wanted."

"I heard he's the best sleight of hand guy outside of Vegas."

"Then what's he doing working at a joke shop?"

I pressed open the door, wondering who on earth would consider themselves the best palm artist in the world of coin magic, and how a guy named Wendell impressed a kid whose nose was ninety-nine percent blackheads. Then again, my hero was Edgar Vance until I realized he was a villain.

A tiny gaggle of bells rang above me and faded as Tommy Dorsey's band filled the hi-fi speakers with sweet horns and static, while a young Frank Sinatra crooned "In the Blue Evening." The interior of Shirley's joint consisted of a single pathway flanked by two glass cases. They and all available wall space were filled with a cavalcade of wonders: pink whoopie cushions, fistfuls of fake vomit, decks of cards in blue and red boxes that claimed a single trick apiece: "Levitate the Ace!" "Shuffle Magic!" "Vanishing Queens!" Higher up were dusty costumes: headless ghosts touched the ceiling, vampire capes, powdered wigs, Sherlock Holmes tweeds and deerstalker, bandoliers for a gaucho.

Sinatra's smooth tones were cruelly bizarre in a store filled with what I could only think of as the castoffs of cults and caravans of the love generation. Too young for Woodstock, the promise of peace, sex, and revolution had mostly flickered out for these kids before it could become their guiding light. The smell of these guys—and it was all guys—was like a locker room, even though the gaunt faces glaring into the two glass cases lining the narrow store looked like they hadn't run a mile, lifted a weight, or done a hard day's labor in their sixteen or so years upon this spinning rock. Amid the stink of puberty and loneliness, of abandoned hope and vast disinterest, I was hit with a note of reassurance. For all I could smell was the stink of young manhood, plastic vomit, and . . . perfume. Some type of Chanel that I suspect Shirley Martel bought in bulk on the black market.

As bad as the smell was, the flavor was worse—but not one drop tasted of real magic. Whatever chicanery, gags, and illusions were on display, they were for the civilians of the magic world, not the players, like Edgar, who used their power for spite and joy.

I took a deep breath and enjoyed it.

A young rake sat behind the cash register at the far end of the store, guardian of the door to the space in back. His hair was salt-and-pepper and his beard was steel wool mashed onto a sharp chin. The gray hair and old-fashioned beard made him look far older than the age attested by a lack of lines on his sprightly face. A certain clarity of eye could be taken for either the wisdom of years or a lively lack of them. He was working three red balls in his hand with an ease that spoke of mad devotion. Perhaps this was the Amazing Wendell before my very eyes.

"See, it's not just about what I'm doing, but what I'm having you look at." He snapped his fingers: a flash of light and bang of sulfur exploded in the room and everyone took notice. Except me. I'd long ago trained myself to not eye the distraction and watched how expertly he squeezed the balls into the sleeve of his double-breasted blue blazer, then plucked the coin he'd been palming the whole time. To the untrained eye, he'd snapped his fingers and transmuted three balls into a single coin, solving a problem alchemists abandoned long ago.

"Thank you, thank you," he said, like an annoying carnival barker. "But my private jet doesn't run on applause, so either buy something or get out!" The blend of confidence and disdain was rather charming and the kids were giggling as they approached the register to chat with their hero.

The back door opened.

"Wendell! You pull that cap gag again and the beauty parlor will have the cops or fire department on our hides like ticks on a swamp hound. Now you boys stay in line and let Shirley make sure you are well taken care off. Wendell, get that blazer back where it belongs and work on the tux and tails or so help me God."

"Right away, Shirley," Wendell said, confident as all get out, as if this had been his plan all along. "Just showing off the merchandise." He cackled like a career witch and then slipped through the back door.

And there stood Shirley.

The shade of her peroxide-blond hair likely cost a cool hundred in chemicals; its upswept waves defied gravity. Her skin was bone-white and shining like a marble tombstone under a harvest moon. Then the magic began. Eyelashes as long as a mermaid's tail seemed to sway with her blinks as if she was under the sea. Her lids were a shimmering turquoise, and her eyeliner was thicker than ink in a Jim Steranko panel showing Nick Fury's stubble. A glossy pink enhanced the sagging beauty of Shirley's lips. She wore a gold chain around her puffy neck, and its pendant of a cat fell between pushed-up 34Ds. The package was wrapped in a leopard-print mini-dress that clung to her hourglass figure like a desperate child.

Among the ogle of boys, the throwaways of magic and pretend on the walls, Shirley appeared to be a princess of Mars as imagined by Russ Myer rather than Edgar Rice Burroughs. She looked at me as if I was John Carter and she was Dejah Thoris.

"By the grace of the Holy Ghost, James Brimstone! Sorry, boys, the store is closing now, but we'll be back open real, real soon. Just leave your wares and they'll be here when we open. Now shoo!" She wiggled her long fingers as if she had charmed them all with a spell. The boys booked out in a hustle while I rode against their tide, hearing the mutters as they looked at me.

"Who the hell is this lounge act?"

"He's old enough to be her father."

"Is that Wendell's dad?"

The little bells stopped ringing, and yet I was only halfway to the counter.

Shirley crossed her arms under her ample breasts and tilted her head to one side, voice a cloying falsetto. "Aw, is Baby James Brimstone still so shy?"

"Didn't realize I was important enough to clear a room of devoted fanatics."

Her head tilted back. "My harem is legion, and they always come back." She winked and I swear to Odin that I felt a breeze. "Don't they?"

"Lovely to see you too, Shirley."

"Same here. And looking at that outfit, I'd guess you've traded in magic for crooning. God, you have a nice voice in bed, but I'd never pay to hear you sing beyond my bedroom walls."

I smiled. "And you're doing gangbusters."

"Oh, magic never goes out of style, James." She sighed. "How long has it been since your first look at me?"

I grinned. "I'm old enough to forget the date, but the memory is unforgettable."

She shivered. "You're too handsome to be so charming. It's just not fair to us girls."

"Wish this was a social call, Shirley, but I need something."

"Everyone does," she said. "And unless you've got leprosy or are voting Nixon, you can come closer than that to me, James. I won't hurt you." Her purple-nailed finger crossed her heart. "Come to Shirley."

Believe it or not, I had to will myself forward to this black-hole beauty who had done what only one woman ever could.

Back then she was a showgirl for one of Edgar's rivals, a civilian magician named Stark Firestorm. And by rivals, I mean Edgar despised this "civilian" who was very good with illusions. He sent me to his show, incognito, to ruin his act with a mirror gag, reflecting light into the poor guy's eyes as he was pulling a dove from his hat. Because Edgar is a monster, he didn't tell me that Stark was prone to seizures when hit with blasts of bright light. In the dark of the Egyptian Hall in London, the grand-daddy of them all for illusionists, I screamed as the crowd gasped and Stark hit the ground like a loaded gun, every trick in his suit blasting off in all directions, his secrets revealed, his career ruined, his reputation a joke . . . all because of me.

I'd wanted to run home, but I knew I'd have to endure Edgar's gloating laughter at the cruelty he'd involved me in, so I ran the other direction, cold and terrified, to the backstage of the Egyptian Hall. Sneaking past security that looked like Pinkerton strikebreakers, I found the dressing room door with Stark's name on it. I ran in to confess to the old man . . . and found Shirley. On stage, she was beautiful, but up close, her glamor was overwhelming. She sat clad in fishnets and a pink tutu, legs crossed, and no top—breasts magnetic to my eyes—a bottle of whiskey in one hand and a phone receiver in the other, screaming to her agent to get her "out of this goddamn country where they still ration milk like Hitler's waiting outside the shithouses they call homes. Get it, Marv? Get me out of here!"

She slammed the phone down, saw me, and smiled.

"Ain't god great? On a shit day when things are ugly, he sends me a present. What's your name?

I muttered *James* and said I wanted to see the magician.

"Oh, precious, he's gone. And he ain't coming back. But you're crying. Are you sad?"

I wasn't allowed to be sad with Edgar. Ever. Angry? Cynical? Disdainful? Of course. Sad was "for the weak and the dead."

I didn't say a word. Tears just fell. She said three words that woke me to the wider world.

"Come to Shirley."

I blinked. Shirley was beckoning me toward her not in the hazy days of my youth, but the heat of 1970. I sauntered forward, over-exaggerated, and she laughed.

"You look ridiculous and handsome in that outfit," she said. "If you got rid of it, you'd be all handsome."

"You read my mind, Shirley," I said, amazed I was looking down at her instead of looking up. She had to be five-eight in heels. "I need a suit. Something classy that could pass for a high roller in this decade."

"And here I thought you wanted to touch base with your old girl." She mocked disdainfully.

"There are many bases I'd like to touch with you, Shirley," I said, and that revved her motor. "But I have an engagement that requires finery and you are the only woman whose style I trust."

"Making you the smartest man in Mira Vista." She did a calculation under her eyelashes. "I don't know what you need, James, but I know what you want. Wendell!"

A second later the salt-and-pepper hand-palmer supreme—with dressmaker's pins between his lips—pulled open the door. "Shirley, my dear, I'm in the middle of a masterpiece."

"Stick a pin in it, handsome. We got a red alert for an old friend."

That's when Wendell took a look at me and realized he saw his future, just as I was looking through a cracked mirror into the past. At least he was far closer to being my age now than then, which gave me hope that she'd changed her tune on the elixir of life being the love of *very* young men—but who was I to judge. "Well now, friends of Shirley are friends of mine." He grinned, pins sticking up and out as if in a defiant sneer.

Shirley lifted the arm of the cash desk and ushered me into the back room, flipped a switch, and I heard the front door lock.

18

"STRIP."

I dropped Jack Lumber's gym bag and did as I was told.

"Well," Wendell said with a roll of his eyes as he focused a standing lamp to bathe me in jaundiced yellow wattage. "Someone fell off the fitness tree and hit every branch on the way down. Who's your father, Jack LaLanne?"

I unbuttoned my shirt. "No. A dock worker from Oakland."

Wendell's attitude was playful, but not happy. He had to respect Shirley's old friend until there was no need to keep up pretenses. Once I was gone, he could shit-talk me to the cadre of teens who called him 'God.' "What do you need? Formal? Elegant? Timeless?"

"I need to look like I fit in at the Hilton in Venice."

Shirley took a half-empty pack of Kools from a worktable with a Frankenstein's monster head tilted to one side. "Hilton? You finally become the gentleman escort I always thought you were born to be?"

I hung my shirt over the head of a faceless mannequin. "I'm a private eye now."

Shirley clapped her hands, smoke perched on the edge of lips that sparkled in the weak glow of the lamp. "Oh, my! Bravo! In what movie?"

Wendell drew his tape across my shoulders. "No. Not an actor. A real private investigator."

Her mirth sank into gloom and she cut the applause. "What? That's the dumbest thing you could ever goddamn do."

Wendell's breath was heavy on my neck. A clear sign of approval of the drop in the temperature of the room.

I grinned. "We can't all be entrepreneurs of gags and magic."

She pointed the tip of the ciggy at me. It shook with her stream of words. "Don't try and make this about me, handsome; I'm good at what I do. I live my life the way I want to live it, and I don't give a damn about other people's dirty laundry. But you? You're sniffing around people's garbage, poking your nose in their bedrooms, collecting the dirt we forget we leave behind." She tapped her ash with enough force to make the flecks fly like windborne glitter. "Wendell, stop."

Flummoxed, my arms dropped and Wendell whistled the *William Tell* Overture.

This was bad. I'd tried the truth and it had sunk me like a freshly dug grave after a monsoon. Fiction would have to do.

"Shirley."

"Get out, panty sniffer."

"You got it all wrong."

"What part of you being a bloodhound of misery makes me off beam?"

"Look." I dropped to my knees, opened Jack's bag, and ripped out the mask.

That shut up further discussion of my heinous character flaws.

Wendell gazed at Shirley, but her dance hall lashes were flapping only for me. "What the hell is this?"

"The truth. I'm a wrestler. A pro wrestler."

Wendell gripped his tape around his neck like a country lawyer's suspenders. "You mean a fake, phony, a conman."

Shirley turned, then tapped more ash. "A wrestler? Like at the Olympic?"

"That's where I'm headed tonight, but I have to meet the promoter. He wants to meet at the Hilton and they have a dress code and my dress code has been S-L-O-B since I was a kid."

"Good thing you've always been handsome," she said, and her firm pink lip started to curl. "Why the fuck would you say you were a panty sniffer?"

"Believe it or not, Shirley, not everyone thinks wrestling is a bonafide career choice and, well, wrestlers are kinda secretive about the code."

She shook her head. "Days like this I'm glad I'm no longer traveling the circuit. Code? As if there were honor among those thieves and shirks. Bunch of dirty old men selling lies for fun and profit." Her lips softened. "But I can see why you're attracted to it. The spotlight. Mystery. Travel." She snatched the mask from my grip. I let her hold it. "But hiding that pretty face under this foul material? That, James, is a crime."

I held out my hand and she gave it back. "Keeps it pretty and out of harm's way."

"Well, thank heaven for small miracles." Wendell laughed, and it seemed genuine. Shirley took a long drag. "Okay. Let's get my boy ready to look like a million bucks of hammered gold."

I never much cared for tailored clothes. Seemed like a waste of everyone's time. But Wendell's fingers weren't just geared for coins, dice, or cards; he was a legit tailor working at breakneck pace while I made gentle suggestions. Shirley watched me standing in my briefs as if the peep show window got broken and she was getting a sneak peek.

"I've always done my best when wearing browns and blues," I said.

"Sounds like a lost track from Robert Johnson," Wendell said, halfway between my legs. Shirley half-laughed with a career smoker's nicotine gurgle.

"My boy's a stand-up comic. Big draw at Ciro's on the Strip."

Ciro's was a legit nightclub and they hired headline comic talent. "Didn't know I was dealing with comedy royalty. Where did you get your start, Wendell?"

He finished measuring my inseam, then ran a quick gait into a sea of clothes. "Like all true artists, I came from nowhere and nothing and wait in limbo for my overnight success. More exactly, I was in a Christian revival family act. I loved show biz, and they threw me off the covered wagon when they realized I was playing with balls at night."

Then his hand snapped out of the pile with the three collapsible felt balls.

"Until they turned red and grew a friend!"

Shirley clapped. "He just makes this stuff up on the spot, can you believe it?"

I could. "Shirley, you don't have to wait here. What about your adoring fans outside?"

She walked over, trying to look sultry in the yellow light, but what she looked beneath the makeup was sick. Worse was how she sounded. Without the noise of the store, you could hear her breathing was ragged and haggard. She used to move like a swinging blade onstage, legs like iron wrapped in fishnets, and she was strong enough to toss me around the way she liked. But those memories were lost to weak lungs, a sore heart, and a desire for denial to be a cure for whatever was ailing her. There was a taste—not magic, just life—of something crossed that could not be undone. She was a startling vision of life before the next station change on the radio we call mortality. But there was no tear in my eye or pity in my heart as she drew close enough for me to feel her breath. Right now, before me, Shirley Martell was a terrible beauty who still made me want to surrender. "Boys always wait for me, James. You know that."

Then she took a kiss. And I surrendered. Smoke and life, hard wet teeth, and for twice in a lifetime my arms didn't know what to do as she took that kiss and made me her own, swimming together as she placed cold fingers on my ass and pulled my crotch to her belly, hips dancing with me like I was her puppet and the show was completely in her hands.

"Save it for the ten o'clock show!" Wendell said, tan trousers over one shoulder, navy jacket over the other. "What if America sees that love knows no age! We'd be having babies dating grannies." He grabbed his head and mocked tearing his hair out. "That is madness!"

Shirley's chest heaved with a giggle she was trying to keep from turning into a cough. She pulled back. "Was it worth the wait?"

I looked down at my member, giving her a righteous salute. "On behalf of all of us, I can say without a shadow of a doubt it was."

"Smart gang," she walked to the office door and darkness enveloped her. "Wendell? This is on the house. Just get the rags he was wearing and burn them."

Shirley coughed with the turning of the door's latch, as if to hide it. She exited and closed the door behind her. Soon thereafter, the shop bell sounded and the lost boys of the love generation were rushing down the aisle to worship their beloved.

"You know she's sick, right?"

Wendell sat at a little desk with a Singer, lining up the bottom of the tan trousers under the needle.

"How long?

He shrugged. "She won't say."

"I get it."

He gave me the stink eye. "Get it? That's rich. Might as well be talking about napalming babies and why it's bad. I get it. I don't feel it. I don't see it. I get it, like a brochure or a commercial of a real feeling. It's different when you're the one cleaning up the bloody tissues."

"I'm sorry."

"Death is easy, comedy is hard."

He started to press the treadle to operate the machine, but something was stuck under it: the brown toe cap of my wingtip. Wendell leaned back, scared but somewhat defiant. My voice chilled. "You're an asshole, you know that? And the only thing keeping me from giving you a lesson in impossible contortions so that you might, indeed, be able to fuck yourself, is that you're the one giving Shirley joy." I yanked my shoe free. Then I held out my hand. "Thank you for making her happy."

He took it. It was neither strong, nor weak, but the opposite of his appearance: completely controlled. We broke off and he told me to sit. "Turning a cocktail napkin into a magic carpet takes a solid ten minutes."

He was ridiculously correct.

I abandoned my favorite suit for tan slacks, a navy blue double-breasted blazer, white shirt, and burgundy tie. I looked like the kind of putz who enjoyed the links and a par four, attended senior executive functions (whatever that was), and fucked his secretary in Palm Springs while his wife fucked her gardener in Cabo. The guy who shit on the man in the gray flannel suit. The boss. The operator. The clothes fit perfectly, and in the glare of a full-length mirror, circled by boxes full of gags and magic, I felt like even more of a pretender than when I handed Shirley the wrestling mask. A complete and utter phony who thought the world was his pleasure yacht and used everyone else like toilet paper.

"Now you look fit for the Hilton," Wendell said from behind me. I turned.

"Thanks. You're really good at—"

"Everything, I know, it's a burden, but I bear it like Jesus on Easter."

I rarely want to punch someone in the face *that* much, but the mirth and more he was giving Shirley was an invisible shield protecting his mug. Plus, I'd already shaken his hand. "Word to the wise, Wendell?"

"You're preaching to the choir as it is."

"Don't quit your day job."

"And what do you know—"

"I mean the comedy. You're a decent magician, and this store is a great way to keep sharp, but you've got a gift for making people laugh that other comedians would kill for." Of course, I kept that case of a mad sorcerer trying to steal a comedian's talent all to my bad self. "Don't get lazy just because you have a captivated audience between recess and the final bell."

I turned to leave.

"You won't see her again," he said. I stopped. "Will you."

I turned and smiled. "You never know. We live in a world of wonder. The impossible is always strongest when it's being watched. Never would have thought I'd see her today and yet, here we are."

I left as he made a witty retort involving Descartes' famous aphorism, and perhaps some Schiller, as if to make clear to yours truly he was actually the smartest cock in the yard. I denied him the victory of recognition, shouldered the gym bag, and yanked open the door.

The burning daylight radiating through the glass gutted my eye, so I only saw the darkened specter of Shirley turn around with a gasp. "Ladies and gentleman, may I present Mr. James Farnsworth, a great patron of the magic arts and owner of several islands in the South Pacific." I briefly held the attention of the boys, who realized they could now stare at Shirley's bosom without her noticing.

I bowed graciously. "Sorry to dash like this, Shirley, but my meeting is minutes away. Thanks so much for being the number one supplier of Magic Incorporated's worldwide network of performers and establishments."

"Not at all!" she said, young and joyous, the phlegm in her throat cleared as if by grace. "But you come back when you're in town next, James. You still owe me tickets to a wrestling match at the Olympic. I just love those masked men. So mysterious!"

"It's a date."

I got outside. I opened the cab door, climbed in, sat, and swallowed my heart.

"Right on time," Hector said, then looked in the rearview mirror. "Hey? Hey, *lucha*, are you okay?"

I wiped my face dry, then smiled. "Just not used to clothes this fine."

He read my expression and shifted gears. "Hey, you win enough, you will wear clothes like that all the time! You any relation to Gory Guerreros? I hear he has a son wrestling in Japan."

"No relation. Tell me more about your uncle as we head for the Hilton."

He did, without looking back at me, and by the time we pulled into the entrance of the mansion of a hotel—a great white gold edifice against the glow of the early evening, the Pacific at its back like a beautiful slave—my ducts were dry. I might be dressed like a millionaire, but I was reminded of something Shirley once said when I apologized for wearing the same shirt twice in a row to her place. "Honey, I love money and what it can bring, but what matters is what you keep in here." She'd tapped her head. "Make memories so beautiful and rich that when the Grim Reaper comes for you, you'll show him things even that old fuck has never seen."

"You need me for another run, *lucha*?" Hector said.

I grabbed the bag. "No, but thanks for the family history." I handed him a ten. Before he could protest, I added, "Take it with gratitude; I loved hearing the stories."

He shrugged, took the ten. "See you around, *lucha*."

"If you get off early enough, I'll have you on the guest list at the Olympic. Tell them the Assassinator said it was jake."

"Gracias! I hope you banish the villain in the ring!"

I smiled, nodded, and hoped the same thing.

19

HECTOR'S CAB GAVE ME A WHIFF OF EXHAUST THAT I found soothing before I faced the glitz.

Gilding the lily must have been the mantra for the school of architecture that birthed the sandy towers of the Venice Beach Hilton. If Dracula had been a beach bum, he'd have a penthouse suite there with the windows blacked out. There's a certain kind of opulence in L.A., a particular brand of gaudy that came in with the white people and the money they minted with their white moving pictures. The face of this flashy monstrosity was, at first blush, the exterior of the Aragonese Castle. But all faces have a skull beneath, and from what I'd heard, there were bones in this place from Chicano labor. Conrad Hilton made a fortune by turning graveyards of the working class into palaces for the chosen. I had a hard time washing the taste of that out of my mouth as I saw a couple in their sixties exit the silver-and-gold front door. He wore a red ascot and sailor cap, she a gold and black dress with liver spots beneath her diamonds and pearls. I walked across the driveway as they strutted out.

"Bring the car!" he said to the young black man in the red bellhop outfit.

"Right away, Mr. Stringer."

"And careful what you touch."

"Really, Aubrey," said the woman. "They can't afford to have proper bellhops."

I set the gym bag down. "And what might a proper bellhop look like?"

Aubrey stood in front of his now-tarnished-by-age trophy wife. "Watch your mouth, smart guy. Nobody talks to my wife like that."

I grinned and spread my arms. "Then you must still live in the Confederacy. Welcome to the twentieth century, time travelers! Enjoy our indoor plumbing and emancipation."

"Do something, Aubrey!" Mrs. Stringer said. "He's worse than your son."

The snarl on his face was not meant for me, but Aubrey was not the kind of man to back down. He took a boxing stance. "Say something else, junior, and I'll feed you some golden gloves."

"Sorry, friend," I said, hands up. "I live in the era of non-violence. Your mastery of the sweet science is wasted here. But if you want to see the modern gladiators of the ring, I invite you to the Olympic, where you will see an enlightened crowd enjoy a fight that is actually about cooperation."

Mrs. Stringer pulled his arm. "He's one of those crazy people from the Strip."

"He's a bum who found a suit in an estate sale." He dropped his fists. "A bum. You have it written over your face. Some blue-collar hood who works out and doesn't know the meaning of class beyond the one he was born into. Enjoy your crazy routine, loser. I've seen better from worse."

The Cadillac approached. The door cracked open with just the right amount of pressure to leave no one any doubt that the owner was outside the car and not on the handle.

"Thank you for choosing the Venice Hilton," said the bellhop.

Aubrey dove his hand into his blazer, took out a wad of cash and threw it behind him. "Consider this reparations."

The two miserable creatures piled into their car and vanished down the driveway while I helped the bellhop chase the paper birds in flight. When the last spinning green was snatched from the air, the entry door opened again, and a man with the cruelest combover I'd ever seen came running out with his own red coat, single breasted, buttoned on his belly. "Roger! What on earth are you doing? You look like some contestant on *Truth or Consequences*."

Roger sucked in air, because he knew that if he told the truth, it would sound ridiculous, and that might be fatal to his livelihood.

I intervened. "The problem was mine, mister . . . ?"

He adjusted his combover. "Duncan." He looked at me. "Are you a guest of the Hilton, sir?"

"Yes, I'm a friend of Alan and Veronica Carruthers, and I'm meeting them here."

The name Carruthers carried enough weight to sock Duncan in the jaw and turn his frown upside down. "Wonderful to have you with us. Any friend of the Carruthers family is an honored guest with us. Now, Roger—"

"As you can see, my hands are real Snickers bars," I continued as Roger looked on in resigned terror. Two white men battling for his future? God alive, it did make me feel shitty. "I was getting out my wallet when the big digits just went pure Butterfingers on me. Off the bills flew until this helpful young man took it upon himself to help someone he didn't even know and hadn't checked in. A selfless act and I'm grateful."

Duncan smiled, top lip glistening with sweat. "The Venice Hilton is always happy to serve the community."

I folded the stack of bills that Stringer had released and placed them in my pocket, Roger's eyes registering that I was one rotten son of a bitch, taking the money another man had thrown at him, making me lower than dirt on a worm's ass. "Now could you see if the Carruthers are here?" I regretted it as soon as I said it, but I was playing the friend card, and even if it alerted Veronica, I didn't have to see her.

"Of course, right away." He smiled, but gave a batting look at Roger, then doubled back, adjusting his blazer as another bellhop opened the door for him.

Roger was pure suspicion, and I couldn't blame him.

"Sorry for acting like such an ass." I handed him the wad, folded down the center so it looked like a single bill to anyone looking on. "And sorry those Stringers are such shithooks."

He took the bills with long fingers and pocketed them in his jacket with a smooth, controlled motion similar to the way he'd opened the door. "Thanks," he said. "And what the hell is a shithook?"

I grinned. "An asshole's kid brother."

He smiled. "I better get back to work. Duncan is impossible to keep happy."

"I bet. Say, you know anything about the perfume shop El Dorado?"

He exhaled with a *whew*. "Place always smells wild."

"Ever see funny characters in there? Guys who might not fit in a fancypants place like this one?"

"No, sir," he said, formally, and he was now so guarded I realized that a friendly chat with any white guy always carried with it fears and assumptions about consequences for his words. "Mostly just women in there. Never seen a man go there alone."

"No boyfriends or husbands buying presents?"

"If they are, they are with their girlfriends or wives. I think the place makes men . . . uncomfortable."

I nodded as if this all made sense. "Thanks again, Roger. Take care."

"I will," he said as a Jaguar approached. I scuttled toward the door, which opened to reveal another young black man in red, stockier but just as respectful-yet-wary, which made my skin crawl.

"Welcome to the Venice Hilton, sir."

"Thanks. You friends with Roger?"

He looked quickly at Roger, then me. "Yes."

I smiled. "Tell him to buy you a beer when you're done work. The amount of crap you guys put up with, you need all the breaks you can get."

He nodded as if he'd been scolded, and I realized he couldn't join in the festivities of my words. "Okay, sir." Again, my privileged position made me feel like a shit, but I was burning daylight and hoped I'd done at least a little good. I'd just have to learn to do better.

If the face of the Hilton was a skull, her brain cavity was a gilded nightmare, as if class and garish had fucked themselves silly and sired only one spoiled child—and she was a screamer. A vast gold-and-white foyer glittered with faux elegance, but all of this was drowned out by the thundering rush of a green fountain the size of a kraken's sex organs and almost as ornate. Dusty cherubs lined the inner spire and peed in every direction at the ritzy glitzy clientele who wore sunglasses inside and tried to outdo the look of bored command that they'd practiced since private school.

It's not that I hate the rich, per se. But run around with the underclass long enough and you see the kind of desperation that would make the life of a Dickens character look like a permanent vacation. The barrios of East L.A., the slums of Harlem, the combat zone of Boston, the Street Without Joy in New Orleans, 9th and Hennepin in Minneapolis: places where families are cutting an egg six ways to eat on Christmas morning and one bad decision can leave you jailed, raped, dead, or all three. Live with those folks long enough and you develop a chip on your shoulder as dense as a king upon his incestuous throne. I'd never wanted to rule the world, which had infuriated Edgar to no end, but those who did, as that Greek fascist Plato noted, were likely the least capable of doing so.

The Hilton smelled of aftershave, perfume, and exploitation. White summer suits and tan leather shoes made in Italy. Men strutted with models only slightly past their prime who were fighting aging with Estée Lauder in one hand and a surgeon's scalpel in the other. Edgar joked once that someday you would be able to buy the face you wanted and have it replaced like glass eyes. When I foolishly asked where the faces would come from, figuring they'd be made in some science-fiction vat of green jelly, I had to endure Edgar's snark. "Oh, you know, the usual suspects. The masses carry within them occasional gems and those girls will be commodities, sold like pig skin and rubber to the highest bidder. Imagine the fads! Swedish faces this year, Boer the next!"

The Hilton had no such facial bootlegs, just the usual range of flawless tans and lush hair, liver spots and bald pates. Thus far, even the rich couldn't buy their way from the tag team of gravity and entropy. I cut through a swath of them, imitating their indifferent poses and never making eye contact until I saw the marble of the main desk, where a man in a sleeveless T-shirt and shorts only a runner would wear was moving as if he'd been cattle prodded.

"I will not be quiet! My reservation was made weeks ago! Do you know who I am?"

Behind the desk was a black-haired, doe-eyed, maybe-twenty-year-old who looked like she'd been on the stage or screen since she was a child: her back was straight and her nose tilted, and she was clearly "acting" the part of a hostess. Back home, she'd been told that she was beautiful and talented and could do anything she wanted, and yet her half-life in Hollywood was already decaying. She was holding her countenance as firm as a soldier grips his balls in his bunk. "Of course, Dr. Stephano."

"And yet you are too stupid to have made my reservation and will not give me a new key. Mine was taken by your lousy staff, and if it weren't for the great run I just had, I'd be even more furious at this thievery, and yet you're treating *me* like a common criminal instead of doing the right thing and giving me my key. Tell me, girl, one good reason to not get you fired today?"

Her name tag said *Candice*. Her eyes said, "I'm terrified."

So, I tripped over my own feet. This sent me spilling onto the reedy Dr. Stephano, who was maybe five-foot-eight and skeletal. I hit him with the kind of force I'd normally save for goring someone's stomach, lifting them off their feet and driving them to the ground, a la Lou Thesz, NWA heavyweight champion. Since I hit the doctor's back, his chest was driven forward, ramming his sternum against the marble counter, effectively stealing his breath and sending shooting pains through his entire nervous system.

Dr. Stephano bounced back and I caught him, dipped him back while sensation to his arms and legs was AWOL, then said, "Oh, sorry about the left feet, old man."

His face was a pinched graveyard for happiness. Creased forehead and dark eyes dominated a face two times too big for its body. And it was turning a shade of red reserved for radishes. The best part: he couldn't speak or move. I had about five seconds.

"Sorry, Candice," I said. "Back in a flash." I then led "Dr. Stephano," most of his deadweight trying to resist me, to the fountain.

When his ass hit the fountain's edge, his voice snapped back with a bark. "How dare you. I will have you locked up so fast—"

I tapped his sternum with two fingers. He shut up.

"No. You won't. Because you're pulling one of my favorite cons."

He didn't blink, which was unfortunate. It meant he was concentrating under threat, instead of being scared and blinking reflexively. He wasn't as slick as I thought.

"I love that you found Dr. Stephano's itinerary somewhere and are literally trying to fast-talk your way into an evening of elegance. I truly do. I'm a member of the same union."

He gasped and I raised my fingers, his mouth closed.

"But you're taking it out on the wrong target. That girl doesn't deserve your shit. If scaring girls to get what you want is your actual thrill then, brother, we got a real problem. So here is the play. You're going to leave in a huff, as Dr. Stephano would. You'll get in a cab and ask for another hotel that would have a Dr. Stephano or his ilk losing their keys. If you're truly good at the game, you'll be in the lap of luxury before dinner rolls are served. But if you stick around, I'm going to poke you until red turns to blue." I raised two fingers and he flinched.

The conman jogged out on weak legs as I turned my attention back to Candice and walked back to the desk. She met my eyes. The blush from the recent hijinks warmed her features and kept her smile formal. "Welcome to the Hilton, sir. Are you checking in?"

I dropped my gym bag. "No. I have an appointment here but need to buy a gift first. Can you tell me where I can find El Dorado?"

"Of course," she said. "It's the centerpiece of our patron's market, one of our most popular features. Just take the hallway to your left, then follow your nose." She said this while tapping her own slim New England snout.

"Thank you, miss." I kept the formal tone she seemed to need, perhaps defense against the prying eyes of managers like the one monitoring the bellboys. "You've been most helpful."

I turned to the left, and her right hand breezed against my shoulder. In it was a key. "Complimentary services are available in a half-hour." Her smile brightened. "We know you have many choices when traveling, so thank you for choosing . . . the Hilton."

I grinned. "It's a first-class operation."

I pocketed the key and walked away feeling righteous, but creepy. Sure, every Lothario since Casanova believed the Fountain of Youth was found between the legs of young women, and Candice could have flipped every switch in these elder sheet warriors. If Chaplin was within ten miles of the Hilton, he might dust off his Little Tramp to get a bit from Candice. But the Fountain of Youth was an illusion, and I liked pillow talk that didn't involve the words "groovy" or "boss" or "Led Zeppelin." The key would not be used.

The arched hallway to the left beckoned with gold letters above: *Les Market*. How European. I expected I would find lutefisk and café au lait on the room service menu.

"You can take the boy out of the trash," a wispy voice said behind me.

I turned to find a bushy mustache of the walrus variety stuck on a wrinkled face. Aaron Piper. L.A.'s other low-rent PI. The guy who didn't take weird cases but had been trying to steal mine since the ink dried on my license. He had scorch marks on his cheeks from I don't know how many years under the West Coast sun; white tufts of hair filled the V of his brown polyester shirt's open collar. Brown was one of the few colors not in the plaid of his jacket.

"And you can take the hack from his sedan," I said. "Nice to see you, Aaron. How is Wendy?" That would be Wendy the Actress Whose Dad Is a Cop so She Dressed up in His Uniform to Harass Me for Leads on Aaron's Behalf. That Wendy.

He sniggered while dragging on a half-spent Marlboro. Each chortle smelled like an ashtray in a cheap bar. "Quit me after she saw you. Thanks for killing my action, J.B."

"You know it's a woman's prerogative to change her mind, even with such a fine specimen as yourself, Aaron. Now, as much as I enjoy our friendly rivalry—"

"You're on a case," he said, just quiet enough that the nearby richies did not hear. "It's the only reason you're not dressed like a has-been crooner begging for another chance outside Harvelle's Blues Club."

"By that logic, you're tonight's entertainment."

"Who is it? More trolling for sex-film stars?"

My anger coiled. I'd already had my fill of Mr. Piper. "Aaron, why are you here? I'd presume you're on a case, but every time I see you or your associates, it's because you're scrambling for leads."

"I got friends in high places," he said, taking a wet drag. "You're also abysmally easy to follow."

No time to be nice. "Good thing, too, or else America's Sherlock Holmes might get lost on his way to the bar."

He poked a nicotine-stained digit straight at my right eye. "You ain't so big, J.B. But you're cutting into my racket. I made a steady check before you showed up with your goddamn movie-star hair and chiseled jawline." Which made me wonder if Aaron couldn't see those features in others, like some abandoned critter from the nethers. "And now the well is going dry. So, it's time to be a mensch."

"That's good Yiddish for a Swedish Lutheran."

The finger was back at my eye. "You owe me. I opened the door to the skids of this town before your ass ever settled at the Thump & Grind. Hell, I worked for Queen Bee once. You're a parasite, building your home on my grave!"

Aaron was livid. He was also scum. And lower on the rung than me. I hated him even more because he was right; I'd crashed into the house that he'd built. All of this made what I said next a thousand times worse than if I'd told him to fuck himself with his own skull.

"I wish I could, but I'm working pro bono. I won't see a dime, even if I find who I'm looking for. I took a personal case, and my only reward is doing the right thing."

Aaron went apoplectic. I thought I saw mushroom clouds steaming from his ears. Then he started laughing. "I knew it. I knew you'd welsh on any deal I offered. You're high rolling now, you useless mick. But you'll fall. We all fall. And when you do, I pray to Christ I'm there when you reach up for a helping hand."

"James?"

Damn it.

Veronica Carruthers tapped her pumps quicker and quicker without losing the stride she'd learned in finishing school. She was no longer dressed in the blood-spattered outfit from earlier. She was Holly Golightly's uptight older sister, little black dress minus the fifty pounds of cheap costume jewelry. Veronica accessorized with a string of tasteful—and probably priceless pearls—and the rock I knew was on her left hand even though she was covering it with her right. Her hair now hung down one side of her face in a gentle wave, eye makeup subtle but effective. "You got my message?" Then she took in Aaron, and the horror of her disdain was obvious. The same look I'd seen at the hall—before I saved her life and changed her tune. Then it muted with a head nod. "I'm sorry, I'm interrupting."

"No," Aaron said, taking in big gulps of air through flared nostrils thick with gray hairs. "You are not. We're done." He dropped his cigarette, ground it into the immaculate marble floor. "Always nice to chat with my good friend James Brimstone." He smiled, each yellow tooth telling me how long it had been since he'd seen a dentist (the square root of never). "Hope you get a case that pays soon, buddy."

Aaron walked away on heavy, worn, and cracked black loafers that had seen more miles than many cars, much to the relief of Candice and the other staff who had been watching our chat.

Aaron's sad form turned right and headed for the door, weight shifting from one side to the other.

Veronica stepped closer so we were shoulder to shoulder. I half expected her to weave her hand through my arm. "Who was that?"

If I wasn't careful, the Ghost of Christmas Future.

20

"I ALMOST DIDN'T RECOGNIZE YOU," VERONICA said, smiling, as her eyes executed judgments about my clothes that I assumed were in the affirmative, as her disdain of my earlier suit was now replaced by a quiet note of acceptance. Getting past her class bias was no mean feat. I'd have to send Aaron a "thank you" card. "I . . . also thought you might not . . . accept my invitation."

"I'm grateful for you checking up on Cactus. And offering to help. That means a lot." I would have said more, but I hoped that truth was enough to imply I had, indeed, accepted her invitation. Now I was stuck with Veronica Carruthers. "Tell me, do you like perfume?"

A joyous surprise lit her face. "Of course. What girl doesn't?" I smiled easy. "But I don't want to interrupt your case."

I could not blow her off without risking Cactus's life and my soul. She and Alan were the reason Cactus was getting first-class treatment. Being beholden to the rich was enough reason for me to refuse their tentacles of obligation, but a good man's life was

in the wings. "You're not. I'm not a classy fellow, but I think a
'thank you' is in order. But I need your help. Would you mind
escorting me to El Dorado? It will spoil the surprise, of course,
but we'll get to spend time together before I follow my next lead."

"Is that what the gym bag is for?" she said.

"You study investigative science at Harvard?"

"Cornell, actually. But no. It is just that you've already
changed clothes." Her lips parted a bit.

I took a deep breath. Whatever scent she was wearing, it
was sweet with a lingering savory note. The kind you wear on
first dates when you're at the country club, or so I've been told.
"A clean suit is less conspicuous than a rumpled one covered in
blood. But I've tucked my previous attire into the bag. Maybe a
good dry cleaner can get the blood out."

She smirked, then shook, then stumbled.

I caught her shoulders and held her up. "Veronica?"

"Sorry, I . . . just felt faint. Let's walk. Walks help."

Fainting was so common she knew the remedy was walks? I
deferred to her expertise, though I wondered if she was faking.
Arm-in-arm, we walked under the arch, heading for El Dorado. I
ignored what I expected to be Candice's glare at my backside, and
hoped she viewed what was happening as me helping a woman in
need. No bad ever came of that, surely.

The beat of her heels was rhythmic but muted. "James," she
said, a little breathy. "I can't stop thinking about it."

I nodded, as if I knew exactly what she was talking about.

"It was so sudden. How did . . . why did you do it?"

Her weight was a light drag on me, just enough to keep me
close but not so much that it would cause anyone to think I was
assisting someone who had taken too many Valiums that afternoon. "Instinct. Training. Same as Cactus and every other man
in that room. I protected what was closest to me."

She squeezed my arm as if that had been the most romantic

thing she'd heard since reading Byron at Cornell. "You did. I would have been a victim of those freaks if you hadn't."

"We don't know what kind of freaks they were," I said. "Political freaks. Hippie freaks. Freaky freaks."

She laughed away my joke. "Is it wrong to want them punished?"

"I just catch 'em and release them to the justice system."

"That's enough for you?" she said, voice soft, as if to slip it in closer.

"There are guys who you could pay for such services, no doubt. But punishment requires a degree of certainty that requires too much work and isn't that much fun." I'd known men and women who got off on punishment of all kinds, from the pretend kind you saw in Betty Page's photos to harder variations that left permanent scars.

Her sharpened tone kept time with the patter of her pumps. "You don't want the men that put your friend in a coma punished?"

"Never said that. But the price of doing it myself—"

"I'd want to."

I began to realize that, for all the affection of her arm around mine and how tightly she held it, Veronica was in a one-woman play with me as a prop in the shape of both foil and audience. I stopped bothering to answer her questions and focused on what was important.

"Tell me what you'd do."

She stopped and looked straight at me. "I'd hurt them for trying to hurt me. Like you do with a dog that won't obey. I'd hurt them worse so, as you say, the price of disobedience would be so high they'd rather be docile at my feet."

A part of me was very dark; the remaining sliver of the man I used to be. The one who almost believed Edgar's world view. That sliver flexed when it heard Veronica. A gash of black desire opening so quickly I didn't realize I'd woven my fingers in hers and that the huge diamond on her finger was leaving a mark. I relaxed my grip.

"Your dogs must be very happy."

She leaned her head on my shoulder. "They never complain."

We walked down the golden-lit hallway. The scent of her perfume gave way to something stronger and sweeter. The store was just ahead—dark brown, almost black—adorned with silver lettering that spelled out EL DORADO above the doorway. The scene refreshed my mind and snapped me back to remembering I had a married woman on my arm, one whose husband was a pharmaceutical kingpin and Vietnam war veteran *in a wheelchair.*

I straightened up. "Do you know the store well?"

She lifted her head, straightened her spine, and assumed the mien of the Queen of New England. "El Dorado is a retreat for me, a Venetian spa without all the boat people. They take care of you as you should be taken care of."

My psyche cringed. "Charming."

We entered a vast store full of golden-silver light. Mosaic flooring reminiscent of ancient Rome, glass shelving and pedestals with sparse goods that spoke of their high cost: creams, elixirs, maquillage, and, of course, perfume—all making the store smell like the sum total of avarice. I tried not to vomit. The place did make me uncomfortable.

"Every breath is like being born," Veronica said.

To the left were five buttery chairs with stools and towels, like barber chairs without sinks behind them. Two of them were occupied by older generations of Veronica, feet soaking in tubs as two Latinas in black uniforms sat on low stools working on their nails with emery boards. Acoustic guitars and flutes played softly from hidden speakers.

"Isn't it just perfect," Veronica said, but it was no question.

"Why don't you take a seat while I get your present?"

She gave me a dour look. "I don't mean to be impolite, James, but you can't afford anything in here."

I smiled. "You're basing this on my previous attire?"

"Among other clues."

She was rapping her heel into my last nerve. "You'd be surprised at what I can save wearing clothes that hobos abandon." Then my voice hardened, like I was commanding a mutt. "Take a seat."

She bristled, then smiled, and did as she was told. "I love the scent lounge."

I wanted to escape, but Cactus was still alive, and that meant I still had a chance not to owe the dead lifelong service. I approached a small desk made of marble pedestals and a glass top that stood before a door. Behind the desk was another dark-haired beauty. This one was regal with almond eyes, high cheekbones, and a long nose. She reminded me of an Argentinean I once knew, a woman who would have still been hot in Antarctica. La Bellaza wore a black blazer over a red silk blouse, her lips a splash of Spanish red wine. "May I help you, sir?"

"I'm looking for Margarita Diaz."

She smiled with a confidence that almost made me blush. "And you have found her in El Dorado."

I smiled, nodding my head at Veronica, who was saddling up, stockinged-knees close together. "See that woman? I need to buy her a gift that won't put me in the poor house."

Margarita Diaz grinned, started to open her mouth, and I finished my thought. "But I'm also here at the direction of Isabelle Caylao."

Seamlessly, Margarita switched to a knowing nod. "A friend of Isabelle is family. Which makes you James."

"She called?"

"No, but she has spoken of you. There are only so many Americanos who fit her description of you. I take it you are looking for something not found in stores?"

"Unless you have a time machine to ancient Sumer."

Her confident gaze almost shook. "Exotic."

"And deadly. Black Lotus."

She nodded if I'd said Reese's Peanut Butter Cups. "Best we talk in the office." She snapped her fingers twice. The two girls taking care of the three ladies stood and, lifting perfume bottles from trays at the ladies' elbows, sprayed them each in the face.

And I tasted it.

Magic. Not strong. Not deadly. But real.

"They'll be no concern to us for a few minutes." All the woman were smiling. Veronica's eyes were open, lips twitching.

"Is that real Spanish fly?"

Margarita smiled without showing her teeth, then tilted her head to the door.

The office was small, filled with a more serviceable desk, an ancient Meilink safe ("Guaranteed Fire and Water Proof"), and a brass coat hook. "Tell me, Mr. Brimstone, what do you know of Black Lotus?"

I dug into my pocket and held my specimen before her as she sat, legs crossed, in a plush, cream-colored leather chair.

"First, I have one."

Her eyes finally betrayed something other than control: wild desire. She didn't realize her hand had been reaching out until I put the flower back in my suit front pocket. "Now, now, looks are free, but touching is extra."

She blinked away the bliss. "How do you know it is really Black Lotus?"

"The shape of the petals, the white skull of the center, and the way it tastes."

She tilted her head. "Tastes? You tasted Black Lotus?"

"Not like regular people."

"So, you're not like regular people. No wonder Isabelle finds you amusing. And she's not alone." Funny how having something someone values raises your own stock by proxy. "Tell me all you know."

I gave her the sit-rep of what I'd gathered and where, including the Legion Hall attack, Weasel's rambles, and Jack Lumber's death. "Can you tell me how in the name of all the gods and their bratty kids a flower that has not been seen since the days of Gilgamesh could be at in L.A. in the glorious year of Anno Domini 1970?"

She gripped her knee and pulled her leg in so I could see the slit of her skirt pull itself open. "People have searched for it for centuries. The last plant was said to be buried in the carcass of a Cimmerian warrior-king whose name was lost because all of his enemies were murdered, including all their wives and children and parents and siblings. There were no family lines left to immortalize his terror. Mr. Brimstone, this is astounding."

"I hear that a lot. But I must admit you're making me sad, Margarita. I thought you'd know more than I did, and it seems I'm the one telling stories of dead muscle men and crazed hippies. I need to know who was responsible for bringing it here."

"You don't care about the flower itself?"

"I don't care about anything other than finding the man or men who did a job on my friend."

"Then might I have it?" She shifted her knee, then rested it. "Please?"

Then I tasted it. Damn it, with all the perfume in the air, my senses were blinded and my tongue had lost its sense of direction, but there it was on my taste buds, as distinct as rotting gumdrops: deeper magic. Charm magic, no less. It was in the air. Thin and drenched in perfumes that scattered its scent. Smelling it late changed nothing. Thanks to Edgar's tattooing of my aura with masochistic knifework and old sorcery called Aphrodite's Tears, the charms here that led to massive sales of junk perfume and overpriced services meant jack shit to me.

But that didn't mean I couldn't have fun.

"Of course," I said, and pulled the petals from my pocket, offering it just out of reach. She stood, defiant and smug, as she reached for the Black Lotus.

I palmed it and made the flower disappear.

"*Bendejo!*" Her hands drew back as if I'd been made out of sparks.

"Lovely scents," I said as she leaned down with her hands on the desk. "Bet the normal gringos and gringettes are just fools for it. I love it. Please, keep up the work and drain their Fort Knox. Like you, I'm pretty fed up with rich white people." I leaned down and mirrored her stance. "But try and play me like a puppet and I'll make sure Izzy knows about your influence among the rich and damned. You know how she loves people who abuse her friends. Hell, there are folk tales in Manila about the little girl with the red left hand."

Margarita's hands trembled, once. "I'd very much like to avoid that."

"Then talk. If I like what I hear, Izzy will have no reason to think you tried to charm her old boyfriend."

Margarita stood up, head back, arms crossed. "My family has been hunting Black Lotus for generations."

"The Spanish part of Sumeria?"

"Turks by way of Anatolia," she said, voice now commanding from a stance of defiance. "Warriors turned herbalists and healers."

"Every family needs a trade. Could you skip a few centuries so I can leave before my lady's done in the Scent Lounge?"

"I almost forgot." She tapped her desk three times, as if steadying her nerves. "My apologies. The trail of the Black Lotus was lost on the Silk Road in the eighteenth century. We hoped to find it when we discovered the research on ley lines."

I gritted my teeth. "You believe in ley lines?"

"If something's real, you don't have to believe."

"I don't have time to debate the secret lines of magic that supposedly cross the Earth. Suffice to say I spent two years running around old rocks and desert wadis and found they meant nothing except to those who believe in the Loch Ness monster and that aliens built the pyramids, and some kids who thought Elvis was dead and replaced by a lost god of Egypt. Imagine the king of rock and roll, dead already."

She sneered. "You never found anything because you don't know how to look. Only one man did."

"Oh god, not Alfred Watkins."

She raised an eyebrow. "Do you want to talk or listen?"

I shut my trap.

"Watkins was a fool, but he was also right in one regard: Ley lines are real, but they move, as surely as we move through space and time. The only way to find them is with a device of his own making. An encoder."

I crushed my molars together. "Don't tell me. You have one."

"Yes. And it only works with a sample. Hence, it's been useless."

"And your price?"

"One leaf. Just one."

"No chance. You'll use it to find the plant it came from and I'll never see either one again."

"Mr. Brimstone, if you cannot find the Black Lotus plant, you will not find the men using it to hurt your friends. Just allow me to test what you have. If it is true, and you are a friend of Isabella, then you are worthy enough to fetch the plant."

I felt the itch of having magic in my pocket. "Why do you want the whole damn plant?"

"It is ours by birthright."

"What will you do with it? New deodorant for maniacs? This stuff is lethal, like LSD mixed with Sterno."

"It is a great elixir for healing those hurt beyond the reach of common root and herb lore. Who would you rather see have Black Lotus: the men who tried to kill your friend, or little old me, sole proprietor of a perfume shop?"

My jaw tensed, then relaxed. "When can you get me the encoder?"

"After work. Are you at the hotel?"

The weight of the bag in my hand seemed to triple. "I'll be at the Olympic. I have a show to do."

She grinned. "Oh, are you a wrestler? Will you be in the ring? I love wrestling. It keeps so many simple people happy."

"Let's just say I'm part of the show. Meet me there. Bring the encoder."

"We have a deal. So long as you give me one petal. Now."

My lips shook, then I snapped my fingers and made the flower appear between thumb and index as if to say things were okay, which was a lie of epic proportions. She gasped. "A wrestler and a magician. You are, indeed, a jack of all trades."

I plucked off a black petal. "Swear our deal is jake."

She put her hands together. "I swear on the graves of my elders."

I released thumb from index finger and held out the single stygian petal.

She reached into the desk, pulling out tweezers and a small bottle. She plucked the bladed petal and put it in the bottle. When she capped it with a squeeze bulb and tube, I realized it was an atomizer like those used for her fancy perfumes. Well, she had plenty available.

"You should see how your lady is doing, shouldn't you?" she asked.

"She's not my lady."

"Even better."

What did Margarita mean by that? Puzzled, but pleased to

realize I'd soon be getting out of this aromatic emporium, I made my way back to the scent lounge to find Veronica the only woman left sitting. Her knees were together, pumps on the edge of a stool, pressing up and down, handing over a wad of twenties to the woman at her feet. "I cannot fathom how I didn't buy more of this fragrance before, but I will take whatever you have in stock." Then she noticed us. "James, you are missing the moment of the century."

Charming. Veronica equated her vapid, doped joy with the Nineteenth Amendment, passage of the Civil Rights Act, and man walking on the moon. "Seems like you've had enough fun for the both of us."

"Now where is my gift?"

Damn it. I forgot.

"It's here, Mrs. Veronica." Margarita had emerged from her office behind me. "A very special blend." Then she squeezed the bulb of an atomizer she held and elbowed my side. I inhaled out of instinct.

Raw magic hit the air between me and Veronica, who inhaled deeply.

When we exhaled, desire seethed to life like a dormant dragon being electrocuted. This was magic strong enough to affect even me.

Veronica's wrist was clenched in my right hand and all I could see in her eyes was the mirror gaze of lust that wouldn't be denied.

"Get up."

She did.

Margarita said something about thanking her, but all I could feel was a bottomless pit of fucking that I needed to fill.

And the old James Brimstone was back in the saddle like a bandit with a badge.

21

WHAT WE DID COULD NOT BE UNDONE.

I'd slept with another man's wife.

Savagely. Give and take brutality and lust. The kind in tawdry paperbacks. What they didn't describe was the bottomless pit of guilt that sawed through me with the serrated edges of a feral child's teeth.

Good guys didn't do that. I'd avoided it with Mandy Jefferson. I'd turned down offers for key parties from some of the regulars at the Thump & Grind. Some lines, once crossed, become scars you carry into every minute of every day and long into the dark night. They itch, wanting to be reopened, torn off like a scab so you can feel the transgressive thrill.

But then comes the bleeding.

Because what we did wasn't sex, and sure as hell wasn't love. It was all thanks to Black Lotus. Margarita had somehow quickly distilled the petal's essence—magic? chemistry? physics? all three?—and we'd inhaled. Mucho mojo was definitely involved for the fragrance to work so effectively on magic-resistant me.

Evidently Black Lotus was a hell of an aphrodisiac. We'd devoured each other with power, dominance, submission. Her skin was beneath my nails. Blood from my lip reddened her mouth. Adversaries trying to break each other's bodies and will, to make them submit. Until she'd won, hands around my throat, choking me out as she rode me on the slashed and dirty floor, clenching my neck as she came and growling at me with disgust and calling me a "dirty peasant fuck" and "slave cock" until the thunder stopped. I took what I wanted in her afterglow, hammering her against the wall as she swallowed the scream of lust I'd reignited in her, breathing in her ear that "no matter who fucks you next, all you will think of is *me*."

We dressed in silence, blood moving from boil to simmer to one degree above ice as she slid on her pumps with her ring hand. The one she used to tend her husband's broken body.

I choked back bile. She spat on the floor. "I can't wait to wash you out of me."

I nodded. But it would take more than a hot shower to clean the stink of the old James Brimstone out of my scared and gutted aura. Black Lotus may have released him, but he vanished as the guilt of being a shithook ate my conscious. He'd never stuck around for the cost, just the benefit, until I'd exiled him years ago. But I could hear his voice whistling past the graveyard of my heart, letting me know "banished" didn't mean "dead." And as much as I wanted to blame Black Lotus, it only made me do what I wanted. I just had to keep what I wanted locked inside a deeper casket.

With the last button done up, she was already out the door to the suite, making it damn clear that whatever happened in this timeless zone of dark lust, she was never anything but herself. I'd been alone my whole life, but it had been a long time—the dark days of my youth—since I felt so empty.

Minus, of course, a full glass of shame.

22

VERONICA'S BLACK BENTLEY SUCKED AT THE DWIN-
dling sunset as she pressed her foot down on the gas, adjusting
herself in her seat every now and then as we kept a steady six-
ty-five on Washington Boulevard. She drove as if she was playing a game of chicken. We were headed to the Olympic, back to
the case I needed to solve before Cactus's tubes were ripped out
in the morning and I became haunted, hunted, and otherwise in
debt for my failure to find his assailant while he was alive.

But that was functional information.

Neither one of us could escape what we'd done. What we'd
said.

As a rule, my first inclination with women is almost always
wrong. I wanted to tell Veronica about magic perfumes and
Black Lotus and the horrors it can render and how I was going
to have a stern talking to with Margarita for why she dosed me
with lust-tinged magic derived from Black Lotus, why she'd waste
a petal—surely it would have taken the entire petal to produce
a perfume that potent?—on me instead of holding it for herself

and her family's thousand-year journey to reclaim a drug that fed the soldiers of the lost ages who fought dragons and demons like Batman fought villains.

So, I said nothing.

Because I'd fucked another man's wife.

Worse, a good man.

And the words I'd uttered with such confidence in the dark now stabbed me in the back during the dying moments of sunlight: *"No matter who fucks you next, all you will think of is me."*

"He doesn't have to know."

Veronica kept driving. I was astounded when she'd told me to get in her car and asked where to drop me off. It wasn't kindness. Perhaps fear of being alone.

"You don't owe me anything."

The sunset flared in her rearview. Her chin rose, and she plucked a pair of bug-eyed sunglasses from the visor above her head. "I don't regret it." She slid them on, voice as calm as a spring breeze, ignoring what I'd just said.

"What about Alan?"

"As you said, he doesn't have to know. So, what do you want?"

I leaned forward and turned to face her. "Blackmail? You've got me confused with someone else. I don't want anything."

"Don't be naive, or presume I am, either. I wanted you. I had you. What do you want? A man of your means must have a litter of needs."

"Thanks for reminding me why I find you abhorrent."

"Except when inside me," she grinned. "Then I was everything you needed."

Veronica had also been dosed with the sexified Black Lotus. Veronica—always in control—wanted someone else to take the wheel. I just happened to be going the same direction.

But the image of dominating and having and taking was pissed upon by the dark clouds above: a vision of Izzy stretched across the sky and *tsk*ing at the little boy who proposed. The little boy heard "no," and then spent two decades making women say "yes" before he cleaned up his act. He got good with his feminine side just as the sixties filled with the smoke of burning bras and he tried to be a stand-up mensch.

"This lift is payment enough," I said.

"Not good enough. Why do you even need a lift?"

"Someone stole . . . it doesn't matter."

"I can have a new car to your office by tomorrow. Name the make and model."

I wasn't driving around in a vehicle that screamed *Hush Money for Fucking a Mogul's Wife*. "A bus pass would be just fine."

Her cheeks flushed with annoyance as we dodged a pile-up in the left lane and gunned it through a yellow. The hulking concrete block of the Olympic Auditorium would soon be in view.

"You can trust me, Veronica."

She huffed. "You even say my name like a slob."

"And you took my dick like a pro." I closed my eyes. "Sorry."

"I'm not. I did. You know what you are? Meat. Good meat. Fit for a Sausage King Party Pack, which I hear the denizens of the suburbs consume by the truckload under the fireworks of Independence Day. But that's it. You're a miserable detective. You have no resources. You have no intellect. And that's why your apology doesn't mean anything. Your life no longer means anything, other than how it impacts mine. So be a good boy and pick out a toy you'd like and let me buy it for you, then I'll know you won't come back begging like Oliver Twist for more."

"No."

"If you don't, I may tell Alan."

My guts clenched.

She smiled. "And I'll leave out the part where I begged for it."

I exhaled.

"You really are terrible at your job, James. Good at being a human shield, good for rutting, but when that's done you're a husk without reason or calculation. Now, tell me what kind of car you'd like."

I ground my teeth.

"Oh, if you'd like an upgrade, I'd be happy to do it. Given your outfit this morning, I assume anything would be an improvement. A Bentley? Rather like putting lace on a sow, but you'd be the one driving, not me."

I stewed looking at the hazy orange horizon, mind sore and body aching from the doped-up rush of Black Lotus and rough sex.

"Tell him."

She sighed. "Don't use reverse psychology with someone who reads Jung's work in German."

"*Sag ihm*," I said, with the harshness German brings out in all who learned it first from reels on the rise of the Third Reich. "Tell him I forced myself upon you. I'll wait. I'll take the hit. I'll go to jail, then prison, because I won't stand a chance with a public defender while you open your purse and buy the law to be on your side. I'll do a nickel. Catch up on my reading. And think of you every day."

The lifelines around her mouth shook once as she tried to regain her composure. "There are other fates than prison."

I snickered "Then kill me."

Her cheeks flexed in frustration.

"You heard me, Veronica. Pay off a hit man. Best be someone with good aim, because I've been known to catch a bullet. Then cover the trail that leads from him to you. Did Jung cover the finer aspects of 'cover your ass when hiring a contract killer?' About the loose ends you'll have when *they* have something on *you?* And if you think finding an intermediary will save them from finding the primary, you have no idea how the shadows of this world can taste the smell of money off of people like you. If your best-case scenario is to have me killed, realize you'll inherit the loose ends of murder that you can't even begin to consider because, sweetheart, you've never tasted the darkness you're bragging about. I've seen men torn apart with machine guns. I've killed men with my own two hands. I've been tortured by those who thrive on suffering and whose appetite for misery is bottomless. So, if that's what you're playing, princess, get ready for a thousand sleepless nights in which every cicada, every grasshopper, every moan of your mansion sounds like your payback coming to slap your ass before it caves in your skull."

I put my hands behind my head. "You know what your problem is, *Veronica*? You were born rich, you'll die rich, and you think of everyone around you as a toy, a chess piece, a servant. No one can touch you. But that's blinded you to a harder truth. Wanna know what it is?"

Her fingers wrapped around the wheel so tight I could see early-onset osteoarthritis gnawing at her cartilage.

"Let me tell ya, babe. You have everything, so you assume that's power. You live in a glass house that makes that clear. But you're outside the garden gate now, and the rules are different. Not to mention your powers are fading, just like your looks." That bit her like a viper. "Out here, you can swing a money sack and get shit done. Absolutely. But eventually, your arm gets tired. And those that you've been hitting? They've been waiting. For a wrong turn. A bad decision. A misstep. A moment alone. Because as powerful as you are, there's something even stronger." I stuck my feet up on the dash, making sure my heels made a dent. "People with nothing to lose."

She inhaled so hard I thought she'd black out.

"So, let's call it jake. And you'll have to do something else to make you feel safe."

"And what might that be."

I stuck out my right hand. "Trust."

She groaned.

"I'm no fan of Hemingway, but that suicidal drunk made a good point: 'The only way to know if someone is trustworthy is to trust them.'" She shook her head. "Or live with the knowledge that we could both make each other's lives miserable."

She pouted, and it was so cute I almost didn't hate her.

Her slim hand grabbed mine.

We shook.

"Now, admit it. You're impressed I can speak German and quote Hemingway."

She groaned. "Any moron watching *Hogan's Heroes* can pick up German, and any man with a dick has read Hemingway. You'll have to do better than that."

I laughed. She grinned. We drove in silence until we reached 18th and Grand.

23

THE LIGHTS OF THE OLYMPIC MARQUEE WERE somewhat dimmed by the haze of a heady cloud made by the smoke rising from a score of tiny joints. But it was plenty bright enough to read:

TONIGHT: ALL AMERICAN WRESTLING!

Underneath that it said:

TOMORROW: THE PRETTY THINGS!

And, in much smaller letters:

AND THE BILLY MARS BAND

I chuckled at Billy's lack of headliner status, then proceeded toward the stage door.

"You're actually going inside?"

I'd not given Veronica an invitation to join me. Hell, I had expected her to drop me off like I was her juvenile delinquent son. But here she was as I made my way around the plain square block of concrete. She kept up, looking ten times better than the freckled gals in hip-huggers and glazed and confused eyes.

"What, not a fan of wrestling? You like big strong men."

"It's fake. You know that, right?"

"Sure. Just like Hamlet's fake."

"Grown men pretending to punch each other for those who think it is real is hardly Shakespeare, and you know it."

"Your class bias is showing. Also, the top of your stocking." She adjusted her dress without an ounce of composure slipping from her stride. "Also, this has to do with the case."

"Wrestlers attacked the Legion Hall? That's a headline for the *National Enquirer*."

"I miss their old format of crime and horror stories from around the world. Now it's just another celebrity-hunting rag that thinks aliens live in Nixon's jowls."

"You didn't answer my question."

I stopped and turned to give Veronica my full attention and the last vestiges of the beast of old James Brimstone shook the new bars but was too weak to rattle a Christmas bell. "No. I didn't. And it's probably best you don't follow me from here on in."

She raised an eyebrow. "You're . . . wrestling? What does this proletariat trough have to do with your dying Indian?"

"Apache. Believe it or not, it's complicated." And involved the drug that had sexed her up enough to choke me like pit fighter. "If you want to stay for the show, you can have a seat. There are two reserved under Jack Lumber."

"Clever name, for a six-year-old held back a year."

"I've always loved hate from a pretty face."

"It's not hate, James. It's honesty." She turned on her heels and assumed a queenly bearing as she walked back to the marquee.

I turned away, trying not to care if she looked back. Her voice pierced the night air.

"James."

I spun around, half-prepared to toss the gym bag full bore at her million-dollar glare.

Her hands were clasped as if in prayer, regal expression slightly softened but not entirely humbled. "I hope you're a better detective than I think you are."

I grinned. "That makes two of us."

Around the corner was a stretch of gray wall that housed the meat of muscle and pain. A couple of large Buicks circled the area as if to keep the hordes of fans—who had not appeared—from crushing the mighty men of the squared circle.

At that door stood a friendly giant clad in chinos and a Lacoste tennis shirt, all six-foot-seven of him looking fiercer than the little alligator on his baby-blue chest. Cigarette smoke haloed his head. "Was starting to think you were the shithook Sam thought you were."

"Nice to see you, too, Achilles. And I apologize for my tardiness. My car was stolen and—"

He waved off my excuses. "Just get in there and talk to the booker so you don't screw up our night. We're starving for asses in seats and you stinking up the joint will cost us all money while you vanish. But don't think you won't get a receipt." He took a deep drag of his smoke to show off his massive chest. "Receipt" was carny slang for "returning the favor to those who fucked you over." He opened the door.

"Thanks for the pep talk, coach."

Pot gave way to Cuban smoke thick and blue. Cutting my way through the fog, I saw a female form. Male voices were muttering low, sweet, unlike any locker room I'd ever had the misfortune to stumble through. The voices cleared and the smoke thinned as I walked down the concrete corridor, but the words kept rolling, the croaky voices of tough guys trying to soften and these words falling out.

"Condolences."

"Sorry for your loss."

"Real shame."

"Jack was a good worker."

"Anything you need, Sam."

Achilles shut the door. The woman who thought I murdered her husband during a skateboard race was now coming into focus.

The bikini was gone, replaced by what must be the West Coast wrestling version of widow's weeds: black mini-skirt, tights, and boots topped by a bright-pink peasant blouse. Fresh makeup starting to run. Samantha Lumber, or Lumbowski, or whatever his real name had been, stood embraced by a crescent of muscle and beer fat, bronzed men with mashed ears and a range of haircuts from bald to balding to buzz cut to thick manes of black and blond and blue. Eyes like a ferret, Sam's gaze darted at me as I walked out of smoke with her husband's bag, his costume, and his legacy. Her head shook. "You."

I nodded. "Me."

"I want to talk to him in private, Shemp."

Shemp was a thick cut of beef in a canary-yellow and lime-green jacket that was stretched to the limit. His red face and ears told me two things: he was a former grappler, which meant he had enough real wounds on him that he could probably stretch most guys until they screamed, and he was the booker. Everyone else seemed allergic to shirts.

"Use my office, Sammy. But we need him. And don't worry. We'll make things right."

Threatened with murder before a weak crowd, I smiled at everyone and introduced myself while Sam strutted through the men, who parted like a fleshy Red Sea and glared hate. "Hey, James Brimstone. Nice to meet you. Great wrestling tongs.

Looking forward to working with you. Kayfabe for life, carny code in effect."

Snorts and threats dropped behind my back as we pulled right and took the door labeled MANAGEMENT in blue and white.

Inside, I relaxed to take a punch or kick to whatever part of my body she felt like swelling until it popped. Instead, Sam kept her back to me. The tiny place smelled of ancient urine and the Budweiser that made the urine. There was a paisley couch ripped at all the edges that might as well be used as a biological weapon. On the edge of my awareness, I could feel the ghosts of glory days past, the ringing of bells and ears, the fights and bets, the sex and drugs and stains of a thousand punches, hammerlocks, and stampeding elephants.

Sam stood like a dagger, so I remained still and silent. My mouth had been the *least* reliable piece of meat on my body for the past day, and if I'd opened my yap and slapped a widow on the day her husband was on ice there was a good chance that karma, if it existed, would toss me in a sack and drop me in an abyss. She turned, claws digging into her forearm. Tears hugged her eyes, the cheeks below already wet. "They told me."

I had no idea who *they* were or what the question was, so I didn't move a rat's itchy ass and held loose, still waiting for the salvo of suffering from her red, raw knuckles.

"Heart attack. Had nothing to do with you. And everything to do with . . ." She shook and the tears dropped. "My daughter is sick."

"I heard."

Her thin lips flatlined. "You're going to do Jack's job for him."

"I will."

"You ain't taking a dime of the purse. I get the purse for both jobs."

"Right. Wait, both? I just have his outfit for The Assassinator."

"They want you in the exhibit, too. And you'll do it. And you'll make it look great."

I took a deep breath and exhaled. "Of course. Thank you for letting me try and make things right—"

Her finger cut the air between us. "Shut the fuck up, mark," she said. "I don't care about you, or what you want, or what you do when I don't see you." She blinked, and that was enough to make her tough, frantic energy shimmer and simmer down. Her boots stumbled back. I charged to grab her shoulders. "I wouldn't sit on that couch unless you've had a tetanus shot. Can you stand?"

Sam jerked away from me like my hands were burning holes in her skin. Her boots found balance and she gathered herself. Her eyes met mine. "He came back to life."

My jaw hung a legitimate three inches slack. "Jack?"

She looked dazed. "Like something out of a movie. A monster on a slab. He tossed the ambulance guy into the wall and thrashed as I jumped on him. But he was dead. They said so. His pulse said so. His heart said so. Then his eyes bugged out and he grabbed his chest." She shook, and then shook her head, a dizzy test pattern of grief. "I could barely make out what he was screaming."

"But you could?

She sucked in breath.

"What did he say?"

The words resisted her first attempt before she spit them out. "Black Lotus."

The door opened and Sam smacked my arms down. Shemp's sweaty five o'clock shadow was like a warren of frozen black ants on his face, barely a smidgen apart. "Hate to be the boss," he said in a greasy voice, "but this is showbiz, Sam. The show must go on. Is your boy ready?"

She strutted. "Jack was my boy. This is some idiot in a suit. He'll do it. Both matches."

"Then he better get smart with the boys he's working with.

Now. You," he said. "You're doing a squash for Kodiak Slim. Then you're putting on the Assassinator for a tag with Kodiak against Bikini Atoll and the Dynamite Hippie." Names had changed some since I was trolling for work as a stick with the carny. There were always wild characters, but these ones sounded like they'd fallen out of a Hanna-Barbera cartoon, hit the gym, and found their home in the ring.

"Got it." I nodded to Sam and kept my mouth on silent.

She grabbed my arm. "Do not fuck this up or I will break your goddamn neck."

She released me and I went into the lion's den of wrestlers.

Down the hall I could hear guttural laughter, grunts, and the sound of cards being flipped. Disinfectant, Bactine, and other salves of the trade created an aroma that screamed "boys who fight like men." I'd been a lone operator as long as I could imagine and thought sports were the opiate of the masses, but wrestling, boxing, and other gags and fights of small cadres or individuals did have a certain pull. Still, this was not my world, and never would be. I'd need to prove myself as soon as I turned the corner, or these wolves would devour me whole.

And then I heard a scream.

24

I RAN, HOLDING BACK THE GYM BAG AS IF DAVID had upgraded his slingshot since beating Goliath. I turned the corner, hard, and even started to mutter *Tyger Tyger* in case I'd need a joyride to take on a room full of fake and real fighters.

But the sight stopped my fears.

A card table lay knocked over, four hands of mixed value at gin rummy splayed near the shining boots of six wrestlers. Near the table stood more muscle per ounce than even Achilles had to brag about. His abdominal wall was an eight-pack of lean muscle, surrounded by hulking lats; his broad chest was crisscrossed with throbbing veins. His left hand—which could have gripped a small meteor—was attached to a thick cut of a wrist, leading to a biceps bigger than my head, and rolling shoulders made of solid rock. His right hand was trapped behind his back, and whoever was responsible was hidden by the titan's muscle. Atop the thick neck was a mop of long, blond hair that hung down to his chest where each pectoral slab was tattooed with a mushroom cloud. I was a lousy detective, but would have bet against the odds at Cactus's casino that this was Bikini Atoll.

"Get off me, maggot."

Most of the six beer-guts-and-biceps crew were smiling, laughing, and pointing. Amid the muttering jibes, I could hear what I'd already deduced. The big man couldn't counter a hammerlock. Dr. Fuji would have laughed as Bikini tried in vain to reach behind him. As I watched Bikini struggle, a hand slapped my shoulder. The hand belonged to a guy with an enormous black beard and wild curly hair, who stared down on me from a height nearly a foot above mine. "Betcha he calls for momma before he cries uncle."

I smiled. "I never bet on the misery of grown men."

"Then you must be new."

"Shemp!" Bikini said. "Get these animals off me!" Then his arm was free, and by god, those biceps had to be twenty-three inches all the way around.

The big beard laughed. "You dodged a bullet."

I smiled. "Better than catching it." I offered my hand, preparing for ten different kinds of wrist locks or stretches to tear me apart. Instead, the callused bear paw grasped mine. "Kodiak."

Bikini shook off the pain. "Laugh it up, has-beens. You guys just made an enemy today. I'm the only one these people are coming to see. You wanna see who's got stroke with the boss? You'll be walking my bags to the airport before we get to San Diego."

I noticed a little guy in a referee's uniform in the corner. He caught my eye until Bikini paced over, stood before me, and blocked the view.

"Who the fuck is this pipsqueak?" There it was: an ashen aftertaste under his beer breath and the cloying scent of tanning oil on his hulking frame, a taste of magic. Black Lotus. Just under the surface.

"This here is Jack's replacement for the main event," Kodiak said, smug. "A real shooter." He didn't mean good with a six-gun, with which I was passable. A shooter was a wrestler who knew real submission holds, guys who could break your wrist as easy as a desiccated chicken bone. "Probably knows more holds than you."

I smiled at Kodiak. Thanks a lot for the invitation to the initiation, I thought.

Bikini shook his mane. "No way. Not this vanilla midget. Not funny, Kodiak." His finger was the size of a bratwurst and jabbed me with malicious intent. "Who trained you?"

"Dr. Fuji, master of a thousand holds," I said, grinning from ear to ear like a complete mark.

Another poke of his bratwurst hit my chest. "Who the fuck is that? Some no-account Jap from the carnival circuit?"

My grin hid, I hope, an intense desire to rip out his tongue and staple it to his head like a fleshy combover. "Oh, you've heard of him!"

The grapplers chuckled and hooted, except one. "Teach him some discipline, Bik!" His hair was thinning beneath his beaded headband, and he wore a suede leather vest that ended in fringe. He wore tights so baggy they looked like a skirt, and across his strong but less-cultivated chest in the faded blue of prison tattoos was a lightning bolt. Ladies and gentleman, the Dynamite Hippie. "Learn him," the Hippie said, as if he, not Bikini Atoll, had the confidence of a real fighter.

"Try a hammerlock!" someone yelled out, and the laughter crashed.

Bikini grabbed my imitation luxury jacket, yanked me close. I dropped my bag, flexed my knuckles until they cracked.

"What the fuck are you faggots doing?"

Shemp filled in the door and everyone shut up and went back to pushups, stretches, or lacing their boots. Bikini's nostrils flared like a dragon's about to spit fire before his mammoth mitts popped open, oh so dramatically, and he extended himself back to stare me down. "Just do the job, mark. Take the bumps. Do what you're told. And keep your smart mouth shut. Or you'll see what kinda hell I can unleash."

"Great promo," I said. "Too bad the cameras weren't rolling."

"Zip it," Shemp said. "Go in the cooler and take a load off." Bikini walked past the booker, Dynamite Hippie in tow. Shemp glared at me, thumbing his jowls so the sweat dripped free. "Kodiak? Smarten the kid up before I just give Sam her money and drop this guy where he stands. You got twenty, then you're squashing this bastard in the ring."

"Got it, Shemp,"

He turned and headed down the corridor to the "cooler," which was apparently reserved for the ruling elite, leaving the rest of the area for the boys who filled out the roster. And in here? Not a lick of Black Lotus, which made me feel good for their hearts. But worry bloomed that Bikini would explode in the ring like Jack on the boardwalk.

Kodiak slapped my back. "C'mon, kid. Time to put you through the paces."

"Kid? He hasn't been a kid since I was breaking chains!"

The ref who had waltzed Bikini behind his back walked over to me. He was tall, thin, jaunty, walking as if he carried sixty more pounds than he really did, face shaved clean . . . that's what threw me. That, and the gray hair, and the fact he wasn't wearing the chains he'd worn on his shirtless, godlike physique thirty years ago.

"Hercules?"

He popped his muscles in his ref outfit as if they were still like Bikini's, his Greek accent played up for effect. "The Original Greek God!"

Kodiak laughed. "You know this mark, Leo?" Even I didn't know Herc's real name was Leo.

"Of course! He was our stick!" He gripped my shoulder, hands so soft they'd be confused with a baby's cheek in the dark. "But don't let the son of a bitch-bitch fool you! He can work and shoot and yes, oh yes, he was trained by a bastard named Fuji!" His eyes welled up with tears. There are a lot of romances on the road, but the one Herc and Fuji had was the kind you had to keep hidden from the prying eyes of the world and management. Edgar had laughed about the two "bastards who buggered each other." All I could see was two outcasts who found solace and happiness in a world that would rather they kill themselves.

"Great to see you, Herc."

"Why you trading in your cards for tongs, James?"

"Long story, old friend."

"And we don't have time," Kodiak said, then pointed at a bench with a stinky pair of black-and-white tights and bright-blue boots. "Get dressed and I'll tell you how this ends. Leo, you, too."

As I undressed in the humidity of other men's stink, Kodiak ran through the set.

"You come out first, because you're the baby face, a hero, because you're pretty."

"Aw, shucks."

"I'll come out second, because I'm the heel. It's better to start the match with them hating me, going nuts, and then watch you try and fail. We'll play the crowd like a cheap violin until we get to the main event. But I'll spare you my philosophy on how to book a good show. What name should we give this victim?" Kodiak said to Herc.

Herc laughed, hands on his hips, a geriatric Superman. "Ha! There is only one name for him: Icarus! He came to close to the burning sun of Kodiak and fell twice as hard!"

"Good enough," Kodiak said. I pulled on my jockstrap, not loving the moist snugness where another man's crotch had been slung. "Just think of yourself like the school hero. You're coming out to beat Goliath. Ha, ha! Get it? I know, I'm George Carlin. Now focus, so I don't break your neck. When the bell rings, start swinging wild. Hit my arms with open palms or an empty fist." He demonstrated. I was to hold my hand as if I was holding an invisible bar. "Put a little Irish on them, but don't potato me." I deduced that meant "keep the blows from leaving potato-sized marks on his skin," proving once and for all I wasn't as bad a detective as everyone thought. "I'll grab you by the throat, lean down, and when you feel me spring up, jump with the momentum. I will lift you up then push you down. But kick up your legs and try to land with your arms extended." He pushed his out like a modern Vitruvian Man. "Land like Christ on his cross, and the pain will shoot across all of you, not just one point."

"Just like a bed of nails," I said.

"Heh! See? He is one of the boys," Herc said.

The rest of the match would consist of me being tossed around like a sack of peat moss that needed to be tenderized before it could be freshly packed in the dirt. Kodiak's "finisher" was, go figure, a bear hug. "You'll thrash about until Leo here sees you scream, then I'll drop your carcass, walk back, and you get rained with boos and sharpened pennies. Got it?"

"Throw wimp punches. Jump when you say how high. Land like Jesus. Jump around and make each move seem like it's rearranging my spine. Scream 'uncle' when you give me a big hug."

I stuck up my thumb. "Got it."

"We go on in ten," Kodiak said, leaving me behind. "I can't be seen with baby faces or it'll ruin the game. You're doing a good thing, helping Sam. Just take the bumps and your check. I'll walk you through the main event with Bikini and Dyna. Time for a smoke before the shift begins." He waved me off, said bye to Leo, and then wandered back as the other bad guys, all older wrestlers with crunched faces, filed in to do the last of their makeup and lacing.

"He's good people, James," Herc said. "Kinda friends with everyone. Reminds me of you, back in the Electric Magic days."

I smiled and we caught up quick, but my mind was on the taste of magic around Bikini, and I switched to a quieter voice and a loose carny code that was common with guys like Herc and me.

I laced the boots, shoving my wallet in the right one. I'd folded the eight remaining petals together and slipped them between two dead credit cards. After all, without the flower, I'd never get the encoder from Margarita. "So, ever see Jody rousting about?"

Jody was our word for trouble from without, a bad railroad dick or a mayor or local shithook who was sniffing around to make havoc. Herc's big grin stayed still, but he nodded his head. "Not Jody," he said, and that meant *yes*.

"I heard he was looking for work," I said, *work* being the nature of trouble. "Soda Pop." *Drugs*. "He used to sell them out of his car."

Herc shook his head twice, meaning he was talking true, but the tone was reversed. "Not here, but I remember they made every kid happy, so alive and strong," he cackled. "Hell, the way Jody sells it, it's like he's making them young."

He slapped my shoulder and I had to choke back the flinch. Herc was what you called a physical culturalist. He turned his body into a vision of perfection with a combo of ancient Ikarian exercises and a cavalcade of concoctions that almost always included egg yolks and castor oil. He was a purist and believed the body was a temple that required worship, devotion, and dedication. He was also a teetotaler who once chastised me for enjoying a cherry brandy at Christmas because it "invited the three imps." These were sloth, gluttony, and weakness. Drugs of any kind would have been the fourth horseman of the apocalypse for such a fine human specimen. And the bang he gave my shoulder made it clear there was some bad mojo here and Herc didn't like it one goddamn bit.

"I always loved Jody's soda," I nodded once, so he knew I hated the idea. "Especially black cherry. Can't get it anywhere else."

He nodded twice, pulled his cauliflower ear, so everything that came next was to be followed in reverse. "Don't bother looking here. All these guys, like the champion who didn't know a hammerlock, they hate that stuff. Poison for the body they would never touch. It's never here."

That's all I needed. "Then I'm glad I'm not a full-time grappler. I'm going to find a cola."

"Concessions will give you one. Just don't let Bikini see you. He'll have a heart attack."

No code was needed to know Herc wouldn't mind if Bikini's chest imploded. Herc was a strongman first, but along with Dr. Fuji, he knew enough holds, hooks, twists, and breaks to keep the Marine Corps from storming an enemy beachhead. "See you in the ring, Herc."

He waved me off, then looked into locker room mirror and adjusted his bow tie. A warning. *Be careful.* This place wasn't safe for an outsider.

I strutted by two guys arm-wrestling on the re-set card table, one dressed all in black with curly mutton-chop sideburns, the other wearing tights striped like a barber pole, face red and nose crunched. Their arms were thick from the labor of their job, not cut or cultivated like Jack or Bikini. If Black Lotus was here, it was only for the elite.

"Hey fellas, which way to the concession stand?"

"You can't go out like that," Mutton Chops muttered, hand still clasped with his opponent.

"There's a cooler by the entrance," Stripes said. "If there's anything left, mark, it's there."

"And you'll need a belt," Mutton Chop said. "You're too damn small for that tong."

"Hence the need for a cola," I said, heading out while the immovable hair and the irresistible test pattern battled for supremacy. Leaving the locker room, I feinted right and headed left.

At the end of a hall, a thin man in black jeans and an unassuming chambray work shirt stood at the closed door of the private VIP lounge of the gods. Under a distinctly sinister and certainly sizable nose, he sported a thick mustache styled with pomade. Dark eyebrows and the sheen of a beard made him stick out from the ragged company. Over one shoulder he carried a weathered leather satchel. But it was his tiny size that betrayed him. No one backstage was smaller than me.

I did my best to look bigger than I was, then strutted toward the man I was sure was Mick Butler, the pusher who bought out Billy Mars. The son of a bitch handling Black Lotus.

25

MICK LEANED AGAINST THE WALL NEXT TO THE door of the elite dressing room, sucking at his cigarette like smoke was the fuel that kept his lungs running.

His ferret-like eyes darted to me as I approached and raised a finger to my lips. I puffed myself up to look even more pathetic and threatless.

"Hey, Mick?"

He nodded but didn't acknowledge I'd known his name.

"Hey, you got a pick-me-up? I'm on soon and am dragging my ass."

That's when I heard Bikini's annoying voice from behind the closed door. "No way, Shemp. No way. Don't welsh. We're going to flip me today. I don't care that Jack's dead. I don't care that some monkey is wearing his mask. Tonight, we go atomic."

Mick exhaled smoke, looked at me. "You don't have pockets, fella. You got cash?"

I lifted my right boot and gave it a slap. "Always prepared. Like the Boy Scouts."

He smiled and the best I can say for it was that it didn't drip slime. There was no taste of magic around him, just the sour-mash smell of a filth peddler. "Come on," he said, turning on his yellow Cuban heels. "My office is this way." Dragging his heels as if his boots were too taxing for his legs, he slid away from the office.

I was awful at first impressions, but, seeing him push open the emergency exit with a spidery hand, I couldn't drum up anything positive to see in a guy pushing drugs that killed people, especially since he seemed to have been enjoying the mayhem of his work.

I followed him into the night air. We were in a back lot, around the corner from where Achilles's eyes would have spied us, for which I thanked Glycon and other false gods. The ground was littered with the yellow corpses of a thousand smokes, one of them still lit.

A black Lincoln Continental Mark VI sat amid the cheap wrecks that the wrestlers piled in to haul ass across country. I was less than a step behind him as he started to slither toward the Lincoln. "So," he said without turning, "what you be needing, big guy?"

I punched his kidney, sending a shock of pain through his entire body. Before pain gave way to reason and causality, I locked my arms around his neck and pulled him back with a real sleeper hold—a blood choke. Mick's rubber legs gave way, fingers digging into my forearm before dropping.

I grabbed his backpack and riffled through it. Mick was stirring so I applied some blunt-force trauma to his head with a wingtip. The concussion should keep him out for several minutes.

There were three wooden cases, each covered in tourist-styled Yin-Yangs or Buddha faces, each a different color: red, black, and blue. Nothing tasted of magic. Red? Hundreds of scattered bennies. Black? White horse heroin, by the looks of the powder in the little bags.

Blue?

I opened the case and licked my lips.

It tasted of nothing. Not air. Not nothing. "Charmed," I said. Fucker had a hex on it. Inside was a single baby blue bag. In it was a dried leaf.

"Where the fuck is he?" screamed Shemp, and the door opened with a gust, sending the tiny baggie into the air. I palmed the one burning cigarette from the ground, stinging my knuckle before I could snake it between my fingers.

"Why are you out here? What the fuck are you doing?"

"I came out for a smoke," I said, standing. "Found this guy. Guess he got mugged. Want me to call the cops?"

"Cops? Are you insane? Get the fuck back inside."

"I feel kinda responsible."

Shemp grabbed me by the throat and brought me eye level with the brown buttons stuffed into his mashed face. "You owe Jack. You owe Sam. Go, and do me a favor? Die. Just make sure it's in the ring. Or else I'll do it back here later." Brick fingers released me. "I'll handle this guy."

I coughed, as I was supposed to have no choice in doing, and let Shemp know he was still the master of the iron claw. I ambled off, quite aware that as soon as Mick woke up, they'd be having my ass.

He was my only connection to Black Lotus.

But if I fucked this up, a widow might lose her kid.

I ran back inside. I needed to lose quick, get back to the soon-to-be-conscious Mick, and finish up our business. They'd surely not stop the match to accommodate his assault complaint against me.

I hoped.

26

FROM THE AUDITORIUM CAME A BOOMING VOICE
wired with tin:

"And now, our first match! Coming to the ring, hailing from
Syracuse, New York, and weighing in at two hundred and fifty
pounds . . . Kiiiiid Icarus!"

A young guy in a striped shirt yanked the curtain open and
I ran out into the tepid embrace of a lukewarm Olympic crowd.

The first beer hit me at a steady thirty miles per hour, exploding on my face with a wet gush and turning my breath into a spray.
I raised my arms and flexed as much as I could, since I'd gained
about fifty pounds when the announcer gave my baloney stats.
Perhaps they couldn't see my heroic physique without heroic
poses.

"Victory is mine!" I screamed at what looked like a confetto
of people tossed into a darkened hall and began a light jog. That's
when the second beer hit my back like a giant's golden shower. I
smiled and rolled with the punch, spinning around so the beer
twirled off my skin and back into the people lining the aisles.

Teenagers seethed over the top rail while a bored cop shoved them back.

"Faggot!"

"Go back to New York!"

"Eat shit, you big faker!"

I ran past them, sure that more adoring examples of humanity awaited. And lo, there sat a matron of about sixty years with her friends in Sunday hats. Old school fans, with old school values. I ran over.

"Tonight, I dedicate my match to you ladies!"

The fascinator veil on the head matron's lilac velvet chapeau trembled as she growled and thrust a hat pin the size of a shark's tooth toward me. "Don't touch me, you swarthy Greek!"

I smiled and muttered "go to hell" to everyone in general, while I spun the rest of the beer off and made it to the ring steps. My soaked body cut through the ropes to the kind of applause has-beens receive when the MC belts out "half-price chicken wings in the China Room."

"Now, coming down the aisle, from the Aleutian Island in Alaska, weighing three hundred and fifty pounds, Kodiaaaaaak ... SLIM!"

The crowd didn't have time to register their disgust, because Kodiak ran out like he was a real mamma bear and I was kicking her cubs. His close to three-hundred-pound frame shook with the vicious intent of a career criminal with nothing to lose. He slid beneath the bottom rope, slick with sweat and no beer. The crowd was cheering for the bad guy as he pulled himself to his feet and I saw his dead smoky red eyes. And worse: the fetid magic scent of his breath.

Black Lotus.

"Keeeyah!" he screamed, throwing a wild haymaker with closed fists, the kind that would make your dentist cheer and a neurosurgeon cancel his golf plans.

I dodged, feinting left and right, ducking and diving as every wild throw missed me, but not for lack of trying. Sweat replaced the beer as Kodiak reared back his head and yelled, giving me time to drill his liver with a savage kick.

The audience *oooowwww*'d as the pain paralyzed Kodiak for a second, long enough for me to catch my breath.

"Slow down!" I yelled, giving him the bird, keeping up the illusion that this was in fact a bullshit wrestling match and not a real one. "You're off book. I don't mind if you squash me but I don't want you to kill me!"

Clarity returned to his hazy red eyes, but not the sober kind. His long arms grabbed for my neck. I ducked and ran under his arm, much to the joy of the crowd, who hooted at David avoiding each blow from Goliath. Me? I was grateful he was so jacked he was fighting like a monster and not a fighter.

I ran around the ring and laughter smacked me from all sides, along with fistfuls of peanuts as I played the wuss, puss, wimp, and mollycoddle while a six-foot-six monster chased me. But I had to keep the match alive, or Shemp would welsh my deal for Jack's pay and Sam and her daughter would be out of their papa's last payday. Thank god for the ref.

Herc finally thrust himself between us and pressed me back with ease and Kodiak with seemingly similar ease, but he'd given each of us a knuckle-punch to the solar plexus, stealing my breath and making even Kodiak stagger. "Come on!" Herc said, then turned to Kodiak. "Stick to the match! Kodiak, squash him now. Do it." Iron laced Herc's voice. But my vocal cords were stolen. I tried to scream out "Herc, no!"

But Kodiak's eyes glazed with rage. His hands clutched Herc's throat. The audience was howling, loving the attack on the ref, a completely vile bit of sportsmanship. Herc fired out his arms to reach for a hold, but Kodiak yanked Herc into the air before his iron fingers could find purchase. The one-time masterpiece of cultivated muscle and viciousness hung in the air, blocking out the spotlight, before Kodiak rammed him into the mat. Thankfully, his reflexes were still good, and he extended his limbs in a Jesus Christ pose to keep the impact divided among his skin and organs.

Silence. The crowd might as well have drowned in blood. Kodiak rose from his knees and I tossed a spinning heel kick to the back of his skull. He stumbled back onto his knees and I leveled an ax kick to cut him down to size. But the slippery giant had dragged Herc to his feet, and I nearly hit my old friend. With his hands under Herc's arms, Kodiak waltzed with a human shield. I couldn't tell if Herc was alive or dead.

"Looks like the ref is back in action!" Kodiak said.

"Put him down!" But the audience howled, dark and guttural, loving this macabre turn of events. I was just glad to see Herc start huffing and puffing. "Put him down now!"

"Or what, mark? What you got? What can you make me—"

Tyger Tyger, burning bright, asshole!

I slid into a joyride and moved faster than even Kodiak could sense, and then I ran like a soul past hell's gate, leapt, and drew my fist back for a haymaker that, if it connected, would have felled a redwood that had stood for a century.

Pain jolted through me as the joyride taxed every nerve into submission, bleeding my aura as if I were in a mystic iron maiden. Damn it! *Tyger Tyger, burning bright!*

I snapped back to reality, but with the momentum of the joyride carrying me like a train. My fist clocked Kodiak's jaw before his eyes registered me as a lethal weapon . . . and that big mouth unhinged. Literally. I'd broken his mandible just below his ear.

Kodiak screamed and hit the ground, and I hugged Herc to keep him afloat. Around the ring were officials, Shemp included, staring at me as if I'd done something wrong.

"Herc? Can you count?" I said, a plan forming just in time to save my hide.

He shook his head and he muttered death threats in Greek until he said "Yes."

"Then get ready to drop."

Herc hit the ground as Kodiak roared with his jaw hanging off its hinge amid the crowd's vicious screams. Kodiak was not entirely impervious to his injury, however, and hunched over in pain as his hand began to explore the damage done to his jaw.

I ran and jumped on his bent back, landing with my arm hooked around his neck, his jaw hanging loose against my forearm as I locked the same blood choke that took out Mick.

Boos and hisses hit me right before the lit cigarettes sparked off my wet skin. Kodiak lumbered around the ring like Frankenstein's monster being drained of his life-force. He bolted to the corner and dropped to his knees. Next thing I saw was the turnbuckle coming at me like a perfect bull's eye was painted on my skull.

My head crashed into the turnbuckle, which had all the give of a boxing glove filled with sand. But the shock of pain did not break the choke I had vice-gripped on Kodiak, who was finally starting to fade. Outside the ring, Shemp and the cronies were circling like starved piranhas. If I fucked up the match, I was doomed, and "I didn't want to be killed" wasn't going to cut it with carny management, regardless of the era. Kodiak lunged up, running on Black Lotus fumes, aiming to go to the well for one last drink. As he surged forward, I let go.

Kodiak boned his half-asleep noggin at full speed on the turnbuckle, his nose going *crunch* while his jaw swung like a drunk pendulum.

The crowd *eeeww*'d! as he staggered backward and tried to straighten his back. All the while I ran around inside the ropes with Shemp yelling, "What the fuck are you doing?"

I had no breath to say what I was thinking: *Need to land in a Jesus Christ pose.*

I climbed to the top rope, glad my feet could grip them like a prisoner's fist around iron bars while the warden works the whip. Crouched on the top, I rose. The audience glared at the man at whom they'd tossed pennies, butts, and beer, not believing that Davey had a slingshot's chance of destroying Goliath.

I raised my arms in victory, knees bending as Kodiak shook his head and Herc shook out the cobwebs, looking at me like I'd lost all of my marbles down the drain. "Never regret thy fall, O Icarus of the fearless flight," I yelled, then jumped into flight, arcing my spine, thinking of Oscar Wilde's last line: "For the greatest tragedy of them all / Is never to feel the burning light."

I leapt into a roar of adoration that I'd missed since being a stick for Herc at fairgrounds and parking lots. I crashed into Kodiak's chest with my knees. I hadn't twisted enough to make it look good, but the big man toppled with me on top of him. Awkwardly, I covered Kodiak's chest and whispered. "For the love of gods old and new, stay the hell down!"

Herc dropped a hand as the crowd chanted, "ONE!"

Kodiak's glazed eyes re-focused and his mouth swung wide without his jaw. Then his feet started to rumble.

"TWO!"

I elbowed his already-bashed liver, his eyes nearly popped out of their sockets, and he screamed, "Arroooga!"

"THREE!"

Every member of the crowd was on their feet screaming so loud it drowned out the bell as I struggled to bring myself up to my feet, sweat pouring out of me by the pint. Herc followed, and I looked in his eyes. I pulled him close so Shemp and his crew could not read our lips.

"You okay?"

"Yes."

"Great, because I'm screwed. Shemp is going to tear my arms off."

"No. He won't." Herc pushed himself off me as the bell rang through the din and grabbed my wrist, not an ounce of his strength having been drained by age or the chokeslam that would have killed a younger man. The bell rang and Kodiak still lay on the floor.

"The winner of this bout as a result of a pin fall . . . Icarus, the Great!"

Herc yanked up my arm and I sucked in the wild applause from the same drunk bastards and old nuts who had wanted me plastered not ten minutes ago. Now I could probably get them to vote me in for mayor.

I waved and did a short run around the ring as three mugs pulled out Kodiak and led him down the aisle on giant legs made of sand and dying fury.

That's when all the pains in my body hit. Herc slapped my back, so I stood up straight. "Parade for them," he said while looking at Shemp. "Sign autographs. Buy time for the son of a bitch-bitch to be tossed in back." I did as instructed.

"That was so boss, man!"

"You got less insurance than Evel Knievel!"

"Here I thought you only skateboarded."

Front row, with a girl under each arm, was Kevin.

"Well, I retired after having my ass handed to me by a kid. So, I started a new job. How'd I do?"

"It suits you, man. It's a trip to watch you hit that guy. I always thought this stuff was fake."

"Never trust anything but your own eyeballs," I said. "Enjoy the rest of the show."

"It will be hard to top a guy losing his jaw," said one of the girls, auburn hair in two thick braids.

I bowed and then looked through the ring ropes. Kodiak was away. "Take care, Kevin."

"You really know Icarus?" the other girl said with soft surprise. Kevin laughed and I waved goodbye as my brain scrambled for a plan once I left my adoring fans for a dressing room filled with men keen to break my ribs.

Rounding the ring, I saw Shemp waiting at the curtain. I walked with purpose, big smile on my face, as I passed by the hatchet-faced granny with the hatpin. She tapped her hat. "You live to fight another day, sissy," she said.

Shemp sat before the curtain, cracking his chubby fingers and preparing to chop me up like mutton. The closer I got, the more obvious his anger became. His pockmarked skin and the heavy veins in his hands almost glowed with rage. Shemp was a shooter. And thanks to the joyride and every part of my body feeling like it had been worked over like a government mule, there was a good chance he could cripple me before I could get away or reverse the tables. Either way would kill the money I owed Sam. Either way he'd be harder to get on my side to tell me about Mick Butler. I was close enough to smell his cigar breath, but no Black Lotus. His eyes narrowed, then widened, but not on me.

Behind me, Herc ran up. Backup, as if I'd yelled "Hey, rube" against management instead of the fans.

Shemp made the come-here motion with his finger, then pushed himself through the curtain. We followed, Herc at my side. "I stay with you," he said. "You don't go piss without me."

27

WE CUT THROUGH THE CURTAIN AND FOUND THE dark corridor filled with mountains of meat and fists ready to give the new guy a once over before dumping him in the trash.

Shemp dug into his pockets. Before I could run my mouth, Herc stepped in front of me. "This man saved my life. Kodiak was bananas. I'd be dead if not for James Brimstone. And, Shemp, if you think of a double cross, I'll stretch *you* and *all* your boys."

Shemp exhaled through his nostrils like a dragon with a deviated septum. "Relax, Herc," he said. "I ain't aiming to screw nobody but the concession stand tonight." He pulled his fist out of his pocket. He held a bunch of twenties. Hopefully enough to pay for the medicine to help Sam's little girl. "That was a hell of a thing you pulled," he said. "You turned the crowd around like a tangle of Christmas lights when things went screwball. I don't impress easy, mark, but you earned Jack's pay." He stuck out his fist.

I smiled, then took the twenties out of his grip. But the last one stayed locked in his meat-fist. "That's for the main event. You still got another job to do."

"What?" Herc said. "Kodiak can't wrestle. He lost his mind."

"Then our baby face here just earned even more chances to prove his gifts." Shemp smiled. Brown baby tombstones hung from gummy graveyards. "Go enjoy the hospitality of the boys."

"What about the mugging?" I said while I was in a room full of witnesses with more leverage. "That guy I tried to wake up in the parking lot?"

"What guy?" Herc said. "What mugging?"

"The guy around back with the backpack," I said while Shemp coughed. "Did you guys see him?"

The glances, shaking heads, and awkward silence made it clear everyone knew who Mick Butler was, and they were sworn by the carny code to keep things mum. "He's gone," Shemp said.

Gone? Was Shemp lying? Maybe not. There was no sign of an enraged Mick Butler calling for my head on a platter, so maybe he *was* gone.

"He the one who got Kodiak crazy?" Herc said.

"Kodiak's always crazy," Shemp said.

"Maybe you gave it to him, then?" Herc said. "Spice up the act?"

Shemp growled. "Don't know what you're insinuating, but I don't like it."

"Bullshit. You know these guys are full of drugs."

"Why would I damage my number one commodity?" Shemp said, making a compelling point until you realized that Shemp thought of people as commodities. Sure, Kodiak was huge, fast, tough, and smart, with natural charisma, but that didn't make him unique like a true giant or a midget or a pretty boy with a high-school athlete's physique. Kodiak was what we call an attraction, and only worth as much as his draw. But even within that, Shemp had no ire on me. Someone else made Kodiak a victim of Black Lotus, but it wasn't management.

"Did that mugged guy know Kodiak?" I said. "Maybe he did something to him that made him nuts."

"All wrestlers are crazy," Shemp said. "Now go rest and wait for Bikini and Dynamite to walk you through the match. Herc, you're on water cooler."

"Fuck that," he said. "I'm reffing the main event."

Two forces met each other behind the curtain. In their heyday, each man would have been a holy terror. Now in their golden years, they were no less fierce, but terrorized quietly.

"You pulling rank, Herc?"

"I'm doing my job. You going to fire me, Shemp?"

I wasn't sure if Shemp had sent Kodiak to kill me in the ring to make blood red or dollar green, but I wouldn't put it past him to make Herc's last days numbered, miserable, and long.

"I'll be fine, Herc," I said. "I mean, it's all fake, right?"

Now all the ire was on me. Nothing spit in the eye of a grown man who plays pretend than telling him the emperor has no clothes. Might as well have yelled, "Hey, rube!" in the Electric Magic Circus and started a donnybrook with the viewing public.

The beastly grapplers shoved forward until Shemp screamed, hoarse as a dying vulture. "Enough! Positions. We got a show to do. Mark, sit your ass in the locker room. And Herc? Let's have a chat."

Shoulders bumped into me like stun guns as I left. The day's soreness crept back on me as the last adrenaline ran out. Heartbeats speedbagged my chest. The world of the backstage halls, concrete, and white light became a parade of shadows. Drained, I realized I was easy pickings for whoever had sent Kodiak to kill me—someone who was still here. That list of suspects consisted only of the two people who disliked me when I arrived, not the world of enemies I'd made since.

I turned left to enter the dressing room where I'd changed.

Every wrestler was on their feet, killing me with their countenances. But they didn't move.

"Boys," I said. "I didn't have a choice."

"They don't care," said a voice behind the wall of flesh. They parted their arms and Sam walked through, straight for me. "Neither do I. You're a shit. A fucking scumbag shit."

My mouth shook trying to find words that couldn't be uncovered.

"Give me my money."

I did.

"Where's the last twenty?"

"Shemp said I'd get it at the end of the night."

"Fuck him and fuck you. I can't believe I gave you the benefit of the doubt." She stormed past me and down the hall.

Mutters grew into threats and threats became promises about breaking my arms and knees, cracking my skull and bending my elbows inside out as I backed out, slow, hands up. "No need to get riled up over little old me. I'll see myself out." I headed to the main-event dressing room, where I'd hoped to find the inane egotistical ramblings of Bikini and his creepy sidekick. Instead there was just a closed door and silence. The grapplers entered the hall as I turned the knob.

Click.

I entered, closed the door, locked it behind me, and enjoyed the darkness.

The main eventers had their own exposed toilet next to a blue cooler filled with ice and Budweisers. Barbells sat on the floor with enough slats of weight to give me an eye hernia. And there sat two gym bags. I perused Bikini and Dynamite's wares. Tank tops, deodorant, a Seiko watch that one of them likely got touring Japan, stray condom wrappers, and a pack of Zigzags.

I shook out a sweat-salted and stained pair of denim cutoffs that exposed more ass than the Thump & Grind Burlesque, and a glassine envelope fluttered and flipped into the bag's mouth. I winced at the flavor.

Black Lotus. But different. More . . . Union Carbide than

ancient Sumerian. The flavor vanished quickly, but there was no doubt who was using this drug.

They *must* know Mick Butler. They must know where he was or where he would go.

And there was no question that those two bastards were going to be jacked on Black Lotus. I had to make them talk. No knockouts. No jawbreakers. I had to force two men who could withstand the pain of a thousand arrows to say uncle and make it look good.

Laughter tumbled out of me. I couldn't stop it. It rumbled and rolled and tickled my ribs and grabbed my guts and shook me like a pox fever as I tried to grasp my breath, but it was useless. Wave after wave of ridiculousness crashed into my funny bone until I was rolling on the ground, in the dark, dressed like a homeless superhero amid the piss, blood, and sweat, and all the while a man who saved my life was in a coma and would be soon be dead without knowing I'd caught the sons of bitches who had killed him. A debt to a dead man is a lifelong mission of suffering, and Cactus was a joyless fellow who hated my card tricks and patter as much as he hated how I cleaned my burp gun, a man whose courage had torn me from death's maw, a man whose only hope for a peaceful afterlife was me—me, convulsing on the floor with unstoppable laughter.

The door opened.

"That's it, you son of a bitch!"

The lights flashed on, then it was over. I laughed as they tore my arms and legs and neck, a cavalcade of holds from faceless monsters who thought I was gloating over ruining a man's life, ripping me in ways almost as bad as Edgar's training, but no man on two legs without a dirt soul could unleash that kind of hell on another human. Not that it mattered one iota, as they made sure I knew these receipts were for fucking with Kodiak, messing with family, screwing one of the boys—and all hope and sanity of convincing them otherwise had flown out the cuckoo's nest. The pain was like a buzzer on a game show and all of my answers were wrong.

"I'm sorry!"

Neeeh!

"He went batshit!"

Neeeeh!

"I just wanted to help!"

NEEEEEEEEH!

It didn't help that I was laughing and screaming in the exact same tone of voice. Someone whispered Shemp's name and I dropped to my knees, streams of blood running like a busted faucet from my nose, turning my chest crimson.

"Uncle," I said with two fat lips that misted the air pink. "Uncle!"

A knock at the door.

I barely got to a standing position before my ankles and wrists, sore from being nearly torn apart a moment ago, began to throb. They were starting to swell and discolor. Hunched over, I opened the door, and smelled the gag before I saw it.

There was my gym bag, mouth open like a torture victim, and resting within was about five pounds of shit sprinkled with liters of piss.

Here was the icing. Beating me was just the cake.

I reached underneath the suit and pulled out the one thing they didn't damage.

In my hand was the mask of the Assassinator. I had to imitate a dead man to make the gladiators of pretend tell the truth about the drug that was killing their kin and my friend.

Holding the mask, the laughter finally died.

28

ICARUS'S BLOODSTAINED BLACK-AND-WHITE TIGHTS and blue boots had to go, but with Jack's costume ruined by wrestlers' excrement, I needed new attire. Poking around the dressing room uncovered some tights and trunks in a tasteful solid black. Didn't equal the gold-and-silver glitz of Jack's mask, but they say you can't go wrong with basic black. The black boots I found actually fit better than the blue ones and didn't smell half as bad.

After donning the new duds, I sat across from the door—lights on, mask tight—and listened for the approach of another attack while my body tried to mend my tattered fleshly coat of many bruises, welts, and one or two bites. But the goon squad must have been ordered to go easy on the mark, because I saw none of the grapplers even so much as peek around the door. Not even the main attractions, Bikini and Dynamite. Wherever they were, they had no more to do with the riffraff or the masked man. After a half-hour, I was able to grab my nose and grip it shut to stop the bright red puddle from growing at my feet.

"James?"

My hand dropped.

"That's . . .you? In the mask?"

I nodded.

Herc was at the door, pale as moonlight on milk. "Oh god, they did this to you?" He craned his head to look down the hall, color returning to his skin. "When I find out which of those son of a bitch-bitches did this I will stretch them like a torture rack and feed their bones to my mutt."

He ducked back inside. "I should have been here."

I waved away his guilty conscience. "Boss had something on you. I get it. Plus, I kinda deserve it."

"No one deserves a schmoz in the dressing room. Chicken-shits should have gone at you one at a time."

"They don't like to lose."

He sat next to me, and I was itching to know just what Shemp had on my friend, but alone time in the backstage of any perfor-mance is a rare and I didn't want to bother with carny slang. "The guy who is pushing drugs. Mick Butler. You know him."

"Yes. Drugged-out mustache and skinny bones."

"Tell me everything."

"He started showing up six months ago. Hangs with the dumb bells." I assumed that meant the weight lifters who were growing in number within the ranks of the wrestling world. "I know he hung at the gym. Those guys, James, they're not real culturists. They cheat with drugs. They pop the pills. They inject stuff like dopers. Or smoke it like hippies." Smoke? Kodiak had gone for a smoke. I wouldn't put it past folks in this trade to use their talent like guinea pigs. Hell, they worked them like dogs and drove them like horses, why not lab rats? "The kind of growth that takes years, especially in pectorals and lats, by god, it was growing overnight. Guys who couldn't press their shoe size were now shaking the weight benches and demanding more." He shook his head. "And in the ring? Lazy, dangerous. Tossing each other around without a care. No idea about holds or how to take bumps. Half the young guys are told to bow before Bikini because Shemp thinks he's the future."

"And he's one of Butler's boys."

Herc leaned forward, cupping his hands. "He was a good kid. Dedicated. Did what I told him and saw results, but, James, this generation wants everything fast, everything now, and they don't care how they get it. Pills. Smoke. Needles. Probably have suppositories."

I chuckled. "Where did Butler come from?"

Herc shrugged. "Don't know. But I bet Bikini knows. Number one customer. They probably have each other on the Rolodex."

"Shemp?"

Herc turned to me. "Yeah. Nothing happens here without him. And I think he's made some kind of deal with that roach."

"Deal?"

"Most of these guys are new. Too many injuries. More and more don't know how to shoot. Which means they're dead in the hands of strong buffoons like Bikini. They want to be Bikini. The next Bikini. And I think they want whatever it is Bikini is taking."

"Jack Lumber was one of them?"

Herc nodded. "He didn't even need them. He could scrap, go long; his cardiovascular system was so strong he could have been the next Verne Gagne, but without a shitdirt personality." His hands shook. "Instead he's dead. And I know why."

"Tell me."

"Ever hear of steroids?"

"Sure. Doctors use them to help you heal after surgery. Took them after Korea while I still had near-torn knee."

"They've been around even longer in gyms and bodybuilding. They're made by big chemical companies. Made from all sorts of things, but mostly testosterone, as if these creatures need more reason to lose their marbles." He leaned back. "But it's not the anger that's killing them. It's not the rage. It's not the giant arms. James, it's their hearts.

"These drugs help all muscles grow. Not just biceps. Not just thighs or glutes. The heart is a muscle, the king muscle, and I think these drugs are making them grow too fast. A friend of mine, a strongman from Lithuania named Zlados the Mighty, he had a stipulation that when he died his body would be donated to a medical school. The miserable Balt made me the executor of his will, and so I had the joy of signing off on his body being torn apart and having them send the reports. I knew he'd been injecting things, the sap, but I had no idea the cost."

He looked at me and I stopped breathing so hard through the mask. His gaze was that cold.

"It was black. Covered in scar tissue. A human heart made of scars, all to win some trophies and die before you turn fifty." He spat, as only the Greeks can, with the accuracy of a career slob and the authority of an Athenian general.

"Heart attack," I said. "That's what killed Jack Lumber."

"No man in that kind of shape should die at his age," Herc said, "unless his heart was made of scars."

Black Lotus was now the steroid of choice for the lab rats of the Olympic. And this new version of the ancient drug had to be refined and manufactured by someone. Someone in the pharmaceutical industry. And who was one of our guests at the Legion Hall? Alan Carruthers, of C&C Pharmaceuticals. If he was the target, the attack was set up by who? Rivals in the big business of solving all problems with a pop of a pill and swig from a sifter? But the agents of destruction had been on the drug. Maybe a black-market lab of Black Lotus? Damn. I hated when clues just made things more complicated. I needed more information.

Shemp's waddle-steps echoed in the hall. He entered, that last twenty in his mitts, his fat face smiling. "Showtime, masked man. Go make me some money."

Herc and I stood together and I blenched from all the ouch and ack and barf that my body was sharing with me.

"Where are the main attractions?" I said. "No one told me the match."

"You're spry," he said, as I walked toward him. "They'll call it in the ring. Just listen, do what they say, and don't you dare go off book again. Whatever Kodiak's problem, we can't have a repeat performance. Get into the launch position and wait for the Assassinator's call."

Nose to nose, he squeezed the twenty, then thumbed the bill into his palm, snapped his finger. He stretched out his hand to reveal the bill had vanished.

"Wow," I said. "A promoter who can make money disappear."

He gripped my collarbone and I could feel the marrow shake. "For my next trick, I'll make you disappear if you fuck with me again." He let go, and I dropped to the floor.

Then he turned to make his exit, but he wasn't as fast he used to be. He never felt my hand dart like a viper's tongue, two fingers flitting into his sport coat sleeve as his arm swung back.

As soon as Shemp was out the door, Herc helped me up. "You were always full of brine," he said. "But now, James, you have a death wish."

I coughed. "Maybe." Then I lifted my closed fist. I unfurled it to reveal the smooshed twenty Shemp had sleeved with his pretty solid vanishing act. "Or maybe I know opportunity doesn't knock if you don't kick her door first. Can you give this to Sam?"

Herc took the bill and shoved it down his shirt. Even Satan himself would think twice of testing the old man's ability to protect himself. "You know they will try and hurt you. Hurt us."

We started to walk down the concrete hallway. "Of course. Which is why I need to hurt them first."

29

ONE MORE WALK DOWN THE AISLE AND THE WORLD
would think James Brimstone was a runaway bride.

"Ladies and gentleman. We are at our final match, your evening's main event!" The crowd was back to piss-warm status and the announcer was trying to ramp them up. "However, there has been a change in the match. Due to severe injury, Kodiak Slim will not be able to compete in tonight's tag-team extravaganza."

A dark *booooo* filled the world. They weren't indifferent. They were hungry for the kind of real suffering I'd given them in the first match. The hunger for blood and pain that helped stain the sands of gladiatorial arenas, fed the Samurai Ikki-uchi, and the spectators around the world's fighting pits.

They hungered for blood and horror. And they were going to get it. Just a different flavor.

"Instead, tonight's match will be a *handicap match!*"

The audience grumbled approval as I tied my right boot tight, keeping my wallet safe for the beating I was about to lay down.

"Introducing first! He comes from Parts Unknown!" A mild

titter. "Weighing in at two hundred and seventy-five pounds."
I thought of Jack's physique of caked-up muscle on an already-taxed frame and figured the announcer was once again full of shit with reading of the scales. "He is the Master of Disaster, the Monster of Monstrosity, the Human Killing Machine. . . the Assassinatoooor!"

The curtain swayed before me. I cracked my knuckles in each hand, then yanked the curtain open like Batman tossing his cape.

"Flex," Herc had said to me as we walked to the launch position. "And keep moving. Jack was best known as a skinny baby face who couldn't sit still, but he was popular because of the muscles he'd injected."

I did my poor-man's Charles Atlas routine while spinning 360 degrees on my heel, realizing how puny my natural physique must look to those who were expecting Jack Lumber. Breathing in the crowd's cheers, I was also smacked with a wave of sickly nostalgia for my last case, where I also ended up in a mask and a pit, on a porno movie set that damn near cost me my life and birthed a demon that would have turned these spectators into an opiate-fed trough of goodies for nightmares yet unborn.

"I love my job!" I screamed, then ran to the ring. I strutted around the floor before reaching for the ropes, the crowd's mixture of excitement and hunger for something with more blood and guts giving me gooseflesh. They were brooding, angry, and lit—a three-day pimple waiting to pop, but holding their time until the juice was right.

I waved to the deadly granny brigade. "Tonight, I dedicate my victory over two dead men to you two beauties!" Three, two, one—

"Fuck you, faggot," said the lead one, hatpin in her brutal fingers, but she was smiling. "And make that deviant Bikini kid and his boy-toy pay for their sins!"

How people could hate men or women whose only crime was

finding comfort with their own sex was something I never understood, except if it was a form of self-hatred.

So I smiled. "Tell you what, Beautiful. I'll do it for you, and for all your *girlfriends!*"

The Century Sam-smoking fellas behind them cackled in delight until the Elder Women's Auxiliary of Wrestling drew their pins and turned their attention to the lesser chromosome before stabbing the space between them. I waddled around doing triceps flexes until I came upon the glazed and confused countenance of Kevin and his crew. "Wake up, kids! The main event is here!"

Kevin, the only lucid one, smiled. "Good luck topping the first match."

I gesticulated wildly with histrionic poses. "Those chumps? They'll only be talking about *me* in tomorrow's sports pages." You know, if local papers actually covered wrestling. "Watch and learn, junior!"

"Our money's on Bikini and Dynamite!"

I slid through the ropes, reasonably certain that Kevin didn't know it was me. Which boded well for the con of the match. Either way, with what I had planned for Bikini and Dynamite, this would be my very last match. It would make Kodiak's jaw look like a skinned knee.

The stains on the canvas were like oil blots on a popcorn bag. A little blood slicked things, but there was no shit-and-ash tang of Black Lotus here. The drug had started and, I expected, would end the night. Herc had come to the ring and pushed me toward the corner, checking my trunks and boots.

"If they turn this work into a shoot," Herc said, "I'll tear them five new assholes."

I nodded, keeping my plan to myself, wondering what the hell I was going to do when Herc saw *me* turn this work into a shoot. I'd had my fill of assholes.

"And his opponents," cried the MC.

The whole place lit up as blazing guitars drenched in more fuzz than a shag carpet in a pimp's five-star penthouse tore through speakers I hadn't even realized were in the Olympic. I couldn't tell if it was one of those spooky metal bands like Black Sabbath or Dust or the ridiculously named Grand Funk Railroad, which some of the gang at the Thump & Grind would sometimes blare while the girls did a busty routine with a lot of ass and shake, but that didn't matter. All the kids screamed louder than the disapproving hisses and *tsks* of their elders.

"From Venice Beach, California!"

I laid my back against the ropes, realizing that Shemp wasn't a bad promoter. He'd saved this trick for the last, and sure as shit the audience was already forgetting the blood and thunder an hour before.

"Weighing in at three hundred pounds of twisted steel and sex appeal."

Music. Rock and roll. The dangerous outlaw image. Rock and wrestling were natural bedfellows, and if Shemp could reach the youth through spectacle that spoke to them, wrestling had a future. Which meant guys that didn't look like their daddy's wrestlers.

Guys like . . .

"And your Western U.S. Heavyweight Champion of the World . . ."

"Western U.S. world champ?" I said. "As if the world needed another non-sequitur from people it considers illiterate."

Herc shrugged. "All the best names were taken."

"Bikini Atooooll!"

I walked to the center of the ring and made the gimmie-gimmie motion, half-expecting them to run out like Kodiak did, Black Lotus running through them like high-octane fuel.

While heavy metal thunder turned every kid into a shaggy-haired victim of electrocution, heads banging back and forth as the song picked up steam, Bikini's massive hands parted the curtain, and before I could yell, "Oh shit," Herc said, "Fuck me."

Bikini walked slow, a six-foot-six slab of muscle, sweat dripping off him as if he'd just stepped out of a shower. Like me, every muscle was flexing. Unlike me, it looked as if each muscle group had been pumped full of cement. He wasn't so much bigger than before, just more solid, dense. The slow, careful walk and the slab arms rustling back and forth like the tether from a stray hot-air balloon gave the impression of a man who flicked Buicks into the sky with his fingers.

The crowd adored this god of concrete and deadlifts. This was how cults started, I thought. Charismatic image, confident with indifference. Bikini's attire had made him the ridicule of the old guard in the back, dressing in a bikini bottom that barely contained his dirty Roscoe. The closer he got, the bigger one part of him flared. Not the trunk-arms or mastodon thighs. Not the bull neck or monster chest. His eyes. Bugged out. Cartoonish. Intense and ridiculous and visible all the way back in the cheap seats.

"His partner. From the corner of Haight and Ashbury, weighing two hundred and fifty pounds, he is the One-Man Electric Kool Aid Acid Test, Dynamite Hippieeee!"

Dynamite ran out wild, throwing his mane and baring his teeth as he circled the slow-walking Bikini, hands like claws, imitating a wild coyote that had contracted rabies. I couldn't help but think of the old French phrase, *plus ça change*.

If our first dance was Davey and Goliath, this was the next chapter: the big man and the wild man. Batman and Robin. Green Hornet and Kato. Gilgamesh and Enkidu. Which made me Humbaba, the monster they came to slay. But unlike that sad sack who'd been made from promises of vengeful gods, they were stuck with a PI who had only one mission: to break them into submission until they leaked the truth.

I yawned dramatically, making loud movements with my hand to indicate how tired, bored, and pathetic I found the two sucking the attention of the room into a dual focus. No one noticed.

Finally, they made it to the stairs. Whatever form of Black Lotus they had in them, it wasn't driving Bikini mad, and I wasn't sure if Dynamite was always this lit or if he was racing on an accelerant. Either way, I didn't care. They were going to talk. Everyone talks eventually. Everyone has a breaking point. Edgar had taught me that.

Herc stood between us as he ran through the patter about a good clean fight, for the unlucky slobs who thought what was about to happen was not crooked.

"And no funny business," he added. "Or else I'll wipe the mat with all of you guys."

Dynamite turned his back, and Bikini stared down at me. "This will be quick."

I smiled. "Like you on prom night."

Herc signaled the bell keeper, then ushered Dynamite out of the ring.

As soon as Herc's back was turned, I landed a quick two-inch punch directly to Bikini's balls.

Stifling a scream, Bikini cupped his family jewels, eyes electrified and wide. "Fucker!"

Seems Black Lotus couldn't completely shield you from all pain.

Then, as he spun to go to his corner, I open-palm-slapped his ass, spanking him.

"What's he doing?" Dynamite said from the apron. "Smarten him up, Herc!"

Herc stood between me and Bikini. "You can't go off script either, you fucking rube."

"Whether you like it or not," I said, "I need to turn this work into a shoot. Now. So, either break my wrist or let me do what I need to do."

Herc grimaced, and was yanked away from me, cast against the ropes, a doll thrown toward his toy box, gripping it with his arms to keep from popping back into the action, all while Bikini's mitts moved faster than sin, grabbing me from a standing position and lifting me above his head like I was his backpack from public school.

"You're going to pay for the cheap shot," he growled from an unmoving mouth, a real ventriloquist. "You're going to pay, big time!"

Then, I was airborne . . . above the ring . . . above the ropes . . . above the crowd, until I reached the third row behind Kevin, where I was gently caught by no one, the audience dashing out of the way like rats from a burning home. I met the floor with my chest.

"Holy fucking shit," said one of Kevin's girls. "Did you guys actually see that?"

"Is he dead?"

"His chest is still moving."

"Then get him back in the ring!"

Herc was counting. "One . . . two . . ."

I got up on my elbows.

"Three."

I looked up. Everyone was a shadow.

"Four."

And only one face emerged from the dark.

"Five!"

"Cactus?" I said. The tough, old soldier was dressed in a blue-and-red suit like he'd wear at the Wild Card Casino. "Are you dead?"

"Not yet, idiot."

"Six!"

"Get off your ass and find who tried to kill me."

"Seven."

I ran for his form and hit the iron barricade.

"Eight."

I climbed on top of it, balanced precariously, summoning all the strength of my hamstrings."

"Nine!"

I leapt from the rail to the apron and dove through the ropes just as Herc was about to drop his arm and count me out.

More howls from the crowd as I looked up to see Bikini tag Dynamite.

The Hippie ran in just as I got both feet on the ring floor, and I immediately found myself in a storm of knuckles and knees. Dynamite was controlled fury and whirling violence without any of the crazed excess Jack or Kodiak had tossed around. This was measured force like I used when on a joyride. Measured, but driven by a manic machine with a single intent: to cut me into pieces before a live festival audience.

I pushed hands, slid between blows, and rolled out of his way, counting my heartbeats as I breathed, just like Dr. Fuji taught me. I slowed my adrenaline rush so it would last longer as Dynamite cut the ring in half like Bruce Lee on bennies. Soreness and stiffness crept up my forearms and shins, as the bastard was pretty well-versed in Muay Thai, making me think even less of him. Not because of studying Muay Thai, but of guys like this who sleaze over to Southeast Asia to learn a few tricks, fuck prostitutes barely old enough to read, and then come back to wreak vengeance on the jocks who once stuffed them in a locker in high school. I know it made me something of a hypocrite—I was a white kid from Oakland taught by a Japanese jujitsu and taiji master, though as Fuji would always say, I was never his best student—but that didn't make Dynamite Sleaze the long-haired creep anything like me.

A straight kick to my balls had me turning to the side.

"You'll get tired before I will," Dynamite said. "You're already getting slow, old man."

An open-palm slap came at my face, and I let it smack me.

The crowd screamed approval as I staggered back to the ropes, Dynamite on the assault. He stuck to what worked and open-palm strikes potatoed my shoulders, chest, face, guts, back, as the wheezing wrestler with the creepy hair unloaded his arsenal without dropping an inch of force, as if he could do this all day.

He battered me into the ropes and Herc stood between us, shoving us both back.

"You need help?" Herc said, checking my face. "You're swelling like a rotten piece of melon."

"I'm fine." Last thing I wanted was Herc involved in my business. That stain stopped with me. "Just protect yourself."

Herc stood back and clapped his hands for the match to continue, then Dynamite drove a straight right hand to my jaw. If I hadn't tucked things in snugly, the impact would have cleaned me out. Instead, the world shimmied before I dropped to my knees.

"You're mine, bitch!" he said, kicking my head. "You fucked with our business? Now we're ending your career."

Herc counted as Dynamite ran over to the ring and tagged in Bikini with a slap. I sucked in air tasting of salt and iron. I had to get the big bastard on the ground. He wouldn't fall for a sleeper like the first match, and Dynamite would just tear me off him if that was the case. I had to deliver a major dose of agony.

Fist gripping the middle rope, I got to one foot as Bikini slowly, slimily, grandiosely, and yet indifferently, stepped across the ring, hands in front of his crotch. "You had one shot, loser," he said. "And now, it's night-night." He put his hands together as he laid his face down upon them like he was going to sleep . . . then dropped them fast to protect his pant weasel as he came within grabbing distance.

I shot-putted myself into him, ramming my shoulder into what felt like a wooden writing desk: whatever fat had once been on him had long since vanished. I hooked his leg and lifted, proving strength can't stop momentum as we both hit the floor. He landed like a marble statue that refused to break while I scrambled on top of his body and dropped an elbow across his nose.

The anger in his eyes didn't soften one bit.

He grabbed both my arms in his hands and started twisting them as easily as a kid would Play-Doh.

"You have no idea what you're messing with, mark," Bikini said as the tendon connecting my biceps to my shoulder joint threatened to snap.

I wedged my right leg between my body and his and stomped on the mat, pulling myself away as I centered my stance. My arms slipped out of his paws as I twisted my legs around his arm, locking up his wrist and forearm, then slammed myself on the canvas. I'd executed the deadliest arm lock that Masahiko Kimura ever used: the combination leg-wrap and hyper-extended submission that made him the master judoka of Japan and the teacher of a legion of great disciples, including Dr. Fuji.

The only problem was that Bikini's arm was stronger than a starved German shepherd's bite. Here I was, wrapped around his arm, trying to dislocate his elbow, and he was lifting me up and hammering me down against the canvas while the crowds chanted:

One!
Two!
Three!
Four!
Five!

Six!
Seven!
Eight!
Nine!
Ten!
Ow.

We were on our backs, me still locked to his arm but my spinal nerves were flashing DANGER! DANGER! DANGER! But that wasn't all. Neck? Overloaded. I half expected cartoon birds tweeting around my skull. Blood from a half-dozen little mouth cuts drooled out of my lips. I hung on to Bikini's arm tighter than the ropes strapping Odysseus to the mast of his ship to save him from the Sirens. The whole time he'd been ramming me like an angry spatula, my every muscle, sinew, bone, and slab of fat was angling against this arm, sneaking for the right combination on his iron-hard muscles to finally perform a move that didn't care how big and strong you were, had no care in the world about your muscles, and felled all men equally.

I was still searching as Bikini took a knee and, to the delight of his worshippers, stood. I hung upside down from his arm like a wayward bat while he strutted around the ring dunking my head against the canvas. I just needed him to stop bending his elbow. If it was at rest, I could snap it back.

"Ain't no way you're going to win, chump. You're weak, you're lame, and this crowd will eat you alive if you pull anything." Dunk, then he dragged my face amid the blood and spit and stains of long-lost matches. "You're out of your league, I'm out of this world, and now we're going to make sure you never, ever come back."

Dunk.

Ow. My grip on the hold loosened and Bikini lifted me up as if I weighed less than a bag of groceries. "Say goodbye to showbiz, mark." He puckered his lips to give me a kiss—and I bit his lip so hard my teeth clacked together.

Bikini screamed, but I hung on to his lips with my teeth and wrapped my legs around his head. Gushing blood turned the mask crimson. When my nose sent out a spray of pink mist, the crowd ate it up with relish and mustard.

"Le go ah me!" Bikini screamed from the red shower. Herc came close, but I growled and he backed off, slapped his hands, and said "the match continues!" The audience howled in sick delight.

"Fall back!" I said, meat in my teeth. "Or I will tear your whole lip off!"

Bikini seethed, ran around the ring, selling the move, and then slipped and fell.

On the way down, I released my teeth from his lip and prepared for the one chance in hell I had of pulling off this plan. Bikini's unwavering control was wildly staggered and the grip he had on his muscles loosened for a fraction of a second—because his arms extended to take the bump, as all wresters do—and his arm went straight.

I grinned red. Perfect.

We hit the canvas and I locked his elbow a split second before he regained command of his muscles. Thank god for the power of tradition, repetition, and body memory, because thanks to that brief moment I was able to act against his muscles. Legs fastened around his arm, locking his hand under my chin, I did something Kimura might find unethical: my fingers splayed out like spider legs and found the secret pressure points of life energy in Bikini's arm. They dug into his flesh like in a move so vicious Dr. Fuji said it was like ripping a man's soul from his skeleton.

Bikini screamed like a girl in a scary movie. The son of a bitch couldn't take the pain. The crowd hushed. I didn't ease up. "Tell me about Mick Butler!"

Bikini gasped and waved over Dynamite. His partner jumped in the ring but found Herc in front of him. "Get out!" I yelled, catching his eye. "Or I will turn his arm into a ghost limb."

I pulled back, and a worse wail, like a kid lost in a department store, sent weird chills up my spine. Dynamite bared his teeth but went back outside. I eased off the armbar. "Tell me! What's Mick Butler giving you?"

Bikini rolled around. "I don't know. It's new. It's good. Packs on muscle. Gets you high. Not scared of nothing. Shit for pain right now—"

"Is that what he gave Kodiak?"

"We dosed Kodiak," Bikini said. "Old stuff. Worse. Made you crazy. Mick gave me the new stuff."

"What's he call it? Tell me!"

"They call it *Barbarian*."

Clever and cute and annoying. "Who is his supplier? Who's making Barbarian?"

"How the fuck should—" Bikini covered his mouth, but another wussy scream pierced the eardrums of the now-silent crowd. Whatever stroke he had with the people of L.A., it was starting to fade. Slippery with sweat, I readjusted my grip, spit some of his lip blood back in the air, then pulled back to the edge of what he could handle.

"Who makes the drug?"

He punched the canvas with his free hand. "I don't know! I never ask who makes it. But they have to be real big. This isn't some garage chemistry set shit. Barbarian I take now? I got density and strength and focus without the wildness."

"What about Dynamite?"

"He just takes speed. C'mon, brother, I don't know much else."

"Where is Butler?"

"In his car, probably with a young piece of ass."

"If you're lying, and you know who makes it—"

"I told you! It can't be a local head with access to the high-school lab. This shit is industrial-class muscle builder. That takes crazy money. Most of the drugs I take are shit, but Barbarian is worth the price."

"Including the guys it drives crazy?"

Bikini squirmed on the ground. "I don't care what happens to others. I do this for me. I take the risk. My body. My career. Kodiak and these old timers can go fuck themselves because they know I'm the future and they just can't compete."

"Perhaps," I said, then yanked so hard his elbow damn near popped out of its skin in reverse. The wide eyes of Bikini Atoll went even wider, his bronze skin now a shade of bad milk. "But neither can you. Say 'uncle.'"

Herc ran over.

"Say it!"

Bikini shook and nodded, blond hair covering his face. "UNCLE!"

Herc screamed, "Ring the bell!"

30

FIVE BELLS TOLLED AS I KICKED MYSELF AWAY
from Bikini.

"The winner of this contest," said the MC. ". . . the Assassi-nator!"

Herc had barely raised my arm when I saw Dynamite coming through the ropes. "You're a dead man walking!" He jumped on top of me, hands gripping the mask, tearing at its lacings on the back of my head.

"Get off him!" Herc said, wedging his body between us.

"Not this time, old man," Dynamite said, and kneed Herc in the guts, stealing his wind. The old grappler pulled himself away while the bell rang and rang. Dynamite refused to get his fingers out of my mask.

I pulled back my arms, fixed my feet in an ugly stance to grip the weight of the earth, and drove two punches into his ribcage with the force of a Mack truck hauling ass from Tijuana. Dyna-mite pulled away, but his hands were still tangled in my mask's spaghetti.

He yanked the mask off my face.

I sucked in the now-cool Olympic air, sweat streaming down my forehead, lips still red from chewing on Bikini, body essentially a stitched-up punching bag with a few thousand more miles traveled in the last ten minutes within the ropes of the squared circle.

My second breath woke me up enough to recall where I was and the kind of con job that I'd pulled on them. Before I could conjure up a solution, someone called out the fakery.

"Hey! That's Icarus! The Assassinator is Icarus!"

"That's not the Assassinator!"

"Rip off!"

Cups of beer took flight, trailed by half-empty boxes of Lucky Elephant, the candy-coated popcorn trailing out the spinning boxes like a bright pink comet's tail. Cigarettes were next, then spare change. Herc and I had our hands up fending it off.

"Oh shit," I said.

Herc nodded. "You know Shemp is coming for you, right?"

"How do I get out alive?"

Herc yanked off his ref shirt, bow tie left around his thick neck, physique a cut and dangerous sixty-year-old diamond. "Cover yourself and get the hell out! Not the aisle. They'll murder you for what you did." Sure enough, Shemp and the goon squad were running toward the ring, along with gray-uniformed security guards from the Olympic. "You ain't got a friend in this hell hole besides me."

But I did.

I turned to the side of the Olympic where the main entrance glared back at me with an inviting eye. I thought of the carnival circuit preachers—evangelical con artists—pounding the pulpit for a crowd that was both audience and target, cash and mass. I remembered Hector's adoration of the *luchadores*, human flying machines. The only idea worth having crystallized. After all, I was Icarus.

Shemp and the boys were almost at the ropes. Cutting across the ring, my strides long, I reached the Shemp-free side. Using the middle rope as the first rung of a ladder and the top rope as the second, my feet grasped a precarious balance.

I yelled, "Kevin!" to make sure he and his crew were watching. They were—with mouth-gaping stunned attention.

"Catch me!" I screamed. "Please!"

Kevin hollered something and the gang got their hands up as I threw out my arms.

I launched myself straight into the crowd.

Unlike my earlier airborne experience with Bikini as my launcher, this time I made a softer landing. Crashing into the kids, they partially collapsed but, amazingly, they all pushed back and up. I rose from the crowd to even more applause.

"The main door!" I shouted and they caught on. I rode their palms as more gathered to help bear me away from the ring while Shemp watched from it, screaming so loud I thought he might explode. But his booming rant was swallowed in the mass of the crowd who'd seen a night of wrestling unlike any other and were moving their savior-killer toward the door, a leaf carried by a thousand ants, draining from the seats, ready to take him to the street for who knew what.

I rode atop the wave of humanity and reminded myself that when the bout had started, they had worshiped Bikini and craved my blood. This is why victorious Roman generals rode through the streets of Rome in triumph accompanied in their chariot by a slave who continuously whispered, "*Memento homo*"—Remember you are only a man.

As we approached the door, someone grabbed my hand from below: Margarita, wide-eyed in a trench coat.

I got my disciples to lower me and held onto her hand as we continued up the aisle, on foot, as part of the crowd pushing its way to the door.

"You are full of surprises, James," she screamed in my ear. "Here." She shoved a heavy canister in my hand, a scrunched-up telescope covered in dials. Watkins' encoder. My divining rod to Black Lotus! "Find it! Bring it back!"

"I will. And why the hell did you dose me?"

She dropped my hand and laughed before being swallowed by the crowd. "There is a rumor you can't be charmed, gringo. Another customer of mine was curious if it was true. Looks like it is, though you can be influenced. Hope you enjoyed your time at El Dorado."

I clutched the encoder to my chest along with Herc's torn shirt as the crowd pushed me away from her, their sheer volume releasing the doors. Another customer? Interested in me? Edgar? Maybe. He'd made me immune, even to his own charms, but given his recent offer . . . Maybe he was looking to see if anything could break his own spell. Perhaps the petal wasn't as precious to Margarita as she had made it out to be? Right now, none of it mattered.

In the drained seats, I saw one couple before being pushed through to the concourse. A big guy—who clearly enjoyed Bud as much as dumbbells—was working his hand up a very familiar skirt as his mouth nuzzled the neck below a very familiar face.

Veronica's mouth was agape amid the spectacle of violence and mayhem. A dark part of me wondered if her closed eyes were filled with me.

Damn it! *She* was my ride.

My procession spilled out into the street. Two words ended my triumphal march and the abrupt stop tripped me up, landing me on my ass. Red lights swirled all around.

"The fuzz!"

31

SANDALS, WEDGE-HEELS, BOOTS, KEDS, AND BARE feet stamped around me as I completed my rapid descent from messiah to possible pariah. Hitting concrete finished off whatever was left of my pop demi-godhood thoughts. If that artist Warhol was right, I still had about ten minutes of fame left, but not today. Remembering the dying man in the hospital and that the weight I carried was the Watkins encoder wrapped in a sweat-stained blue ref's shirt—my way to find Black Lotus—killed any idea of godlike outrage at my demotion.

A hand came out of the scramble as I wiped blood from my mouth with my forearm. Kevin smiled. "You are the coolest adult I've ever seen." I took his hand, and he did a fair job in pulling me up to my feet.

"Praise from Caesar," I said. "Thanks for not letting me become a stain on the concrete, but we gotta go. This place is too hot for even the innocent. Any chance I could crash at your guys' HQ?"

"You want to come to Tumbledown?"

Then everyone's favorite wet blanket, Austen, showed up. "They took our boards!"

"What the fuck do you mean?" Kevin's attention was high-jacked by the immediate emergency.

"The cops, they just grabbed them from me and Garth. They thought we were Brown Berets."

"The Chicano activist group?" I said.

Austen scowled. "The Berets were in the parking lot handing out flyers. We were helping them. Then the cops showed up and grabbed us, took our backpacks, our boards. We got no axles."

But I might. "Okay, help me get around the building and I'll help you guys get home, deal?"

"Not this guy!" Austen said. "I'd rather go to the joint than deal with him."

"Speak for yourself, Austen!" Kevin's loyalty was, no doubt, inspired as much by the lack of any alternative as by trust in former demi-god me. "Guys, form a square."

With that I was escorted around the building by seven kids of varying ages, who hugged the wall as I donned Herc's shirt, the flaps hanging out to further disguise my trunks and tights. While they kept the coast clear, I examined Watkins's device.

It was the kind of craftsmanship I'd only seen in the archives of Edgar's mansion, a well-dusted collection of assorted baubles, charms, and esoterica from around the world of the arcane. Trinkets and amulets carved and polished by patient hands: pre-industrial, pre-colonial, pre-historical, a range of lost relics and specimens of immense influence. All I could do was watch and dust and listen, because for Edgar wielding magic was something for grown-up sorcerers, not their adepts.

The Watkins Exposure Meter—or so the encoder was engraved—was cool and modern, a casting of iron and bronze with a compass on top, sheathed in glass, the needle to the compass missing. This was where I was supposed to put a leaf of Black

Lotus. A combination of nature and industry created by a nine-teenth-century antiquarian who believed that ley lines were the markings of aliens who also built Stonehenge and the pyramids before ditching our rock for parts unknown.

I flexed my ankle to feel my wallet against my wrestling boot. We turned the corner to find a bunch of cops and Latinos arguing near a squad car. Placards reading "Stop the Illegal War," "Peace is a Method," and "Kill the War Machine" lined the ground because all of the non-cop hands were restrained behind their backs.

"We have a right to protest!" said one man with hair down to his shoulders. "All we did was show up with signs to inform the public. How much of a threat is the free exchange of ideas?"

The cop had no response until he saw us. "Hey!" said the sweaty patrolman. "Where do you think you're going? Didn't I see you guys earlier?"

"What?" I said, glad my shirt was now buttoned. "Officer, sorry my son and his friends were making hoopla for you. I had to use the washroom and there they went—causing mischief. Well, no ice cream for them when we get home."

"What's that in your hand?'"

I raised the Watkins Exposure Meter. "Oh, to see from the stands." I put it to my eye and looked through, face distorting. "The kids love to zoom in on the guys in the ring." I was glad that my trunks and tights were covered up by the shifting and restless feet of the crowd.

The cop viewed us askew. "Where's your car?"

I thumbed around the corner. "I won a chance to meet Bikini Atoll, so they said we could use the backstage parking lot."

"Is that your Lincoln back there?"

"Yes, sir." Good. As I had expected, Mick's car was still here. Which begged the question: Where was he?

"Fine, go."

"Hey, *gringo!*" The protestor who had been arguing his First Amendment rights wanted my attention.

"What did he do, sir? He has a right to protest."

"Don't need help from you, just remember what I looked like before you turned away. Take a picture, *gringo*. Take a picture of what a police state looks like."

The cop winced, then saw all of us—witnesses, white as milk—looking at him. "Let's all calm down here."

"I know a lawyer," I said to the young Chicano. "I can call him on your behalf."

The Brown Beret leader snickered. "We got lawyers. What we need are witnesses."

"I'm one," I said. "My name is James Brimstone. Private investigator . . . and loving father. Officer? This was a peaceful protest. If you arrest these folks, there's going to be a lot of paperwork. Save yourselves, your bosses, everyone all that work by giving these kids a break?"

We all stood there, the cop weighing my logic against the indignation of being told what to do by a civilian. Just then, I noticed the deepening color on my right sleeve—blood from the match was soaking through.

Time to leave.

One of cops approached to his senior. "What you want, Sal?" he asked?

Sal exhaled, looking at the sweet innocence of my cult family.

Another cop, one with some *umph* in his voice, said "Let 'em go."

"What?" said Sal. "But we—"

"Just let them go, Weiss. We don't need the paperwork. And you?" he said to me. "Get your kids out of here. Stop wasting your time with this fake wrestling stuff."

"I quite agree," I said stoically. "Children, to the car."

We shuffled off around the corner and the kids started laughing while I tossed a glance back at the Chicano leader. He massaged his hands, free of silver bracelets, then nodded. If I read him right, he'd said: *Thanks, but don't think this squares a hundred or so years of being thought of as sacks of shit by white Americans.*

I nodded in silent agreement, then hustled the kids around the corner.

The Lincoln was there, all right. Achilles was, too. Lying on the ground near the backstage door right next to Mick Butler, both dead as dirt.

32

"RUN," I SAID, QUIETLY. "DON'T STOP UNTIL YOU GET to the car, then get in the car and wait. Go, now, move it!"

They bolted as I ran to the two dead men.

Each had thick bruises around their necks. Strangled where they stood, dead when they dropped. I rifled through their clothes, but nothing, and no taste of magic, either. They were killed and stripped clean of anything useful. As if someone was cleaning up a trail I'd been finding.

"Hey!"

Sal the cop stood staring at a guy wearing a dress shirt and wrestling tights hunched over two prone bodies. "Uh. Whatever this looks like, officer, I assure you you're wrong."

His hand slapped his holster. "Stop!"

I raised my arms, Exposure Meter in my hand. "Easy!"

Vrooooomm!

Tires squealing, engine gunning, a one-car drag race was coming straight at me.

I turned. The Continental blasted forward, Kevin behind the

wheel. "Jump!" he screamed. I stuffed the Exposure Meter in my trunks as I leapt, crashing onto the hood, and rolling toward the windshield. I gripped car's frame before the impact could break the glass. I'd driven Lilith with cracked glass, and I wasn't about to revisit my past so goddamn soon.

Sal the Cop screamed and the gang starting forming a thin blue line as the Lincoln's headlights blinded them all. Kevin—speed demon on any type of wheels, it seems—roared forward like a bowling ball hoping for a strike.

"Move!" I screamed. "The brakes don't work!"

That malarkey tipped the scale as Kevin kept his game of chicken with the cops going, his crew screaming and hollering. The thin blue line went from 3D to 2D as they jumped out of our way. The car skidded, fishtailing so our lights cut across the Berets. The protestors, seeing the pile of cops on the ground, took off—cuffed or not.

Although I enjoyed the L.A. evening breeze from my al fresco seating on the Continental's hood, wrestling boots sliding to and fro, I shouted, "Might be less conspicuous if I was in the car!" just as another fishtail pulled us around the front of the Olympic.

"No time to stop!" Kevin said. "Those Belvederes will be on us in no time."

Honks and steady gas drove people away like citizens avoiding Godzilla's foot. "Then one of you leaders of tomorrow better open the goddamn passenger door!" We swung onto West Washington Boulevard.

The passenger door was opened and the window rolled down. I flipped my body over so I was splashing the windshield, my sack sticking out so I didn't crush the Watkins Exposure Meter, which I was quickly coming to view as the Watkins Pain in the Ass Contraption. The kids screamed with wild smiles. "I got an idea." I pulled myself to the left and grabbed the window frame of the Continental, climbed onto the frame—hand over hand—

thanking the gods for the nights and days of slinging elephant shit and grabbing fire, because as bad as the pain might have been, my calluses had caught bullets and I'd lived to tell the tale.

"How is this better, narc?" Austen said.

I smiled, then said to the girl in passenger seat. "You're going to want to get in the back seat, kiddo."

I lifted my knees to my chest, the Watkins device stabbing into my already-sore abdomen like a sharpened skeleton key. The kids gasped as my legs shot out straight and I looked like a human triangle holding on to the door.

Kevin jetted forward at fifty miles an hour, and I sprang out from the car's frame like a career acrobat, swung in the open window, and let go before the momentum closed the door behind my ass—an ass now snugly in the passenger seat, albeit sharing it with the girl with auburn braids.

"That was some circus shenanigans," said Braids.

"I come from circus people," I said. "Thanks for the chauffeur service, Kevin," I said.

Kevin smiled. "Wrestling. Skateboard. Circus stuff. What don't you do, man?"

"Can't sing, can't dance, but I'd be grateful for your hospitality until the heat dies down."

"No way, Kev," Austen said from the back seat. "No way. You know the rules. He's not one of us."

"Let's see," Kevin said. "He saved me from losing because he stopped Jack in the race. He came in third while you came in nowhere. And he put on two wrestling shows for us while you were losing our boards, and then he helped us find this ride to escape back to Tumbledown. I'd say we owe him the benefit of the doubt."

It was egotistical as hell, but Kevin reminded me of me. A younger, smarter, more charismatic, leadership-oriented, friendly, and handsomer version of me.

With the others agreeing, and asking me a hundred questions about the circus, we carried on into the night. For them, it was exciting. Wrestling got real. They'd faced down their enemies. Seen how the Latinos of this city are treated by their mutual foe. They'd lost their boards but were high on adrenaline and some cloying artificial bubble gum that smelled like a strawberry built by DuPont.

What they didn't see was the split jaw of a good man.

Crowds that worshiped spectacle like a god.

The three men whose lives I'd touched and who were now dead: one by his own undoing. The other two clearly murdered to keep the trail cold.

I still had no real clue where it would lead, except that it would not be a ma and pa operation.

As quietly as I could, I reached into my trunks, yanked out the encoder, and made a prayer to the gods of the ancient world that I hadn't crossed these fires to be given the Golden Fleece, only to find it destroyed by my acrobatics.

But the little cylinder was intact. No glass broken. The small compass area reflected my tired eyes back to me.

"You were wearing a bong?" Kevin said, turning us at a dead light and heading north toward Santa Monica. "Man, that's a trip."

All the kids stuck their heads over the seat to see an old man with a bong. I couldn't say it, but Kevin had given me the best possible cover for the world of the unexplainable. "Yeah. Was made by an old wizard friend of mine. It got banged up being chased by L.A.'s finest, but it still makes a pretty good telescope." I raised it to my eye. "Will try and fix it before we get to your HQ."

As we drove into Santa Monica, I fiddled with the compass's screws, little brass fasteners I could barely angle with my thumb and started counting all the places where my body was aching. After fifty, I gave up. The adrenaline had fallen away from the gang in the back, who spooned each other to sleep as Kevin drove, a picture that was both sweet and troubling. These kids were being trained for something. I hadn't forgot about the cults of Venice.

Whatever I'd find at Tumbledown, it was closer to the truth I needed than anywhere else.

"You're a detective?"

A twist of the thumb, and the barest of movements, the screw began to loosen. "Beats working."

"For real? Far out. I didn't think people actually did that kind of stuff."

"You'll find that when you open your eyes, and see beyond the horizon of your own experiences, the world has every possible kind of work. I've done a hundred different kinds of jobs, and also begged for my supper." I bared my teeth as I delicately massaged the screw back and forth. "Ditch digger. Tent pegger. Short-order cook. Low-rent prize fighter. Sold dictionaries. Sold puppies. Bunked with the army, though I recommend joining when they aren't dying by the thousands for no conceivable goal beyond our president's ego."

"You're anti-war?"

The screw gave, then jammed. "No. I'd have signed up for the Polish army in 1939 when Hitler and Company thought it was a good idea to run the world from Berlin. And I still think we did more right than wrong in Korea."

Kevin snickered. "So, you are like the rest. A good soldier if the war is good."

"Kid, I just spent all day on skateboards or in a wrestling ring, do you think I made a good soldier?" I went back to the screw, adding a little more heat. "How about you? Tumbledown your home?"

He shrugged. "It feels right. Like the place I was meant to be. All those jobs you worked, was that in L.A.?"

"Sometimes. But I'm what you call a retired knight of the road."

"Knight of the road?"

"Hobo. Road kid. Itinerant worker and former JD, that's—"

"Juvenile delinquent."

I laughed quietly, not wanting to wake the kids, especially Austen, for any reason. "You've been through the system, huh?"

For the first time, Kevin wasn't smiling. Wasn't confident. His face was tight, like the good emotions had vacated the building and he'd locked up the doors so the bad ones couldn't kick themselves in.

"Sorry. I'm actually a pretty lousy detective, but I got a lot of respect for those who survive the system. Didn't mean to pry."

"You didn't," he said, and I clearly had. "What case are you on?"

"A friend of mine got hurt. The people who did it want folks to pin it on the hippies and heads, but it's a front, a cover and a wild goose chase. The people who hurt my friend? They're bad mojo. Big time."

"They killed those two guys back there?" I nodded. The confident Kevin of two minutes ago was still absent, the house still locked and vigilant. "Why?"

The screw gave way and I kept my screams of delight inside as I switched to my fingers and gently removed it from its hole. "Truth? I'm getting closer to their identity. They've also got their fingers in the wrestling business. Truth be told, junior, I'm something of a tar baby." I reached into my boot and yanked out my wallet. "If you want to drop me off at any corner, I'll be fine." I plucked out a twenty along with the credit-card sleeve of Black Lotus. "You can take this for gas and snacks as a thank-you for taking command of the chaos I tossed you into." I stuck it on the dashboard, palming the cards and keeping them in my closed fist while my fingers squirmed a single petal out.

"Keep your charity," Kevin said. "You've earned a place at Tumbledown for a night."

I wasn't sure if Kevin's vehemence reflected his disdain for the past that I'd dredged up, or part of Tumbledown's doctrine, which sounded downright libertarian. I hoped to high hell that I wouldn't be introduced to their leader, just to discover he was a science fiction author with a bad back and worse pencil mustache who thought Ayn Rand was smarter than Einstein.

Ahead were the sparkling lights of the Santa Monica Pier; alongside us were art deco buildings with dim lights and sidewalks of increasingly ragged stragglers.

While Kevin stewed in silence during a hard-left turn, I'd lifted the lid of the compass and slid the petal into the needle holder, which looked like a brass chicken foot. I slid down the top and replaced the screw as we turned again. Dead ahead was a gray mansion that looked straight out of a Universal Horror film—or perhaps it was the Munster's summer home.

He flashed the headlights twice while my fingers searched for some kind of "on" switch.

Once I'd found it, I brought the Watkins Contraption to my eye . . . and stopped breathing.

Through the encoder's eyepiece the house was bathed in milky blue light that emanated across the ground and led straight to the car. But there was more. Inside the house were darker, slithering figures; the dim auras of the shadowy creatures showed only suffering and pain.

The edge of my taste buds recoiled.

Black Lotus. Fetid with rot.

"We're here." I placed the encoder in my lap. Kevin grabbed the twenty and handed it back to me with contempt. "You need to meet Sonny Ray."

"He the boss?"

Kevin's face soured. "We don't have a boss. This isn't a work camp. We're free to come and go. He's just the founder. He's a friend. If you can't groove that, perhaps you should split." He tossed me the keys, then clapped twice and everyone woke up and filed out, yawning, sneezing, or wiping the goo from their mouths.

I dropped the keys in a clumsy fashion, and while fishing for them between my thighs, I twisted a knob near the eyepiece. A brass cover dilated over the eyepiece, closing it.

I opened the car door, leaving far less dramatically than I entered. The night winds lashed wounds new and old and the kids walked, single file, toward the creepy house, itself looking blue in the moonlight. Kevin was in the lead, leaving me and the car behind. "Hey," I said. The kids stopped, but not Kevin. He just shot a glance behind.

I ran. "Slow down, kiddos. Uncle James ain't as fast as he once was." Kevin's face was caught between hope and protection. He'd reached out to an old man—old enough to be *his* old man—and new daddy had turned out to be a creature of the road, bound to leave and not stick around. Didn't have a house like Tumbledown.

We walked the crooked stone path up the short hill that Tumbledown sat atop. I knew where we were now. It looked like Tumbledown had once been part of the grand old world of the Pacific Ocean Park. Hard times and creditors had shut the place down two years ago. Most of the rides and games had been auctioned off and the rest had been left to decay. A sun-bleached brown and blue wood sign proclaimed: TUMBLEDOWN: THE HOUSE BUILT TO DEFY GRAVITY!

It wasn't that it was forsaken amusement park housing. It wasn't even the eerie glowing sadness that thrummed in its belly. With night vision, I could tell the lawn was immaculately cared for, shaved down to a Marine's jarhead cut, not a hair out of place. Kids working to keep a place that was no more than junk look clean?

Ever meet a Marine barber? Ever met one who was also a dope-smoking skateboarder? Tumbledown was a host of contradictions—notwithstanding the monsters in its guts—so I tried to be as relaxed as possible for a man wearing wrestling trunks and a stained referee's shirt and bearing a compass for Black Lotus that seemed to be screaming *HERE BE DRAGONS WHO SMOKE THE DAMN STUFF.*

I looked back. A fistful of homeless were eying the car, but everyone was five yards from it and not moving. It was if the house cast a spell of "don't you fucking dare" over the surrounding area, keeping the desperate from taking a chance. We wound up at the door, and I half expected Scooby-Doo to jump out with a monster mask and scare us.

Kevin pressed the door open. It wasn't locked. That that made me more nervous than if it had been covered in a dozen Schlage deadbolts. He walked into the darkness, which I could see was a hallway leading to a weakly lit bathroom at the end of the hall. "Everyone, catch some z's," Kevin said. "James, you need to meet Sonny."

Need? The free-loving hippie commune had a military edge underneath the hair, tans, and attitude.

And I'd been a lousy soldier.

I was amazed at the smell of Tumbledown when I cut across the threshold: bleach. Sure, weed and roses and assorted scents. But bleach most of all. The smell of cleaning the diseased. The smell of covering horrors. The smell that drowned out the stench of life.

The kids took a left. I followed Kevin as he turned right and we entered what was once a dining room.

Kids, judging by the mass, were spooned, snoring, and satisfied on the floor beneath blankets. The bleach smell was stronger here. This must be the cleaning crew. Younger, smaller, perhaps less agile on their boards. Such was the division of labor at

Tumbledown. As we stepped over kids who were almost as young as me when I hit the road, I wondered what other divisions there would be. Cooking crew? Harem?

My fists tightened around the encoder. Whoever Sonny was, he'd made a cult of kids who were making him the King of Dogtown. I thought it was time he had a talk with a grownup.

Despite an army's worth of effort to plug up holes in the cheaply built walls, the stench of wood rot lingered beneath the bleach and wind. Tumbledown was breezy. One good storm, and it would earn its name. The place was a death shack that hadn't yet rolled over in the grave.

I'd slept in worse digs, but that didn't make me see this structure as anything but temporary.

More troubling: there was no taste of magic. Beneath my soles, there was burning proof to the contrary. That meant deeper magic than kids play with.

Kevin stepped around shaggy heads with practiced ease, as if he had night eyes like me, the dark just a different kind of light in the world. He looked back. I nodded in deference, following his lead. His face pursed, as if he didn't believe me, but he had given his word to introduce me to Sonny. He turned a corner and took another creaky step, no attempt to quiet it.

We started up a staircase, walking solemnly upwards, thin wafers of wood creaking on the treads. I swear you could feel the house sway with the Pacific's breeze, echoing the tide. The stairway walls featured cartoon rabbits and dolphins, painted upside down. Then I looked up.

Sure enough—defying gravity as promised—chairs, a sofa, a chinoiserie bureau, and a small writing desk were stuck to the ceiling, hanging like a half-dozen swords of Damocles, all being held up with god knows what beyond nails, prayer, and industrial adhesive.

But the second floor made my shit itch.

It was a barren room, and parts of the walls had fallen—or been ripped—out, leaving the spare ribs of the house's inner skeleton peering through gaps in the thin flaps of old plaster: the ugly interior beneath the veneer.

There were holes in the floor as well. We stayed clear, knowing that any foot pressure on those weak boards would crush the kids beneath and maybe release whatever monsters lived in the basement.

"Come on," Kevin said. "His room is upstairs."

"He gets his own room," I said, matter of fact. "Probably for the best." It was even worse to think this creep was sleeping with these kids.

The encoder rattled in my angry fist and I had to release the tension before I dropped the only thing keeping me on track to find the makers of Black Lotus.

Up the last flight to a large landing. A single door lay on the far wall. It appeared to be new, with a decent frame and clean knob. Kevin opened the door to reveal a dark room. Perhaps fifteen feet away sat a chair containing a single figure cocooned in a blanket, book to his nose, weak candle glowing on a table to his side. "Just listen, don't judge, okay?" Kevin said, holding the door open for me. I walked in.

Then I caught scent. Litholine grease. Fresh. Not covered in bleach. A part of this damn ride was still alive—

"Sorry, man," Kevin said, then closed the door.

"Shit!" The floor slipped away from under my boots. I dropped into darkness, stealing a glance at the figure in the chair. It stood as I fell, a bleached white dummy pointing skeletal fingers at me and screaming with cadaverous recorded laughter.

33

THE CHUTE SLIPPED AWAY INTO AN 85-DEGREE AN-
gle, sending me spinning, grunting, and fearing every bounce
would shatter the encoder—or me. Zooming down the chute, I
banged into its metal sides a thousand times.

I shoved my left hand out to stop my momentum, but my
right was holding the encoder. Trying to brace myself hand-to-
shoulder failed spectacularly.

Bonking my skull three times, I saw stars come out of the
dark while gravity dug its claws into every single cell of my being,
pulling me down to where the blue shadows glowed. The star-
sparks snuffed out before I could hit the—

THE SKY WAS MADE OF DRIED BLOOD AND THE SAND WAS CRUSHED TEETH.
Fingerbones outlined a pathway and pointed toward an onyx tower, sur-
rounded on all sides by a sea of churning mercury. The tower was made of
scales that breathed. I'd seen this place before in flashes of agony: a place
in the nethers where nightmares were spawned—a living structure, a

prison, a place that I apparently could access when I was knocked for a loop in the mortal world.

"NOOOO!" boomed a voice in the thralls of anguish.

I recognized the scream: it came from Cactus.

I ran down the path, kicking up the guiding bones as I followed them to a silver door polished to reflect the distorted horror of my own visage like a funhouse mirror, though I had to admit my hair looked great. I shouldered the door but passed through the silver membrane into the living tower—

—and snorted.

"Oh, for the love of Glycon and P.T. Barnum."

The blood- and sweat-spattered ring from the Olympic was recreated with the twisted limbs of the grapplers who had wanted to tear me a thousand new assholes, faces mashed and melded with arms and boots and legs and tights. Each of the ring's turnbuckles bore the skull of a fan, mouth distorted with screaming insults.

"Die already, you faggot!"

"Rot in hell, Brimstone! Don't care which one."

"Go back to being Edgar's fuckrat!"

The wind that roared within was not from the crowd, it was Cactus, screaming—no— refusing death, fighting for life.

"This is your choice for a champion, warrior?"

The voice. It was white cold. Fear distilled. My bones rumbled. Neither female nor male, animal or human, it was something other. The crushing voice of birth and murder.

"No!" Cactus screamed. "But he's the only one who answered!"

I sighed. "I deserve that. All right, who am I fighting?"

Black smoke sparked from the center of the ring, wispy tendrils of smoke rolled out overwhelming the ring and forming an eyeless face bigger than an L.A. city bus, then bigger than Izzy's storefront. Its snout was best fit for Godzilla's death mask.

"Who?" said the creature. "Legions. Legions of foes await you, James Brimstone."

"You mean cowards who throw grenades at old people?" I said, mouth finding courage that had utterly drained from my heart. "Bring them, one by one, or in a schmozzle."

Below the cavernous mouth a neck grew, then another extended from the top. Tentacles, I corrected myself, not necks. The tentacles begat more tentacles until the maw was the center of some monstrous nervous system. "For every one you face, more will grow. You will fall, James Brimstone. You will fall."

I blinked. "Oh. I get it. You're Tiamat. Or what's left of Tiamat, the great goddess of oceans and creation. Living near the beach. Kinda cute."

The maw smiled. "And you are no Marduk."

"That Babylonian demi-god who crushed you with fire and a magic blanket? Uh, no. I'm barely able to be a good version of me on a bad day." I stepped forward, the oppressive presence of this old god calling me. "But if you're mucking about with mortals of no account like me, then I must be on to something big, something scary. I saw your home when I was saving the world a couple of months ago."

The maw snarled. "You toyed with a girl who had little knowledge of power."

"And now the life of one Apache warrior is worthy of your attention? Why?"

"Mysteries can kill, Brimstone."

"So can soap and a shower to a Hells Angel." I stepped closer. I could see the ring again through Tiamat's smoke. "I remember asking Edgar where all the old gods had gone." I pulled myself up on the apron. "They couldn't all be sleeping or frozen in lost dimensions. Some had to have presence. Impacts. Little fingers back in the world."

I gripped the ring ropes made of twisted sinew. "Figments, he called them. The barest flicker of great powers . . . but you're not a great power. Tiamat was about the baddest mother of all, and here you are, playing chess with Apaches and road kids for street drugs. How the mighty have fallen."

The limbs thrashed toward me and the mouth hissed, but I stayed put. Because things were clicking. "Tiamat created worlds. Drugs *create illusions. Worshippers of false gods. That's what you want. You thought Tabitha could do that with her porn sorcery. Now? You're helping some mortals make a drug that was best known for murder and rapine."*

Each writhing appendage now had a mouth and they all hovered around me.

"But I've tasted Black Lotus. Notice how I don't want another hit?"

The mouths shook. "Tell us."

I raised my hands. "Easy. I can't be charmed. Not by magic, not drugs. Sure, it turned me into the first-class asshole that I used to be. But when it's gone, it's gone. I'm immune to your worship, Tia."

"DO NOT CALL US THAT!"

"And I know what you're wanting me to do: get in this ring where you will taunt me with images of who you'll ruin or who I'll lose if I fail. But here's a secret: no one knows how to kick my ass more than me. I know that if I don't stop you, Cactus's ghost will never leave me."

"NEVER!" Cactus screamed from the shadows of consciousness.

"Thanks, buddy. And I know who's doing your dirty work."

The smoke maws smiled. "Doubtful."

I stepped between the ropes and some of the smoke heaved away. I cracked my knuckles. "I definitely know that I'm tired. Of being afraid. Of losing. Of wasting time with the likes of you. It's time for James to wake up."

I ran through the smoke in the ring, moving at the ghost speed of whatever netherworld rules of nature existed, and heard the hollow screams of the maws, and an older, deeper one.

"You will regret not serving me, Brimstone. Now feed my people!"

Tia's many mouthless visages pulled back, then dove for my face, drowning me in the smoke of hells so foul they burned my magic taste buds so everything tasted like embers covered in piss. I gasped, swinging my hands wildly and touching nothing but acrid mist—

—that hardened into flesh as my hands punched gaunt faces that were screaming all around me. My night eyes brought them into full relief in the dark: creatures that were once human and now something fit for hell's sanatorium.

"He's got it! I can smell it!"

"Give it!"

"Mine!"

Without thinking, I shoved the encoder into my trunks. I stood, a lonely island amid a sea of human misery. Weathered bodies and gray limbs of what you'd guess were junkies but I could taste were something far, far worse. Here were the victims of Black Lotus, modern day zombies minus the voodoo, eyes as hungry as eyeless Tia's mouths; her little head cases, smelling like fecal putrescence and a craving deeper than addiction. A legion of the damned, weak in body but strong in need, thanks to a rotting cosmic sweet tooth.

I spun my arms in wushu moves just to create space, and their various outstretched limbs dropped back. A ragged crew of homeless faces and beach-bum bodies, muscled and hard but withered to poor imitations of their once-mighty selves, now forced into action because they knew I was carrying their only chance for peace outside a long dark night of the soul.

But fuck if their nails hadn't cut Herc's shirt to shreds.

"Hands off the duds!" I said as they reached for me again. "It's a loaner." Exhausted and body aching, I fired a spinning heel kick that made my hamstrings burn and damn near tore out my crotch, making me regret all the mornings I didn't do the stretches Dr. Fuji swore were the secrets to a long and fruitful life of protecting yourself.

But it bought me a breather to take in just what fresh hell I'd fallen into.

Above me was the chute that had been the ride's chief novelty. I'd apparently landed on a sea of sleeping Lotus heads, which no doubt awoke their anger. Around us were broken pieces of Tumbledown: wall paintings of upside down families having upside down dinner, stray bumper cars kissing each other at odd angles, canvas torn to make blankets, and all around me the stink of the skids from loose bowels and voided innards along with the sour tang of ancient urine from days unending. The smell of where road kids end up if they take a wrong turn and follow it straight to a dead end. Gentleman junkies always softened the horror of the needle brigade. I never understood the chic of it all, living in an opium dream while there was so much of life to be had. I had sympathy for the chronics with no money and nothing left but bad backs and split stomachs who could find no relief beyond the next fix.

They inched toward me again.

A roundhouse kick kept what seemed to be about twenty desperate creatures at bay, but I was convinced I'd torn my pooper three inches and promised myself to never avoid morning stretching again. "Sorry to crash the slumber party," I said. "If you can just show me to the exit."

"No exit," one said, laughing before covering their face with yellow nails. "No exit."

"A Sartre fan," I said. "How . . . fitting. Look, I've got nothing you want."

"You have the only thing I want," said a white-haired skull with eyes.

I elbowed his chin and he crumpled like tissue paper. Thankfully, his swollen chest was pulsing. The rest backed off but growled.

"Didn't want to do that. I want Sonny."

The snarls around me were mixed with sounds of anger and confusion.

"He's our friend," a small creature whispered.

"Who said that?"

The little voice scurried in the dark and hid within one of the kissing bumper cars.

A kid.

One that didn't make the grade to sleep upstairs on the floor.

My patience melted like butter under a blow torch. "Out of my way. You get this one chance."

"You're our last chance!" another voice screeched, and I gave its owner an uppercut without even glancing.

The others took a step back.

"Why is he doing this to you? Why is he keeping you here?"

"Rats," said another voice. "Rats, that's what we were. To our family."

"Tests"—another.

"We're all rats here"—another.

"What tests?" I said. "Don't make me drop another one of you."

"He waits," said the kid in the bumper car.

"Move," I said, and they scattered a bit so I could approach the youngest among them.

A girl. No more than ten. Face blue as the moon. Veins tattooed her face like an Escher sketch. "Waits for what, kiddo?"

She blinked. "For us." She blinked again. "He waits for us to die. Lifting things. Fighting each other. He times us." Her hand snuck out of her ragged green sweater. "Click." She imitated a stopwatch.

"He's timing us now," she said. "How long it takes."

Damn it.

They'd all slipped behind me.

"I'm sorry," she said, face shaking, hands gripping her sweater.

"Don't be, kiddo. For anything."

Gummy teeth clacked behind my back, and I totally lost my shit.

I moved with the grace of a ghost, felling each one of the litter of ragged desperate souls around me like toy soldiers before a flamethrower. Chopping the deadwood before me, I was sickened to my guts. These were victims, not predators; they needed medical help, not right crosses and axe kicks. I kept my blows at twenty-five percent, hitting to stop, to stumble, to knock away, not to crush, to kill, to maim. Still, the bodies filled the floor like debris from an overturned trashcan and regrets chewed my moral compass.

When the last fell, my anger was still raging at an all-time high.

The girl in the bumper car cried.

"He's watching," I said. "Isn't he?"

She nodded.

Without the dregs of humanity blocking the view, you could see the basement of Tumbledown was as big as its main floor, except for a partition made by an old P.O.P curtain blaring WELCOME TO TUMBLEDOWN! THE TOPSY-TURVY ADVENTURE ONLY AT PACIFIC OCEAN PARK!

"Sonny?" I said to the tarp, reaching into my trunks. I yanked out the encoder. It was immaculate. "Time to talk."

The canvas parted down the middle.

Through it stepped the Scandinavian giant I'd seen at the Legion Hall, carrying a gas can in his left hand. The guy who had been among the protesters, the one with the calm face and the twitchy hand. This time, the hand was as calm as the rest of him. It held a stopwatch. He clicked it.

"Time's up, Brimstone."

34

I WAITED. I LOOKED AROUND AT THE BROKEN LIVES
at my feet. Then I looked at Sonny.

"Okay, time's up for what?"

"For you. And the people you beat up."

"That's rich coming from a filth peddler."

"I'm sure that's what they're going to call you when they find
the mess here."

I laughed, then marched toward him. "If you think you're
going to pin this on me, hero, you're in for a rude awakening after
I knock you out." I slid so my right shoulder was in position and
prepared to unleash the unspent rage of the day and make good
my promise to Cactus. I shot my hands up.

"Kevin?"

A rustle from the bumper cars.

Goddamn it.

Kevin's left hand held the girl by her shoulder, like any big
brother would, but the large hunting knife he held to her throat
ruined the familial portrait. His face was blank.

Sonny cleared a path, spilling gas until it washed through the stink of the humanity he was preparing to set afire. "You're almost a perfect patsy, Brimstone. When they find what's left of you here, there won't be any further investigation. The weirdo perv detective was running a cult in Dogtown. The place collapsed because of a stray cigarette, lighting old canisters of fuel. You've sped up my timetable somewhat, but we're still on schedule. Only a tad early." His voice was relaxed, in command, as if all of this had transpired according to plan. I hated it like an open sore on my ball sack.

"Nice plan. Love the stopwatch. And the gas can. It's like a tribute to Adolf Eichmann, author of the Holocaust. Efficient inhumanity."

"If you're expecting to be rescued by the Mossad, I assure you they have bigger fish to fry in Argentina than the workings of a petty detective here. We have a better future to plan."

I looked at Kevin. "You believe this guy?"

"Kevin knows that freedom comes with responsibility and sacrifice," Sonny said, kicking two of his victims into a huddled pile. "Tumbledown is more than a structure. It's an idea. And ideas have no prisons."

"Kid, this claptrap is from Brainwashing 101," I said. "Open your eyes, use your mind, and ask when it's *ever* okay to kill a kid who did nothing wrong. Here's a hint: NEVER!"

Sonny finished his circle. "Loyalty is built with trust," he said. "Who trusts you, Brimstone? The Apache who is dying? The married man whose wife you fucked? The dead man whose life you made fun of tonight?" Gasoline splashed my back and I covered my eyes. "If not for Kevin, you would have been caught, and yet you'd tell Kevin to abandon the man who saved him from the streets?"

I shook the gas from my body. "Kid, listen. I've seen guys like this one. They promise you magic. They promise you a warm cot and a better tomorrow. But they don't promise for free. You're a good kid, Kevin. You're a natural leader. Lead by example. Right now. Would you ask your gang to slit a kid's throat?"

Another splash shut me up and had me coughing my guts out. Kevin just held the girl like a frozen puppet.

There was no other choice.

Tyger Tyger, burning—

Black snakes of smoke choked my mind and lungs and deep down, from the dark recesses, I heard Tia's cackle from a thousand mouths. *Hahahahah! How pathetic, you think the doors to such places are known only to the weak? Such places are now denied you, as Tiamat commands! HAHAHA!*

I coughed gas, now on all fours, floored, surrounded by the doomed. Sonny stood before the canvas partition, placing the gas can on the ground.

"Now, Kevin," he said.

But he didn't move.

"Put her in the circle."

I shook my head, blood rolling out of my nose from the failed joyride. "Do the right thing."

"Kevin, I always give people three chances. And this is your last."

"You don't owe anybody a murder," I said, leaking crimson like water from a busted Dutch dike. "Even those who saved your life." I blinked. "Trust me."

Sonny sighed, putting the stopwatch in the front pocket of his striped trousers, then reached for his ass pocket. "This is why we optimize with a Plan B."

A figure emerged from the canvas behind Kevin. At first, I didn't recognize the shadow, but as he lifted his skateboard I realized it was Austen. I screamed, "Move!"

Austen's skateboard crashed against Kevin's skull, and the lights went out in his young eyes as Sonny lit a cigarette with a lighter . . . which clearly displayed the stylized initials *C&C*.

Carruthers and Carruthers.

Austen bent and grabbed the knife from Kevin's limp hand. Pushing the girl to one side, he hurled the blade.

It cut the air between us in an awkward spin.

My right hand shook as it dropped the encoder and I leapt for the blade, sensing its spinning angle of descent, just as I had with a thousand card tricks, knife throws, and juggling pins over the years. The same hand that had stopped a bullet now shook as a hunting blade bit into its callused palm like a starved cannibal.

I rammed my shoulder straight into Austen's chest, hearing his sternum break as I turned in mid-air.

Sonny was already through the tarp, heading upstairs.

From my position atop Austen on the floor, I chucked the blade like a dart toward the canvas concealing Sonny, not trusting myself to do anything fancy.

It soared through the air as flames rose from the floor.

I scrambled to my feet. Air became smoke, and I could hear Tia's laughter in the crackling flames.

No time for gentleness, I grabbed the blue girl. "I'm getting you out."

She nodded and I flung her over my right shoulder.

Kevin became deadweight in my arms.

The fire circled the damned.

And, glowing on the floor, was the encoder.

I knelt, arms shaking, freed a hand, and reached for the compass on top.

"It's mine!" screamed one of the Lotus heads, who grabbed the device as the flame cut under his arm.

The compass broke off, its petal of Black Lotus in my hand.

"No!" he screamed, now wreathed in flame, as the other heads tore at him, assuming he had the leaf that was in my trembling hand.

I turned to the tarp, something in me cringing.

Behind me, Austen was choking and shaking and didn't have a chance.

Good, part of me thought . . .

I sighed, shoved the compass in my mouth, then kneeled to grab his thin ankle.

I dragged Austen and carried Kevin and the girl to the opening in the canvas. Flames lit up the stairs before me.

Halfway up was Sonny, clawing for a door. The knife handle stuck out from directly between his shoulder blades.

Each step shook under my weight as I clambered up.

He reached for the door. "No. I accounted for everything."

"Nope," I said through clenched teeth. "You failed to account for the underdogs having guts, you fucking shitheel. "

I ax-kicked the blade into his back until it punctured his lung, and his breath was a wet release of red. His body slid down into the furnace of screams, C&C lighter still in his hands. The single shred of evidence that would tie them to the crimes they'd clearly committed . . .

But the Blue Girl coughed and I climbed to the door—

—which opened.

Braids. Illuminated by the fire: Kevin's girl. She held a bat.

"Either swing or get out of the way!" I said.

She dropped the bat, took the smaller girl, and helped me Kevin and Austen up and off the stairs before the first flame licked Sonny's trousers. We were surrounded by Tumbledown kids—the cleaners and the cool ones—so many confused faces, both their leaders out for the count.

But there was no time for an epic speech on freedom and such. "Run you little bastards! Run! Fire!"

I glanced back as flames lit up Sonny's backside. All life was void from his sly eyes. The lighter was still clutched in his dead hand. I spat, and the spit hissed into vapor as his skin began to sizzle.

Outside at the far edge of the lawn, the kids went into action like a casualty-clearing station. Someone grabbed two skateboards and laid them down for Kevin and Austen. I did a quick check on Austen myself. "Braids?" I said. "Keep an eye out. He popped Kevin good."

"What?" she said, tossing a winter vest on Blue Girl. "I'll break his face for that."

"Easy, save it for later. Right now, get all who can move to run, take the rest in the car. You need to scramble before the cops descend like flies on a turd."

She grimaced, then nodded, knowing that whatever dream Tumbledown portended to be, it was junk. Worse, burning junk.

The kids of Tumbledown took care of each other and began to vanish. I tossed her the keys and the youngest and most wounded were rolled into the Continental.

Before they loaded him into the car, I tapped Kevin's pressure points until his eyeballs flickered. He was knocked out, but not for good. His eyes opened. Dull, but awake.

"Hey . . . I'm . . . I'm—"

I raised my hand. "You're a kid. And a good one. Just took some bad advice. And when you had your fill, you stood up and took a chance at the right thing. No reason to apologize."

"Wasn't going to."

"Oh?"

"I'm . . . I'm in charge. Of them. Now. I can't let them down."

I smiled. "I bet you won't."

Sirens. Closing. "Better get you in the car."

He pulled himself up, woozy, but on two feet. The kid was made of sterner stuff than me.

"I'll walk." He reached for his board, and almost collapsed. I righted him. "Allow me to carry your board." I thumbed at Austen, the sole man left on the grass.

"He's still one of us."

"Even after trying to kill you?"

"He wanted to be Sonny's boy." He shrugged. "So did I. Who better to help him than me?"

I laughed. "Okay, hero. Let's get you out of here. Braids is driving."

I rolled the board to the car. He looked back. "Where are you going?"

"Need to see a friend at the hospital. The guy whose life is on the line."

I held out the compass. "Over such a small thing do empires die."

Kevin grabbed his board. "Which hospital?"

"Why?"

He smiled. "I . . . want to bring some flowers. For your friend."

35

CACTUS HUNG IN SUSPENSION, AS IF FLYING ABOVE the world that was trying to get rid of him. Tube in his mouth making him breathe. Swathed in more, and cleaner, bandages than Karloff's mummy. Under the linen I knew his back side was a model of No Man's Land, littered with torn flesh instead of shrapnel and barbed wire.

"Hey, Sarge." I said, knowing he'd hate it, but he said nothing. I still wore the shredded wrestling costume, but I'd acquired a white doctor's coat to complete the ensemble. It was a good compliment to his own. "Sorry about the duds, but you hated my fashion sense anyway, and are probably glad that I showed up without a clown suit. See, I had to sweet-talk a nurse to get me in—she got me the lab coat—and I have a meeting to attend, so this will be quick. It is close to noon, which is the time they have scheduled to pull your plug. But I got the guy. The real pusher behind the attack. He's charred in an amusement park attraction's basement. So, my promise has been kept. If you died now, you wouldn't haunt me."

Okay, I was stretching the truth. There was so much more to it. Maybe I'd explain it all to Cactus one day, but for now it was enough for him to know that Sonny, the no-good bastard whose hand had thrown the grenade, was dead. I fulfilled my promise to Cactus. Besides, he wasn't going to die.

I checked the door. "But I'm going to do you one better."

With the deft hand of a career card sharp, I took out the tube and placed it on the bed. Then, I unscrewed the encoder's compass, took out its petal of Black Lotus, and placed it with the remaining petals I'd had in my wrestling boot. "Good enough to heal Sumerian warriors, so I suspect it will do in a pinch for a real Apache warrior."

I placed the leaf in his mouth and closed it.

And waited.

And waited.

"Not sure about the dosage, Sarge, but that's eight times the amount that sent Kodiak over the edge."

I waited.

The door opened and a doctor wearing wire-rimmed glasses looked at me like I'd fallen out of a ZAP! comic. "What the hell is going on here? Who are you?"

I kept my hand clamped on the old soldier—and then his lips twitched. I raised my hands in surrender. "I'm the trustee of Cactus's estate."

"Nurse," he shouted over his shoulder. "Where's that lawyer who's been hovering around?" A reply from outside the room I couldn't make out. "Then find him!"

The doctor turned back to me. "This man's wishes are to be carried out, whoever you are." He noticed the tube. "You took that out? Are you a doc—" He noticed the name embroidered on the coat. "What the hell? That's MY coat. I'll have you—"

Cactus's eyes snapped open. "You touch that man," he said in dusty gasps, "and I'll have you up on charges of medical misconduct for letting an idiot like this anywhere near me. Now get out! GET OUT! I am alive and will kill you!"

He left.

Cactus's body sagged. "I can't believe it."

"What, that you're alive?"

"That you did it." And for the barest of moments, Cactus smiled. "You did good, Brimstone. Now let me rest."

I smiled. "You're welcome, Sarge."

I opened the door and he snickered. "And you're right. You do have the worst taste in clothes for any man on two legs."

"Ain't that a fact."

I exhaled a day's worth of hellish worry, mouth so dry I could drink the Amazon without quenching my thirst. I dragged myself to the "quiet" room I'd been allowed to use, thanks to a sweet nurse.

Inside was a man in a blue double-breasted blazer with immaculate salt-and-pepper gray hair. "You must be Mr. Brimstone," he said, annoyed and unimpressed.

"You must be Foster Carruthers. Alan's big brother. The head banana at Caruthers and Caruthers Pharmaceutical."

"Please make this short," he said. "I was intrigued by the message you left with my secretary, about this case, but I'm a busy—"

"Yes. This case," I closed the door. "See, I know it's you who's behind it all. Oh, not directly. Hitler never signed anything saying 'I am the one behind the death chambers.' Plausible deniability, and all that jazz. But your company is fucking around with something far more dangerous than you can imagine. And you're using the good people of L.A. as lab rats. It stops here."

"Your allegations are as ludicrous as your attire."

"But no less honest," I said. "I'm wearing the gear of a man's whose heart exploded because of you. I rescued a bunch of kids who would have died under the supervision of your guy, Sonny.

See, I asked Alan about his lighter. Really nice. He said people only get that if they're long-term and loyal."

"I suppose you have proof of this man having one of our lighters? Because, even if you did, it's meaningless."

"Oh, in a court of law? Absolutely. But I don't do court cases. Too much ink. And no, Sonny's arson left nothing to salvage but his bones and those of some of your victims. Couple of dozen in the basement, anyway. I'm sure there are more."

"You are talking nonsense."

"You did a fun trick with the attack on the veteran's hall. Your operatives did a clumsy job of making it look like bikers were infiltrating the hippies. Using protests to cause havoc. That's where the cops went, no doubt figuring they'd always be able to pin something on the Angels or the freaks."

He stood. "You are a fool, talking idiocy, and wasting my time."

The door behind me opened.

Kevin stood in it.

In his hands was a large desiccated root, or what was left of it. It stank of smoke. Black Lotus smoke.

Foster couldn't disguise his recognition completely. His jowls shook.

"Now, I don't know how you got hold of Black Lotus, let alone got it to California. Maybe somebody discovered it somewhere and sold it to your people. Maybe they stole it from Mick Butler, another man you murdered. It doesn't matter, because it is gone. All of it. Every bud. Every leaf. Every petal. And we're going to the incinerator in the basement to finish the job right."

"You . . . you have no idea what you've done," Foster growled. "We were . . . Alan was going to walk again."

I swallowed. "Sorry. Your brother's a good man, but his life shouldn't be built on a pile of corpses."

"Ants," Foster said, reaching for the roots, then pulling back.

"You people, all of you, you are ants. When the time arrives, you won't even see us coming before we squash you out of existence."

"Fleas," Kevin said, catching the guy off guard. "We're fleas, Mr. Carruthers, not ants. You see, fleas go where you can't. You can't really protect against us until you start scratching where we have bitten. By then it's too late. We will have spread disease that we're immune to. Try it again, Mr. Carruthers. Try using the people of Venice or Santa Monica. Try, and see how we bite back."

Apoplectic, purple-faced, with eyes nearly spinning, Foster yanked open the door and stormed off just as Veronica arrived pushing Alan in his wheelchair.

"Foster?" Alan said. "What are you doing here?"

"We'll talk at home," he said, and shoved by his brother, then continued his storm, leaving with the kind of impotent rage that leads to an early heart attack—even if you're not a wrestler.

"Thanks for the gardening work," I said to Kevin. "Mind polishing it off?"

"They'll never even find one ash," he said. "I hope your friend is okay." Kevin nodded at Veronica and Alan, turned a corner, and was gone. I felt a tad bit better about the future of the country.

"Friend?" Alan said. "Oh god, are we too late?"

"Easy," I said. "Cactus woke up about five minutes before they were going to yank his cord."

Alan smiled. "You must be relieved. Did you ever find out who was behind it? Is that why you called Foster?"

Veronica was in a lovely green outfit, including a designer scarf that covered the damage that I'd done to her neck. "No. Whoever did it was smarter than I was. Foster didn't like hearing the confessions of a loser detective. Suspect he'll pay someone far better than me to get to the truth."

And that word punched my guts so hard. I wasn't telling Alan and Veronica the truth about his brother's evil or the nefarious deeds he'd ordered, but that wasn't my job. There was another truth hanging around us like a bad smell. Looking at Alan in his chair, his face still bandaged from the shrapnel he'd taken, that I couldn't help what happened next.

I went to one knee.

"Alan? I have something to tell you.'

He nodded, seriously, and Veronica clutched her scarf.

"I'm sorry." I gulped. "I'm sorry for fucking your wife."

His face went blank.

"Oh?"

I blinked. "Yeah. Uh, this would be where you punch me."

He smiled. "She didn't tell you?"

"Tell me what?"

"That she told me. It's fine. James, really. You both almost died. You saved her life. Hell, if I was you, I would have done it."

Veronica scoffed. "Don't talk like that! He's just trying to be modern about such things."

He laughed. "Come on dear, we need to speak to the doctor about my physio."

They rolled away, leaving me shattered, surprised, and unnerved.

Veronica looked back, once, sizing me up, then sighed as if bored with a toy she'd outgrown overnight.

I stood in the hospital hallway, what was left of Herc's shirt falling at my feet with every move, Jack's trunks and boots smelling riper than hell. I fell down laughing.

"You finally gone mad, Jimmy?"

Above me was Detective Dix, and I put out—well, up—my wrists. "How about some silver bracelets, Dicky? I think I need some time on the county."

He shook his head and stuck out his hand. No handcuffs hung from his fingers.

"Get up. We need to talk. And not here."

37

HALFWAY DOWN THE HOSPITAL ELEVATOR SHAFT, his thick finger punched the emergency stop. Bells rang until he pushed the button again, turning the alarm off.

"Tell me."

"Tell you what?"

"Tell me who did it."

"Why? Aren't you the detective and me just a schlub in a barbequed outfit?"

Dixon positioned himself none-to-nose with me. Any closer and we'd be kissing. Not something I even wanted to consider. "The bikers were a ruse. They're a dead end. They don't have a political agenda. Plus, the other attacks we got solid leads on and they aren't bikers or hippies. There's a web here, but the spider keeps moving. Who pulled this operation and why?"

"If I tell you, will you do me a favor? Will you help me find my car?"

"Oh, for fucksakes, say it."

I did. Dixon's hard stare was Medusa-grade stony. When I

was done, he wiped his five o'clock shadow so slow I could hear the burn. "C&C? Dogtown? Exploding hearts? Black flowers?"

"Yup."

He punched "G", then muttered to himself. The door opened. "I can't believe I bothered to even listen . . ."

"Hey! I am not lying."

I followed him out past the gift shop and through some glass doors. His Belvedere was parked at the curb.

And right behind it was Lilith. Electric blue, pristine and pretty, untouched and unharmed, as beautiful as when I lost her yesterday. "Mercy!" I said. "That's my car! Dixon, how the hell did you—"

His straight right fist hit my sternum and I dropped like a medicine ball, breathless and seeing spots. "Because I actually thought you might be good for something. You rattled some cages. There is someone behind all the . . . weird garbage going on, too weird even for L.A., and all roads are pointing at you. For a second, I thought maybe Jimmy Brimstone would be an ally, so I found an olive branch to offer. What do you give me in exchange? A cock-and-bull story so bad it wouldn't make the third feature at a rural drive-in. So, thanks for nothing yet again, Jimmy. I so much as see you near anything weird, I'll take you up on that offer of silver bracelets." He yanked me up by the collar. He held my stare, but there was something in Dixon's eyes.

Fear.

Beating me up, calling me a crap artist in public—nurses, patients, visitors used this these doors, several passing by during his performance—he needed to cover his ass.

Because behind the fear, there was something else.

Belief I was telling the truth.

"Watch yourself, Jimmy," he said, then shoved me back to the sidewalk. Keys, tossed over his shoulder, landed at my feet.

Watch yourself, Jimmy. Dixon wasn't talking about himself.

I scrambled out of the way of his screeching tires, then clawed my way back to Lilith.

I opened her door.

Knife wounds marked her leather innards, chunks of foam hung out of scars, and her radio had been yanked out, leaving nothing but green and yellow wires. Acrid smoke stained her. The barest hint of Black Lotus.

I laid one hand on the dash, hotter than an egg fried in hell. "I'll take care of you, then get the butchers who did this," I said, then gently, oh so gently, placed the keys in the ignition and made a silent prayer to the gods of fallen creatures.

I turned the key.

Wheezing emerged from the engine.

She was pretty, but gutted. And even though they abused her, she could still roll, still do what she could always do—get me home.

We pulled out of the parking lot, two wounded creatures, and I sang her a chanty about knights of the road as the afternoon sun shined over a city deepening with darkness.